"I Want to Live..."

The Story of My Battle with Leukemia,
My Journey of Discovery, and
the Many who Helped in my Healing

by Keith Dorricott

iUniverse, Inc.
New York   Bloomington

I Want to Live

The Story of My Battle with Leukemia, My Journey of
Discovery, and the Many who Helped in my Healing

iUniverse books may be ordered through booksellers or by contacting:

*iUniverse
1663 Liberty Drive
Bloomington, IN 47403
www.iuniverse.com
1-800-Authors (1-800-288-4677)*

*ISBN: 978-1-4502-1654-8 (pbk)
ISBN: 978-1-4502-1655-5 (ebk)*

Printed in the United States of America

iUniverse rev. date: 3/1/10

Why I Wrote This Book...

Once there was a man who was so deeply in debt to so many different people, that to consider even trying to repay them was out of the question. That man is me, and that is how I feel. But my debt is not financial.

I have just been through by far the most trying experience of my life, my almost ten-year struggle with leukemia, culminating in a bone marrow transplant in the middle of last year. To say that I am now "cured" would be premature, and it's not a word the doctors use. But so far, six months later, I am in better health than I have been for years, and there is no present indication of a resurgence of the leukemia in my body - for the first time since 1988.

This is a story that I need to tell. It has not been easy to write. I need to do it for myself; it is therapeutic, and one of the many things I have been learning is how to be more open with others in expressing my feelings. But I also need to do it to express my profound gratitude for the genuine and comprehensive support that I have received from a myriad of people around the world - family, friends, medical professionals, colleagues, even people I had never met. What a difference they have made to this one individual.

I am utterly convinced that they have been instruments in the hands of God, my loving and infallible heavenly father. For it is God who has been healing me. And it is my fervent desire that every one of those people who contributed in some way to my story would themselves have a deep and personal knowledge of "the only true God and Jesus Christ, whom He has sent". I am well aware of the diversity of their faiths and religious views. But I would merely ask each one of you to read this book - with an open mind.

Someone once said that we cannot always cure disease, but sometimes the disease cures us. I have constantly through the years searched for the meaning in my experience. Not "why did this have to happen to me?" (fortunately I have been spared most of those thoughts; lots of people have worse problems), but "what is the purpose of all this?". I have become increasingly convinced that this has been an accelerating learning experience - a journey of discovery - that has irrevocably changed me for the better. Because I needed to be changed, and still do, if I am to come closer to fulfilling the reason I was put on this earth.

Part of this story is the factual part of the disease, the treatment and the suffering - my physical ordeal. Perhaps this will be of some value to others who are going through similar afflictions. It's no picnic, that's for sure. Perhaps the hardest part for me was just the dogged perseverance required, no matter what. It may also help some care-givers, since I found that one of the most helpful things they could do for me at any particular moment was to just acknowledge what I was going through. Another part of the story has to do with my thoughts and feelings, especially in the later phases as my life, and that of my family, was increasingly being overturned. This psychological aspect was at least as difficult for me. And the third part, of course, is the spiritual aspect, which is inseparable from the other two. The story tries to deal with me as a whole person.

My dear wife Sandra went through every step of this with me (as did my children). In her own way this was just as deep and difficult an experience for her, and she and my children have helped me considerably in writing this account.

I do not intend this book to be in any way a prescription for other people. Everyone's experience is unique. Some of you know me very well, others hardly at all. Some of you share my faith; some do not. Some of you are going through serious afflictions of your own. But I do sincerely hope that all of you find it interesting and at least some parts of it to be of particular value to you.

I know you'll understand why what follows is rather introspective. It is, after all, my story.

Keith Dorricott, Toronto, Canada January 1998

(The author can be contacted at keithdorricott@gmail.com)

A Brief Chronology

April 1988	*I am diagnosed with C.L.L.*
December 1988	*We tell our daughters Adele and Jennifer*
August 1989	*We get a second opinion*
September 1989	*I begin Chlorambucil treatment (12 months)*
July 1991	*Dr. Brandwein takes over*
February 1992	*My first round of chemotherapy (5 months)*
February 1992	*We tell Andrew and then go public*
September 1992	*We try Fludarabine (for 6 months)*
December 1993	*Our daughter Adele is married*
February 1994	*We try various chemo protocols (6 months)*
April 1994	*We buy the condo at Grandview*
June 1994	*I begin writing a journal*
July 1994	*I take 2 months off work*
April 1995	*Serious infections and 2 more treatments*
August 1995	*I'm accepted for a bone marrow transplant*
September 1995	*I have splenectomy surgery*
November 1995	*Another treatment*
January 1996	*A final attempt - "salvage treatment"*
February 1996	*I'm turned down for the transplant*
August 1996	*I begin visiting Dr. Nusbaum*
January 1997	*New experimental treatments (for 4 months)*
April 1997	*My worst crisis - the pleural effusion*
May 1997	*I'm re-accepted for a transplant*
July 2, 1997	*The transplant process begins*
July 8, 1997	*"Day Zero" - I receive my new bone marrow*
August 7, 1997	*I'm released from Princess Margaret Hospital*
September 11,1997	*I'm diagnosed with CMV (Day 66)*
October 16, 1997	*The "100 days" high risk period is over*
January 8, 1998	*My six-month anniversary;*
	the beginning of "the rest of my life".

Contents

1. The Diagnosis

(April 1988 to August 1989)

I was diagnosed with leukemia in April 1988. It came totally out of the blue. I was 45 years old, and had gone to Dr. Peter Kopplin at St. Michael's Hospital in downtown Toronto for my annual physical checkup, as arranged by my employer, the Bank of Montreal. Dr. Kopplin was often quite casual in conversation and enjoyed hearing news from the Bank. But when he called me back a few days later he was quite serious. He said my blood results were a bit irregular and he wanted to repeat the tests. I went in to see him again and had them take some more blood. He called again a few days later and said that the results were the same. My white cell count was about 20 (that is 20,000 cells per cubic millilitre of blood); the normal range is 4 to 11. And that's when he first mentioned the word. He said "this can sometimes be an indication of leukemia. I'd like you to see a hematologist".

And so I went to see Dr. Butler, in his office at St. Michael's. Dr. Butler was an older man, fatherly in manner and, I would find out later, only three years from retirement. He repeated the blood test and also performed a bone marrow aspiration and biopsy, the first of several I would have over the next few years. And then he confirmed the diagnosis: I had chronic lymphocytic leukemia ("C.L.L."). Me!

The truth of that Bible verse "Do not boast about tomorrow, for you do not know what a day may bring forth." was never more real than that day. My whole life had been altered in a moment! From that day on it has never been out of my mind. It was April 28th, 1988.

Dr. Butler told me that this was the most common form of leukemia, and that it was largely confined to middle-aged and older men. Leukemia is cancer of the blood - one type of cell growing out of control and not knowing how to die, eventually interfering with the production of other cells. The pace of growth at this point was not known. "Lymphocytic" refers to the type of cell that turns malignant, the lymphocyte. Blood has many types of cells in it but there are four main ones: hemoglobin (red) - for supplying oxygen; platelets (small particles) - for clotting and stopping bleeding; neutrophils or granulocytes (white) - an important part of the immune system against infection; and lymphocytes (white) - also part of the immune system. Neutrophils particularly fight bacterial infections, while healthy lymphocytes work against viral infections. (Of course I didn't know any of this at the time.) Other symptoms included swollen lymph nodes (I'd had a couple of those in my neck for some time, which had been quite noticeable), and loss in weight (which also gradually became more noticeable).

Immediately a flood of questions came into my mind, and so I asked him: How bad was it ? (Not very bad at present.) How fast would it progress? (He didn't know; some people can leave it untreated for many years.) What's the treatment? (Nothing at present, eventually chemotherapy). Can you cure it? (No, but hopefully we can manage it successfully for a long while to maintain your quality of life.) And then the big one - what's my life expectancy? (After a lot of humming and hawing and "it depends", "maybe ten to fifteen years".) That was almost ten years ago.

10 to 15 years! Instantly I did the math. In ten years I would be only 55 years old and Andrew, my youngest child, would be only 18! Far too young to be without a dad. And my daughters Jennifer and Adele would only be 24 and 28, and Sandra would be far too young to be widow.

Immediately, but not at all deliberately, I sized up my life. Were there things I had wanted to achieve in any aspect of my life that I had not yet done? And the answer came back to me quickly - 'no'. Whether it was my family life, my career, or my church life, I did not feel that I had mountains left to climb. And yet I very much wanted to live. Why? I thought a lot about that, and the same two-fold answer always came back to me - to be there for my family - my wife Sandra, and my children Adele, Jennifer, and Andrew - they needed me; and to fulfil the purpose that God has for my life - which is what gives my life its fullest meaning. What I did not know at that point was that this whole experience of my illness would steadily intensify and become very much a journey of discovery for me - a discovery of myself, of my relationships with other people, and of my ministry for God. That process is still very much in progress.

That first night of course I had the horrible task of reporting the news to Sandra, sitting in our living room. She was shocked, and actually felt her heart miss a couple of beats. But she was very supportive and, as became common, full of more questions for the doctor than I had thought of. She wanted to know, for example, why there would not be an advantage to treating this as soon as possible, rather than waiting until it progressed. She began to do research of her own, finding books and enquiring at the Institute for Sports Medicine where she worked. Her research showed average duration from diagnosis to death was seven years!

She also asked Dr. Butler at an early meeting what was the possibility of a bone marrow transplant. He replied that it wasn't possible. I was over the limit of forty years of age, and even then they would only try it if possible when they had run out of all treatment options.

Should we tell the children right away? I asked Dr. Butler for his advice. How old were they, he wanted to know. Adele was 17 and Jennifer 14 - and so he suggested we tell them. But he thought it was still too early to tell Andrew who was not quite 8. It was during the Christmas holidays that year that we told the girls one at a time. They took it better than I had expected (at least outwardly), with just a few questions. Fortunately I was still looking well at that stage and quite active, which helped a lot. But it was very hard. "What a rotten piece of news to have to give to your own kids", I thought to myself. I would never get used to doing that.

Seven years later, in 1995, a young teenage friend of Andrew's, Sara Neely, wrote me a lovely letter telling me how she was praying for me every day. She was doing a school project on leukemia (it was because I had it, I found out later), and wondered if I'd mind answering a few questions for her. I replied "not at all". I was finding it helped me to talk about it to others who were interested. One of the questions she asked me was

"When you first heard you had leukemia, what did you think?".
I had to pause; it had been a long time since I'd reflected back
those seven years to my initial reaction. I replied in part:

*"I was a bit numb. It was almost like it wasn't real at first. I
went home and told Sandra and she was pretty devastated. But we
both had so many questions because we knew so little about it. I
tried to remember everything the doctor had told me and we tried to
concentrate on the positive things, such as: this is the most common
form of leukemia in men; they had diagnosed it early; it didn't always
shorten your lifespan if it develops very slowly; I didn't have to go on
any treatment right away; I don't feel any symptoms. It's amazing
how you can do a review of your life in what seems a few seconds. I
wasn't angry or afraid. I felt totally dependent on God who I knew
had everything in control. I wasn't even tempted to ask why all this
was happening. You can't predict how you're going to react; you just
react. My overwhelming concern was for my wife and my children
because I felt so responsible for them. Telling them was very hard."*

There is no way I could have prepared myself for news like
that. It's amazing the thoughts I had when the reality hit me
that I had a fatal illness - that this could kill me. My perspective
on what was important changed instantly. I realized how much
I took for granted. Now everything else got pushed into the
background of my mind. But I didn't have any symptoms; I
didn't feel sick. I didn't want people other than my immediate
family to know at that time; and I didn't want to be thought of as
an invalid. Apart from a few people commenting on the fact that
I had lost weight, nothing else was said. As I had previously been
on a light diet to reduce my weight from 165 lb. to about 155, I
had a good (if not totally accurate) answer for them.

The proverbial lifetime flashing before your eyes happened to me. I reviewed in split seconds what I had accomplished in my life - my aspirations, my successes, and my shortcomings. And to my surprise, I was generally content with my life at that point. I had a wonderful family whom I adored. I was so proud of them all. We'd travelled to many cities and countries in the world and we'd had some great vacations. I had a full and busy spiritual life, active in the things of God, which I believed to be the things of most lasting value. Career-wise, I had exceeded every expectation; I had reached the top of my profession as a chartered accountant and had been able to provide adequately for my family's financial future. No, there were no great unfulfilled dreams, no great regrets or disappointments. Life had been good and I had enjoyed very good health. My aspirations revolved around my family's futures. I so much wanted the best for them.

And then something else occurred to me. I knew from the Bible that sickness can sometimes (not always) be the result of unresolved conflict and wrongdoing in a person (the verse in 1 Corinthians 11:30 came to me: *"for this reason many are weak and sick among you"*, referring in this case to misconduct in connection with the Lord's supper). And so I turned my attention to a self-examination. Did I have unconfessed sin? But my conscience was clear.

In the summer of 1989 we thought it wise to seek a second medical opinion. Not that we lacked any confidence in Dr. Butler, but a second opinion is often a good thing. As a result Sandra and I met with Dr. Garvey, head hematologist at St. Mike's. She gave a very full explanation and confirmed completely the diagnosis and treatment strategy, which was very reassuring. As we were to realize so many times, it helped so much when my doctor told me the whole story without either watering it down or embellishing it. It's usually better to know.

To that point I had often referred to my disease as "a serious blood disorder", although I began to think that when I eventually told people, some of them might assume I had AIDS. It was Dr. Garvey who said to me: "Yes it's a blood disorder, but it's also leukemia. Say it, spit it out, and get on with it".

2. The Treatments Begin

(September 1989 to February 1992)

In September 1989 Dr. Butler started me on Chlorambucil pills - one a day for 5 days per month for six months. (Later Sandra told me that the text on our calendar that day had been "*I set before you the way of life*" from Jeremiah 21:8.) By this time my white blood count was in the 70's (normal is 4 to 11). The Chlorambucil brought it down to the 20's again, but it stayed there, and then began to climb again. I was having monthly checkups at this point. (I wish I had a penny for every time they've poked me in the arm over the years to take blood or insert an intravenous needle.) In early 1991 Dr. Butler would have prescribed something else but, since he was about to retire, he thought that his successor should be the one to decide. When I pressed him, his prognosis at the time was that I had one to two years to live, due to the advancing rate of the disease, quite a different story from two years before.

One to two years! That changes everything. Whew - it's hard to grasp the reality of a prognosis like that. How could the leukemia have progressed so quickly and we not have realized it? One to two years! Why didn't he tell me before this?

I began to pray and rely on God much more heavily. But my faith in God was no "death-bed conversion". I've been a believer in Christ as my Saviour and Lord almost all my life, and as committed a Christian as I could be. As a result prayer had always been important to me, especially in making big decisions and dealing with big problems. There were going to be none bigger than this.

For some strange reason, I didn't immediately beseech the Lord to cure me then and there. I'm not sure why. I think I was still searching for the reason, wondering if God maybe had some plan in all this, or if there was some underlying cause I needed to discern. It was a little later before I was seized with the need to be very explicit and earnest with the Lord as to what I wanted Him to do. I remember reading the story of the poor blind man Bartimeus in Mark chapter 10 who heard Jesus was coming and yelled at the top of his voice *"Jesus, Son of David, have mercy on me"*. Despite the huge crowd, Jesus stopped and said an amazing thing *"What do you want me to do for you?"*. Wasn't it obvious what he needed? *"Lord, that I may receive my sight"*. And Jesus restored his sight - but he had to ask. So I began to make sure God wasn't in any doubt about what I wanted.

In July 1991 I was assigned to Dr. Joseph Brandwein, who had recently been brought over from Toronto General Hospital as a hematologist with experience in bone marrow transplants. When I first met him he looked so young and reserved; but he was very fulsome in his information and answers to me. I saw him in the Medical Day Care Clinic.

I found that first visit quite disorienting. Instead of what I had been used to, a private appointment in Dr. Butler's office (on schedule), I had to wait a long time in the waiting room with a TV blaring. (I came to realize why they call us "patients" and I admit I wasn't very patient the first few months. It was something else I had to learn.) I didn't know any of the nursing staff at that time. It seemed so impersonal and routine, and this was life and death for me. Over the years, however, as I returned to Day Care on 7F (7th floor, F wing) time after time after time, I came to love those people - Yvonne and Elizabeth and Rita and others - and to develop a huge respect for their ability and dedication. And I came to realize I had been given the best possible doctor for me.

Between 1988 and 1992 no one else but my immediate family knew about my leukemia and life carried on fairly normally, although it was never out of my mind. It was during this time, in October 1990, that I was asked to speak at the funeral of Mrs. Mary Beck, a long-time friend of the family, who had died of acute leukemia. As you can imagine, when her husband Doug and the Beck family found out later that I had leukemia myself at the time, they were amazed. But it was early enough in my illness that it wasn't having a major impact.

I remember one day in particular in September 1991 when I was in Bermuda on business. I was riding a moped after work, and I couldn't get my illness out of my mind. It was one of the relatively few times when I've felt really down about it, because generally I have not felt overly depressed (although I've certainly had my moments). I remember stopping at a bookstore in the little town of Hamilton (beside "the Birdcage") and reading one or two books about it. I think that was the first time I had done that. But to think that it was three and a half years since my diagnosis before I had done any "research" of my own on this illness.

Looking back, I can see that in this early phase I was very accepting of my condition. I wouldn't quite call it denial. I knew I had it and I knew it was fatal, and it was never far from my conscious thoughts during all my waking hours. But I relied heavily on the doctors (they were the experts, after all); I relied on Sandra (who was leaving nothing to chance and checking out every available source, while being a bit frustrated with me); and I relied on God having everything under control (but almost blindly).

In February 1992 I began real chemotherapy intravenously (the "CVP" regimen, each letter standing for a different drug), but as an out-patient. (By this time my bone marrow had been completely replaced by the C.L.L.) Immediately my appearance began to change. I lost weight, my skin became taut and brittle, and my dark hair began to fall out, leaving only the grey. I got to hate the way I looked, and so I avoided looking in a mirror. My voice became very weak and unpredictable. It eventually put an end to my participation in our informal singing group which I had enjoyed so much. And I became very tired and lethargic. (I can remember sitting in my office at work one day waiting to go in to make a financial presentation to the Board of Directors, when I fell asleep in my chair. Normally I would have been quite keyed up. That was a scary feeling.)

I learned that chemo has a delayed effect. I would spend the mornings in the clinic (three to five days a week, once every five weeks) and then go back to work. But a couple of days later it would start to hit me. With these early doses the nausea wasn't too bad, but the weakness and "flu-like symptoms" were severe. But then after a week or so I'd start to recover until I felt human again. Then it was time to do it all over again. I wasn't sure which was worse - the disease or the treatment.

Chemotherapy works like a shotgun, not a rifle. Its job is to kill cells. But it kills all types of blood cells, not just malignant ones. It makes all the blood counts go low, often requiring transfusions until they recover. The drop in hemoglobin causes loss of energy due to the lower oxygen level; the drop in platelets increases the risk of bleeding; and the drop in neutrophils suppresses the immune system and so made me susceptible to infection, which is potentially the greatest problem.

I would sit in the chair in Day Care watching that toxic fluid drip into my vein hour by hour. Sometimes I'd read; sometimes I wouldn't. The patients seldom spoke much to each other, but we spoke a lot with the nurses. I would watch them working - never stopping for a break, always knowing just what to do, always with a smile, so sensitive to how we were all feeling - special people. And I only once in all the years heard a patient complain about it all. There's an unspoken bond between the patients. Everyone's circumstances are a bit different, but everyone is going through their own particular nightmare. But I saw a lot of kindness in that room over the years.

My frequent visits to the clinic at the hospital involved having them take my blood and then waiting an hour or two for the results to come back from the laboratory, while waiting nervously to hear what they were that particular time. We "lived and died" by those counts. My spirits (and Sandra's when I immediately phoned her each time) went up and down with the numbers on those sheets of paper.

One of the more pleasant aspects of my job as an executive at the Bank has been to be on the Board of Directors of the Bank's subsidiaries in Barbados in the Caribbean, which involved travelling there usually twice a year, sometimes with Sandra. As a result we have made some very good friends of the other directors and their wives - Trevor and Sharon Carmichael, Paul and Rachelle Altman, Steve and Bobbie Emptage and Brad and Jane Bellis - all of whom have been very supportive throughout my illness. In December 1991, when Sandra and I were on the island having dinner together alone one evening, we decided the time had just about come to tell our young son Andrew about my leukemia. He would soon be twelve years old. That following February we were planning to go to Walt Disney World as a family, and we decided that this would be the best time to break the news to him. Here's how it happened...

We were booked into the Contemporary Resort on the grounds. As soon as we got there, Andrew said to me "Dad, let's go for a ride on the monorail". I agreed and thought this would be the best opportunity to tell him - alone, and with the whole, enjoyable vacation ahead of us. I had a lot of butterflies in my stomach on that monorail. Telling him my news was "job one"; I couldn't put it off. When we got off the train I suggested we go over and sit on a wall overlooking the lake, as there was something I had to tell him. I could see Sandra watching nervously from a distance. I told him the whole story and he reacted very maturely. He just listened carefully and told me everything would be all right. Whew! That was tough. I hate giving my family bad news but for them, like me, it's better to know.

Andrew had been studying blood cells at school and he said "well you could live over ten years with this". That was almost twice the length of his lifetime to that date, and it seemed long enough at that stage to feel a bit better about it.

The next morning when I got up, a lot of my hair was on the pillow and some more came out in the shower. I had just completed my first treatment three weeks previously. That was my initial experience of hair loss and I found it very traumatic. First my hair became lifeless and brittle, then it started to come out in my comb. (In the future, the speed and extent of hair loss in each case would depend on what particular chemotherapy drugs I had been on.) Then it fell out by itself, on everything my head touched. There were hairs everywhere. Sandra bought one of those rollers of sticky paper that are used for picking up fallen hair from cats and dogs; it worked very well.

I found myself admiring people will full heads of hair. I'd see a shampoo commercial on TV and think "that's easy for you to say". The way I was beginning to look, it was going to be hard to keep this thing a secret any longer. And now that all the children knew, perhaps the time had finally come to let people know. I wasn't looking forward to this.

3. Going Public

(February 1992 to June 1994)

Also in early 1992 I was promoted at work from Executive Vice-President & Chief Financial Officer to a new position as Vice Chairman, Corporate Services. (Corporate Services included all the staff functions across the Bank - finance, human resources, internal audit, real estate, law, public affairs, economics, strategic planning and one or two others.). When I was approached about this by my boss Matt Barrett, the Chairman and CEO, I felt I must tell him about my condition. I told him I would do the job to the best of my ability but that I could not devote any more hours in the week than I already was (which were plenty). He accepted that, and said my health must always come first. He has never relented on that, for which I am extremely grateful.

After telling Andrew, there was a whole communication program we had to embark on to inform people in the right sequence. My appearance made it necessary to let people know. I could see people looking at me, and some of the older ones would ask me questions. (Generally I found the younger people didn't say much, probably not knowing what to say.) I remember at the Easter 1992 church Conference in Brantford, an older lady said to me: "Keith, you don't look like yourself". I replied: "Why, who do I look like?" But I was getting tired of giving evasive answers. Sandra and the two girls were getting even more questions than I was, and it was very hard on them.

The first of all to be told was my mother. We brought her home overnight after the Conference and I sat her down in our family room and spelled it all out for her. She listened intently and took the news surprisingly well. She asked me some questions, encouraged me for what lay ahead, and then left me with one of her characteristic sayings, which she has used subsequently many times: "Go with God, my son".

My illness has been hard on my mother. She lives out of town and doesn't get to see us as often as she used to. She's in her eighties and sometimes the information she gets from us and through other people is confusing to her. She's lived alone since my father died twenty-one years ago and is lonely, because she's a people person. But she's a godly woman and very definitely a woman of prayer. She often reminds me that I'm always in her thoughts and in her prayers.

She loves to reminisce. She's often told me how she prayed for a son who would be a man of God. I was born six weeks' prematurely, as a result of my mother taking a hard fall in the garden in pouring rain. It was the height of World War II and a total blackout was in effect where we lived, the south-west coast of Scotland. With my mother in labour, a neighbour who was a taxi driver had to drive the car at night without lights (or street lights) several miles from our small village to the nearest town, West Kilbride. He could have been jailed for being out of his territory because of the war conditions. The town only had a senior citizens' home; it was impossible to try to get to a hospital. And that's where I was born - on February 6th, 1943. The only person able to deliver me was an army nurse who had just arrived from London, still in her war uniform; she had come up for a break to visit her friend who ran the home. I was so tiny I could fit on a hot water bottle and I was without my top layer of skin. Later the doctor said that I couldn't possibly live because I was "coal-black" with jaundice. He cautioned my mother: "Don't waste any love on that little thing; he's not going to make it!". But Mom is not easily put off. And so the miracles began early in my life. Later when I was leaving the Boys' High School in Scotland to emigrate with my family at age eleven, the headmaster told her "Keith will never amount to much - he's too independent". I attribute a great deal to her motherly and godly care over the years. I honour her and I love her.

I'm named Keith for a special reason. My father had been married for a brief period prior to marrying my mother, but his wife Ida had died of sinusitis within three years of their wedding day. She had been ill for eighteen months and my father spent a lot of time with her at the hospital. Her doctor showed her such care during that time that my father went to thank him especially afterwards. He replied by simply quoting the Lord's words in Matthew 25:40 (which incidentally is the motto of St. Michael's Hospital): "inasmuch as you did it to one of the least of these my brethren, you did it to me". The man was a Christian; and his name was Dr. Keith. My father responded by saying: "If ever I have a son, I will name him Keith". I only learned that story on the day of my wedding, when my father told it at the reception (in the third person). He had experienced suffering in his life, and he would experience a lot more from the emphysema which would eventually kill him. But he had saved that story to tell me on my wedding day. I was very moved by it.

Then I wrote to my two aunts, Aunt Olga and Aunt Sheila, in Britain, and Sandra wrote to her side of the family over there. On Easter Sunday Sandra's sister Jessie "happened" to be having a family get-together in Brantford, at which we broke the news (and the mood). I told my local church elders and then had an announcement made to the whole congregation. At that time I was in the middle of giving my series of Bible presentations to them on "The Eternal Purpose" - God's master plan for the ages. The news then spread like wildfire. In the announcement I asked them not to hesitate to speak to me about my illness at any time, but to be very sensitive in how they spoke with Sandra and the children about it. I also asked for their fervent prayer privately and collectively. They have certainly honoured those requests over the years.

Having a lot of other people know about my leukemia also made it a bit more real to members of my family. It was talked about more openly, and my life was being altered by it significantly for the first time. The impact on them and on me became more evident. That added to our stress.

I continued on the conventional chemotherapy (the "CVP" protocol) from February to June 1992 at roughly 5-week intervals (three days each time), but with little response. Then Dr. Brandwein managed to get a hold of Fludarabine - an experimental new drug being clinically tested in the U.S. Somehow he got permission to bring it into Canada and I switched to that from September 1992 to February 1993 (six cycles). Again I took it as an out-patient by I.V., three days every five weeks. Because it was experimental, Dr. Brandwein himself rather than a nurse had to hang it from the I.V. pole. I remember coming into Day Care on the Tuesday morning for my second dose, after having received the first one the day before, and they all hovered around me wanting to know how I had reacted to it. "Well, I got in nine holes of golf last night", I replied, and so the crowd (and the concern) dissipated pretty quickly. Overall I tolerated the Fludarabine very well; the side effects were virtually nil. My white count came down right away, but my platelet count was very slow to recover. However, after this, I was able to stay off treatment for almost a full year, until February 1994, which made 1993 a very good year.

In April 1992 I visited The House of Masters and got fitted for a full hair system - a customized wig. It took over six weeks to arrive. I was to find out that the whole experience of losing my hair and having to wear a wig would be emotionally very difficult for me.

In August 1992, Sandra and I were able to take a delightful cruise to Alaska to celebrate our twenty-fifth wedding anniversary. I thought to myself: may we have many more anniversaries together. We've since had five.

After the year's respite throughout 1993, in February 1994 I went on an experimental regimen called "2CDA" (from the Fludarabine family), but it seriously depressed my platelets and had to be discontinued after one cycle. Dr. Brandwein then put me on a different conventional regimen ("CNOP"). It contained prednisone, which made me jumpy, hyper and unable to sleep. I had four sessions of that. Blood transfusions and platelet transfusions became common. I normally received two units of blood, which took over four hours to transfuse. I would often look up at the bag of blood going into me and think "someone gave that for me - the gift of life". But I was never, of course, allowed to know who had given it. Platelet transfusions are generally five units but usually take under an hour, but I had to take them with medications to prevent an adverse reaction.

After this I began to get involved at work promoting employee blood drives for the Red Cross, although I explained I was in no position myself to donate. It was also during this period, in a phone call from Sandra to Dr. Brandwein, that he told her that we could begin to expect that I would get heavy infections, not all of which could be cured. She asked when this might be, and he replied "in the next few months". I didn't find out about this conversation until much later.

In June 1994 I began five cycles of another protocol (Adriamycin, VP-16 and Prednisone), but bone marrow tests showed that my marrow remained "packed" with leukemia cells.

It was beginning to look as though I was approaching the point where I was running out of available treatments. My body was building up resistance to the ones I'd already had so that they could not be reused. Everything from now on would be experimental. Meanwhile we were trying to live as normal a life as possible. Sandra and I always made a point of fully informing the children of all developments and including them in all important decisions, but there was no doubt the tension was mounting and the future becoming a lot more uncertain. Then Matt Barrett suggested I take some time off work to give my body a break, and so I arranged to take off July and August.

4. Taking a Time-Out

(July 1994 to March 1995)

The previous summer our family had spent two weeks' vacation at Grandview Inn near Huntsville, Ontario, which we had noticed advertised in the paper. We liked it a lot and Sandra and I went up again for a weekend in the winter time in February 1994. It was then that we first began considering buying a condominium there. The one we liked in particular was unit 1411 - on the ground level with an indoor and outdoor deck, a walk-out door to the path along the lake, a sunken living room, and the best of all views overlooking Fairy Lake. We bought it, and moved in on June 28th. On July 1st, after visiting Jennifer and Andrew at the opening day of Mount Forest Camp, Sandra and I arrived to take up residence for the summer (with two-year old Jordan Kennedy, our first visitor, whom Sandra was looking after for the week to allow his mother Rachel to go to the camp). I was feeling far from well that first day. This was to be our home for my two-month break.

What a God-send that condo has been in the past four years. It has so often been a fortress for us in difficult times and times of big decisions. Not only have we ourselves enjoyed it, as a frequent last-minute get-away, but it's been a place others have been able to enjoy when they need it. Huntsville has a good regional hospital just five minutes from Grandview and several times, with Dr. Brandwein's permission, I have gone there for my blood tests and for transfusions, avoiding the two and a half hour trip to Toronto. The first time was on July 6th, at which my counts were: white cells-90 (normal: 4-11); hemoglobin-66 (normal: 130 and higher); platelets-19 (normal: 150 and higher). I received 2 units of blood, as I was generally transfused when my hemoglobin count went below 70 (or my platelets 10 or below). That's when I felt especially lethargic and dizzy, and my afternoon naps became more frequent. Dr. Brandwein told me that if my hemoglobin suddenly dropped to 70 or 80 from the normal level of 130 or more I would be out cold on the floor, but when it goes down gradually, the body has an amazing ability to adjust.

It was in June 1994 that I also started to keep a journal - not to write in every day, but to record periodically what was happening and my thoughts and questions about it all. I have found this to be very therapeutic, and I have kept it up to the present time. I did it just for me, not for anyone else to read. My first entry was on June 25th (a Saturday): "This is the greatest learning experience of my life", I wrote, "Today, if it were all over, if I were asked (for myself only), would you have willingly gone through what you have gone through so far for what you have learned and gained and the positive blessings you have seen, my answer would definitely be 'yes', believe it or not.".

The next day I received two surprise phone calls of support - from Ian Stewart in Glasgow, an old boyhood friend (the first contact with him in two years), and Charlie Dawn Williamson in Trinidad, Colorado. They both seemed to be messages from God. I have come to realize that God ministers to me in a wide variety of ways and through many different people, if I'm just alert enough to notice it. Marg Smith is a long-time friend who would later undergo radiation therapy at Princess Margaret Hospital; she and I made a deal based on the words of a song: "You pray for me, and I'll pray for you".

In June I had a good conversation with Rose Patten at work and shared my faith with her. She told me her own experience of surviving a serious car accident in 1983. She told me she too believed in the reality of prayer. She also told me the saying "coincidences are God's way of doing miracles anonymously". It's a cute saying, but it's amazing how many things seemed to just "happen", especially as I looked back over them. Like Romans 8:28 says: *"all things work together for good to those who love God and are the called according to His purpose"*.

We had a lot of visitors at the condo that year. The names filled up in the Visitors' Book. Greg and Liz Neely, and their boys, Jonathan and Aaron, were up one day, then Greg drove me back to Toronto for my chemo the next day. We had a good long talk - about the scriptures, about his diabetes, and about my leukemia. He is someone who shows real understanding and concern. He has been such a good friend during this. I've found that the best support is not people telling you things or saying everything will be all right, but instead genuinely asking questions and wanting to hear the answers, and listening attentively. That's what I find it takes for me to open up to people, which I need to do. I must remember that when I'm trying to minister to others,

I remember thinking. Greg is like that, and so is my young friend Shaun Clements.

On July 26th, 1994 I spent the day at House of Masters getting my hair piece fitted. I had lost so much hair in the past few weeks. Apparently 90% of the hair on the head is growing at any one time, and 10% is resting; it's the reverse with eyebrows and eyelashes. It's the follicles of the growing hair that are mostly affected by the drugs. Several times in stores I was being asked if I had a seniors' card! My hair now looked so straggly and lifeless that I was in no doubt that wearing a wig was the right thing to do, and now was the right time to do it, although I hated the idea of it. One thing chemotherapy does is force you to lose any pride of appearance. But God arranges the timing of these things, and I now felt ready to do it. Sandra came with me (thankfully) but she had to leave early. It only took about ten seconds for them to shave my head; now I know what I look like bald - not a pretty sight; I know why God designed us with hair. I was committed now. The whole fitting should have taken a couple of hours but it took over six hours. That's a long time to hold your breath, not knowing what you're going to look like. They had problems fitting it and then they didn't cut it short enough. They have to be careful - it won't grow again if they cut it too short. I felt like I looked like Shakespeare and I was getting very anxious, but eventually it was fine. Wearing it took quite a bit of getting used to. I kept wanting to take it off when I came inside or when I was praying, as though it were a hat. It was tough going out in public the first time. I knew most people could tell, but they acted like they didn't. Sandra's emotional support through it all was invaluable.

Cards and letters kept coming. Reading them reminded me of the constancy of God's care for me, through so many people.

I tried to keep them all, and I now have quite a collection. They were particularly encouraging during those many times when I was out of circulation, or "on the shelf" as I put it.

Early in August we got a card each and an audiotape from many of the young people in the church, singing for us. It was great. Sandra was visibly moved by it. They had made it specially for us. (Later Jeanine Madill in Vancouver, Jennie Thomas in Hamilton, Richard Drain in Belfast and the group at 1997 Family Camp at Mount Forest would do the same thing.) This was another of countless examples that our friends really do care. I prayed "Lord, help us not to get too self-centred in all this. Help us to act the same way to others in need." I think this is one of the greatest lessons for me in all this - to be more sensitive to others' problems; caring makes such a difference. I now tend to be much more sensitive when I see struggling seniors (they weren't always that way) and people with disabilities.

I hated having to give Sandra bad news after a doctor's visit. When my counts were worse she slumped noticeably. But I always had to tell her the whole truth. By August 31st my platelet count was down to 5, the lowest yet (normal is 150 and over); the lab had to count them by hand. I was pretty scared of bleeding or hemorrhaging and it not being able to stop. I also had some cramping in my left ankle. And so Dr. Wilson (at Huntsville) gave me 5 units of platelets on two successive days. (Interestingly, platelets are peach-coloured when they're being transfused.)

I managed to finish my "summer project". It was a booklet called "Uncovering the Pattern", the culmination of a lot of Bible Study over the past few years. Although I had made a comprehensive study of the Biblical position of the churches of God in which I worship on two previous occasions, this particular effort took a different approach. I received some valuable new insights from it. It's so important that if I'm devoting my life to this community of Christians that I be convinced that it's right. Perhaps that's what God had in mind by me starting the project. I know that my calling from God among His people is as a teacher and (small 'p') pastor, and I feel convinced that what He has shown to me and others has to be taught - both to those inside this community (so we'll value it more) and to others (because of the fragmentation that sadly exists among Christians today). Christ said clearly He wanted the unity to be a practical reality, on His terms. The force of that longing of His came through to me as I worked on this booklet.

It's always been important to me to "fulfil my ministry", as the apostle Paul put it. That's when I feel most useful. Merely living a long life but being of no use to God or anyone else is not very fulfilling. In my prayers, the reason I asked for healing and extension of my life was to fulfil God's purpose in my life - as a husband and father, and in my service for Him. Sandra needed a husband; Andrew, Jennifer and Adele needed a father. Becoming a grandfather to their children would also be a great bonus. "O God, may it be so", I prayed.

Although we had been back to Toronto several times during the summer, on September 3rd, 1994 we returned from the condo. Sandra had been at Teen Camp cooking that last week. She had been reluctant to go there this time under the circumstances. Crowds sometimes bothered her, when they were asking a lot of questions about me, and she was having to deal with it. (People often waited until I wasn't there and then asked her about me. I would have preferred they had asked me directly.) There was no question she was suffering at least as much as I was. If I died she'd be the one who'd be left. How would I feel if it were the other way around?

I let her down that summer. I had promised her that we'd have good long regular talks about everything that was going on, and we didn't. I was often too busy with other things. That needed to become a bigger priority with me. She needed to talk about things, and I needed to be better at letting her know what I thought, without reservation. And I found that hard. We tended to protect each other. We were so concerned about making it worse for each other that we each tended to hold back. One Saturday she said to me with a frightened look in her eyes: "I'm terrified that you're going to die"!

Back in May if you'd told me we'd have spent two largely delightful months up north, I'm not sure I'd have believed it. Back then it looked like no treatment was working and that I'd be spending a lot of the summer in hospital. I thank God for the way it turned out - the relaxation and fresh air were marvellous.

I was well enough to make a trip to England in early September to attend the Churches of God Elders' Conference. I wanted very much to go, but if God intervened I would of course have had to accept it (and I know Sandra would have been relieved). However I made the trip, although not in the best of health. Dr. John Terrell was assigned to the room next door and he was very good at looking out for me, and giving me medication so I could sleep a bit.

I went back to work after I returned from England after my two months' leave. I was in an unsettled state of mind, although I had missed the people. I found that when you've been away for a while, you lose your place in things, and the business just keeps humming along without you. I have no particular ambitions for position with respect to secular work, just to do the very best I can do, but there are aspects I enjoy and that I'm good at. I realized that I definitely needed the stimulation and the sense of accomplishment and contribution. It didn't take long I found, however, to be right back in the thick of things.

Meanwhile I always prayed that whatever happened would be to God's glory. It says about Samson in the Old Testament that he accomplished more in his death than he did in life; Peter in the New Testament was told by Christ "*by what death he should glorify God*". Perhaps my near-death experience will be to God's glory, I thought. When Christ was troubled about His own impending death, rather than asking to be preserved from it, He prayed "*Father, glorify your name*". That was the paramount thing. Witnessing for Christ had never been easy for me; I deeply wish I'd done it more. I'd been too private about my faith. I was so grateful for the opportunities that this illness had given me to speak about it in a meaningful way to some colleagues at work. (My friend Fred Marks told me he was praying that through this some of the senior executives at the Bank would come to know the Lord personally.) I wanted my healing to bring great credit to God. I even visualized it happening - the doctors double-checking, everyone amazed. But the thought came to me - could that happen if I was on chemo? With so much prayer going up for me for so long, was my recovery being delayed because the credit would go to the doctors and the medicine? I didn't know. But I wondered sometimes.

I still puzzled over some of the scriptural promises and teaching regarding healing. They weren't completely clear to me, although obviously it was very personally relevant. I did know that God can't go against His own word; He's bound Himself by it. That's why I needed to understand it so carefully. Isaiah 53:4 says "*surely He has borne our griefs, and carried our sorrows*". Literally it means that He has carried away our sicknesses and our infirmities. But would that be fulfilled in our lifetimes or only in the future? And Psalm 103 says that God heals all our diseases. The Lord and His apostles healed many people miraculously when they were here, to give proof of their divine authority. But Paul didn't heal everyone (e.g. *"Trophemus I left sick"*) and he didn't heal himself of his own disability; God said to him: *"My grace is sufficient for you"*. And the Lord Jesus Himself said that those who were sick needed a physician.

Then there were those tricky verses in James 5:14,15 which have had so many interpretations: *"Is anyone among you sick? Let him call for the elders of the church, and let them pray over him, anointing him with oil in the name of the Lord. And the prayer of faith will save the sick, and the Lord will raise him up. And if he has committed sins, he will be forgiven."*. Did it just apply where the sickness was due to sin? Did I have unconfessed sin? I thought a lot about that. But I didn't think so. The anointing with oil that's referred to in that verse was a Jewish custom. Did it apply to Christians today? Or did it just refer indirectly to the use of medicine? There were so many different opinions. I wasn't sure, and this was not just a theoretical question for me. And so I asked God for the answer to that, too. I did know my elders were praying for me. In fact their uniting in prayer for me perhaps brought us closer together than many of our meetings could have. God does work in mysterious ways, and I still had so much to learn about them.

And then I realized: God (alone) has the power to heal me, and He could do it instantly - but to what avail? So that I'd be just the same as I had been before? He had a much bigger job in mind than that - He wanted to change me, and that was going to take time and my willing consent. And it could be painful, as I was going to find out.

29

Keith Dorricott

Meanwhile our short-term prayer was for peace of mind and strengthened faith. Sandra was such a wonderful supporter to me, and eased my life in a hundred ways, and was so very capable. From time to time both she and I struggled to have that peace of mind that Philippians 4:6,7 talks about:

"Be anxious for nothing, but in everything by prayer and supplication, with thanksgiving, let your requests be made known to God; and the peace of God, which surpasses all understanding, will guard your hearts and minds through Christ Jesus."

It sounded so simple, and yet it was sometimes so elusive. It was so much easier to lose than to get back. Sandra would sometimes tell me how she felt Satan was directly attacking her, causing doubts and fears to resurface in her mind. "Remember what the doctor said. You know they can't cure this. You know each time is getting worse, and he's running out of time." Sometimes it was almost unbearable.

5. A Turn for the Worse

(April to July 1995)

By April 1995 my white count was again very high and I was in line for further treatment. As my body's immune system developed a resistance to previous drugs, it made it very difficult to repeat the same protocol effectively. Chemotherapy has a cumulatively damaging effect on the body. (Plus, how many dozen times can your arms be poked to give blood or receive intravenous needles? After a while the veins collapse.) This time it would be for a "DHAP salvage regimen", as an in-patient for the first time. I asked for a respite until May, to tidy things up at work. But before I was scheduled to go in for the chemo I had to be admitted for an infection. I had just finished a Board of Directors' presentation at work and felt ill, so I went home and then into the Emergency Department at St. Mike's. I thought my hemoglobin might be low, but instead I had a high fever. (I had standing instructions to go right to Emergency any time my temperature reached 39C.) It turned out to be "staphylococcal pneumonia".

I was in hospital a week, then home a week, then back in a second time for the treatment. As I was getting into the bed on arrival that second time, Dr. Brandwein came in and asked me if I had a sister called Hilary. A few weeks before he had suggested that both my sisters, Shirley and Hilary, be tested for a possible match on bone marrows in the event a bone marrow transplant became a possibility; both of them had previously volunteered to donate their bone marrow if that option were ever offered to me. When I said yes, he told me that she was "a 6 out of 6 identical match" - which is the best possible match! Knowing how hard it is to find a matched donor, we were ecstatic and saw it as a door being opened by the Lord. Little did we know all that would have to transpire first.

As was so often the case, it was only later that I stopped to reflect on what had just happened. Initially Dr. Butler had ruled out a transplant. Back then the age limit was forty; after that they considered it to be too risky. And there were very few ever done for C.L.L. patients like me, anywhere in the world. And so on the one hand a transplant represented a last resort when I was out of options; on the other hand it represented one shot at a solution. It was almost too much to hope for. And what were my chances of finding a donor anyway? I had heard and read of many cases where no match could be found, despite an international registry of donors. It was a very complicated formula. Dr. Brandwein had told me that if they didn't find a match in either of my two siblings, they wouldn't search any farther. I knew Shirley and Hilary had been tested. But I was almost afraid to find out the result. I didn't enquire. I just waited to be told. And now he'd told me - and I had a match! My little sister, whom I had wanted to be a boy when she was born, might save my life. And I know that Shirley, three years older than me, would have done it just as willingly. Wow!

At this point we were advised that both North York and Brantford assemblies of the church were having several special prayer meetings for us. Then two phone calls arrived from England, from friends John Archibald and Graeme Bennison, to assure us of their remembrance. Graeme's father and mine had been best of friends. At that point Graeme had an advanced case of lymphoma and couldn't have any more chemo until his blood improved. He and I were kindred spirits in a way, and we often thought of them dealing with their own struggle. We kept in touch with Graeme and his wife Jane periodically until he passed away early in 1996.

My daughter Jennifer started her first day of summer interning with the chartered accounting firm of Coopers & Lybrand on May 8th - one week after her final Bachelor of Commerce exam at University of Toronto. That week included for her a cross-Canada drive to Vancouver with her friend Wendie Edwards. A lot was happening in her life too those days. It seemed that whenever she had a big event in her life, such as a tough exam, I wasn't doing very well, which just added to her pressure. She didn't say much about it, but I know she worried a lot.

Like me, Jennifer is a middle child, and she's like me in several other ways (although a lot prettier). She completed her Bachelor of Commerce degree at University of Toronto at age 22 and is now early in her career with Coopers & Lybrand, as well as being immersed in her studies for acquiring her chartered accounting (C.A.) designation. She's done so well. She's athletic, musical, and does beautiful cross-stitch work, and she needs those outlets. She has many friends but, by nature, is quite careful who she opens up to about her innermost feelings. She's very loyal and sensible. She visited me a lot in hospital and was always very willing to help. I love her dearly and am very fond of her and want so much for her to continue to have the best in life. She still lives at home with us; I realize one of these days she'll decide to move out, but I'll definitely miss her when she does.

I was in hospital for a week for the chemo, then home for a week to recover. What a week that was! I felt just awful and time dragged by, day and night, in five minute segments. I couldn't get comfortable sitting or lying. I wished I could have just shut off my mind until it was over. I lost at least 15 pounds and became skin and bone. I eventually dropped to 113 pounds that November (1995). I looked half dead and hadn't the energy to talk, read, watch TV, or listen to music. I found it hard to pray. (Thank God for the intercession of the Holy Spirit because of our weakness - Romans 8:26, and for so many people who assured us they were praying on our behalf.) Laurie Gillespie of Vancouver (we were each "best man" at the other's wedding) was in town and came by for a one-hour visit. We hadn't seen each other for a long time. It was good to see him, but it was a real struggle just to be able to keep up a conversation with anyone. I just had no energy, and Laurie is always bursting with it.

On the Saturday we went up to the condo at Grandview, which was probably a mistake. On Sunday Rodney Falconer and other young people who were at his parents' cottage nearby helped Sandra bring our new boat from Peninsula Lake through the canal to our dock. It was a wild, stormy day and they had a terrible time with it. But apparently I was insistent that it got done. I felt so helpless not being able to do the things I thought I should do. It was a major frustration to see all the burden for the house and the family and caring for me landing primarily on Sandra.

That day my condition got worse and we came home to Toronto that evening. When I got home I had a high temperature and so had to immediately go downtown to Emergency at St. Mike's. Again I was admitted with an undiagnosed infection. This time they were able to diagnose it from the blood culture; it was a strep infection in the blood, which is serious. I was put on the antibiotic Vancomycin for four weeks. I also had pneumonia and fluid around the lung, which had to be drained, by tapping it through my back by means of a needle and suction tube. I also had several blood and platelet transfusions. I reacted to one of the platelet transfusions and went into shock. Fortunately Sandra was there at the time and quickly got Dr. Brandwein who was able to deal with it immediately. They also put me on oxygen as I was "saturating" at less than 90% (normal is 98% and up); that meant there was insufficient oxygen in my blood and so not enough was getting to my brain. I had several chest X-rays.

After the next chemo I got really sick again, with more fluid around the lung that had to be tapped twice more. At this point Sandra began thinking in terms of making arrangements for a funeral (but kept those thoughts to herself).

It was around this time that Sandra first said to me "If ever you've had enough of these treatments, that's O.K.; you just have to say so". In all the many days I have spent in hospital since May 1995, not once has Sandra missed being with me for several hours, meeting my every need, even on the two days a week that she worked at the Institute for Sports Medicine. At times the burden must have been unbearable, running the house, worrying about the others at home. And she suffers from the most terrible migraine headaches. And yet every day she would come in looking her best. What a gift.

I was sent home after ten days on "Home Care". A St. Elizabeth's nurse came into our home at 9 a.m. and 9 p.m. to administer the Vancomycin through a "saline lock" inserted in my arm (which could be connected and disconnected from the I.V.), and also "GCSF" growth factor injections to boost the production of my neutrophil immune white cells. I was also on oxygen for a while, with a long tube stretching through the house to the supply tank. Naturally Sandra learned how to do everything quite quickly and so we were able to dispense with the nurse for the last few days, which also let us get up to Grandview again, this time with the doctor's consent and a referral letter to Huntsville Hospital.

Andrew was an assistant counsellor at Mount Forest Camp that year. It was great to see him and Jennifer carrying on that work that I was no longer able to do after doing it for twenty years. From all reports they're both pretty good at it.

Like Adele, Andrew's birth arrived quite suddenly, and on the way home from the hospital I remembering hearing my favourite poem on the radio - Rudyard Kipling's "If" - spoken by a father to his son. My father had recited it to me at my wedding. Part of it goes as follows:

> *"If you can dream, and not make dreams your master;*
> *If you can think, and not make thoughts your aim;*
> *If you can meet with triumph and disaster,*
> *And treat those two impostors just the same;*
> *If you can bear to hear the truth you've spoken*
> *Twisted by knaves to make a trap for fools,*
> *Or watch the things you gave your life to, broken,*
> *And stoop and build them up with worn out tools;*

If you can walk with crowds and keep your virtue,

Or walk with kings, nor lose the common touch;

If neither foes nor loving friends can hurt you,

If all men count with you, but none too much;

If you can fill the unforgiving minute

With sixty seconds worth of distance run;

Yours is the earth, and everything that's in it,

And, what is more, you'll be a man my son!"

Andrew and I have always had a special father-son bond, which I cherish. He's very focussed on sports and one of the best experiences we had together was when I flew him on a surprise trip to Chicago one weekend in early 1995 to see his hero Michael Jordan, who had recently come back from retirement, at the United Centre. We had box seats, the Bulls beat the Cavaliers, and Michael was the game star. As a bonus, we also happened to stay in the hotel where the Cavaliers were staying and so he got to see some of them in the lobby. Then he visited the NikeTown store on Michigan Avenue, and then we hunted all over town and he finally found what was probably the last available number 45 Jordan basketball jersey. It was a great trip. On the flight home, he asked me: "Was this like that story you told me of the father who took his son to lots of baseball games, not because he loved baseball that much, but because he loved his son that much?" I told him he had it right.

When I was in hospital and Sandra was visiting, Andrew was often left alone in the evenings at home. But he had a circle of close friends and they kept in touch with him. We were always very appreciative of friends of his who would think to call to invite him for weekends - the Thomases, the Anthony's, the

Ramages, the Williams. He also had a support group of other students and a teacher at his school (Toronto District Christian High School) and he was able to open up a bit to them about how he was feeling. He admitted to me that initially he was quite angry about my illness and would rather have gone through the chemotherapy himself than see me suffer. We always tried to keep him fully informed and make him an important part of decisions that had to be made. He's just seventeen even now, but he knows his own mind and is a very considerate person. He has looked after me, often anticipating when I needed some assistance, and I love him dearly.

While I was home recuperating in June 1995 I would often sit out in the back garden, in the shade, and read or just think. I found the constant uncertainty in my life difficult to deal with, but I found I had a heightened appreciation for certain simple things: waking up and feeling good; enjoying a good meal; a sunny day; time spent with good friends; the beauty of nature.

I had two calls from Scotland. One from my Aunt Olga; both she and my Aunt Sheila have been very supportive throughout my illness, both by phone and through encouraging cards. The other was from Andy McIlree, a brother in our churches engaged in full-time ministry. Another evangelist, Allan Toms and his wife Gill from England were in town and came by for a visit. Allan showed real interest in my series on "The Eternal Purpose" for use on both radio and in Needed Truth magazine, and also in my booklet "Uncovering the Pattern" on which he gave me very useful feedback. He felt it was a unique presentation of scriptural teaching and that it should be published or videotaped. While my activities were very confined, I was encouraged by this because it was very important to me to be engaged in doing what little I could do.

The cards and phone calls kept coming. The assurances of continued prayer from so many was almost overwhelming. Surely God would hear. People were so kind. There was inevitably a bit of misinformation from time to time and it bothered Sandra more than it did me, I think. There were two special prayer meetings for two weeks again, this time in the churches in North York and Dundas, and perhaps elsewhere. And I found out that the elders in my local church (Des Clements, Geoff Hydon, Norman Kernaghan, Greg Neely and David Oji) had committed to meeting weekly to pray for me.

To begin with I found it embarrassing when I was present in a meeting when I was being prayed for (and it continued to be hard for family members). But I got over it, and began to realize the love and faith that motivated it. They were appealing directly to their heavenly Father - they weren't talking to me. And I've heard many lovely and heart-felt prayers being spoken for me and my family. It is very humbling. Once at an elders' seminar, Mr. Tom Ramage and I prayed privately together. The scriptures just poured out of that man of God (because he'd been pouring them in all his life). He prayed for us all, and when he stopped there were tears running down his cheeks. He just said "many tears". We often talk about the value of praying, but I've experienced the value of being prayed for. I wondered if it's what Peter felt like in Luke 22 when the Lord said to him: "*but I have prayed for you*"? And then I realized He still is praying for us. What a comfort it was to know that.

At this point, July 1995, I was losing hair again, not in large amounts, but constantly for about six weeks, leaving mostly gray and taking all the body out of it. I hesitated to shampoo it, because it came out in my hands. There were always hairs on my clothes. I hated it. I tried a "dry shampoo" but it didn't work. It takes about four to six months for the hair to come back, but I was never sure what colour or what texture it would be. Brian Steck, my colleague at work, jokingly started calling me "curly". Brian has a bit of a tough-guy reputation, but he's been just great with me, showing real concern.

I had been reading and hearing a lot lately about "alternative medicine" - natural remedies, homeopathics, acupuncture, etc. And many friends had been recommending many things over the years, many of which I tried. Sandra herself, through her own research, had come up with several remedies for me to try. I was told that it's quite a controversial subject, due they said to the bias of the North American medical community towards chemical solutions (supported by the pharmaceutical companies), and the unproven nature of much of these other things. I had an interesting conversation in hospital one day with a doctor from China. I asked him his opinion. He said that because of his background he tended to put more faith in these remedies and had seen instances where he's sure they worked. However, he said, "They're taboo around here". He said that one lady with cancer on the ward where I stayed said she wanted to try acupuncture and was told that if she did she would no longer be under their care. This whole conversation took place while I had a thermos of Tahebo herbal tea beside me, which I had been drinking. Later I did tell the medical staff what I was taking, and they raised no objections.

I asked God to show me which if any of these alternative remedies I should be taking. At that time I was taking several drops, pills and vitamins and two kinds of herbal tea - Essiac and Tahebo. Tahebo is supposed to be particularly good at reducing the toxicity in your system and stimulating the immune system.

In fact it was reported to be working so well that the federal drug authorities took it off the market for a while to consider reclassifying it from a health food to a drug. We had to go hunting around to get it. However, regardless of which methods God would use in my healing, I had to remember it was Him who must get the credit.

Meanwhile, in my periods of forced confinement, I had been studying a lot about the subject of "spiritual life" - the functions of the human spirit, soul and body. One aspect of it obviously was my physical health. Lying in hospital for hours on end gave lots of time for reading and quiet meditation, and I filled quite a few notebooks. (I found that confinement could be very depressing - I had always been very active - but I remembered that the apostle Paul did some of his best work in writing epistles, which have helped so many people, while he was confined in prison.) But there were also lots of occasions when I just didn't have the energy to read or meditate. One of the things I was learning by experience was that a reason for sickness can be God's chastening or discipline, intended for our refinement. Only a loving parent would do that. But it's not pleasant at the time - for either of them. Once the purpose of the chastisement is accomplished, the sickness may go. I thought about that for a long while.

Sandra had been seeing a counsellor (as I would also later) and receiving some help from the sessions. When Adele was here from Vancouver in April all five of us had gone as a family. There were a few awkward moments, and we observed that we had been very protective of each other, rather than letting each other know how we needed them. We had a lengthy conversation together later at a weekend we spent at Niagara on the Lake, but overall I think it was beneficial for each one of us to have the chance to

41

express ourselves in front of the others. It really bothered me to see how all this was hurting those dear people I love so much. But they were all dealing with it in their own way. It was the first time that we as a family together mentioned explicitly that I could die!

6. A Turning Point?

(July 1995 to February 1996)

I spent the last week of July 1995 in hospital again, as I needed several blood and platelet transfusions. I was very restless. (I had always hated hospitals, never thinking I'd be relegated to spending long periods of time in them, and St. Michael's is an old hospital, although the people inside are wonderful.) Instead of renting a T.V. this time (most of which I found to be nonsense, and the repeated commercials were driving me nuts), I read a bit, including "Chicken Soup for the Soul" by Jack Caulfield and Mark Victor Hansen (a gift from Fred Marks).

Some of the things I'd been wondering about were becoming a little clearer, it seemed. It was about this time, while lying in the hospital bed, that I distinctly remember "waving the white flag" of surrender to God - <u>whatever</u> He wanted for me I would do (that's not the same as giving up) and I prayed that He would help me to keep my word. I thought I'd reached that point much earlier in my life, but I had never felt it as deeply as I did now. The words of that old familiar hymn took on new meaning: "But we never will prove *the delights of His love until <u>all</u> on the altar we lay"*. *I wondered what deep experience the writer of those words had gone through to come out with them. I didn't realize it until much later, but I really believe that this was a definite turning point in my journey. A slight turn of the steering wheel and I was heading in quite a different direction.*

I realized that being uncertain about what to pray for or what to be obedient to doesn't seem to be the way God wants it. It's not the way He operates. He wants us to know. He doesn't enjoy keeping it a secret from us. But it does require complete willingness in advance - and that's hard. He's not just out to satisfy my curiosity. God's ways are not my ways, and God's timing is not always my desired timing, but perhaps sometimes the delay is my fault. So I needed to start looking to find out - and I did that this time in hospital. I had lots of time to lie and think. I had some great times alone with God, and later I felt better able to express the richness of what I had been given when I was able to get out and attend worship meetings again.

One day after I was discharged, while waiting for my blood test results at the hospital, I went for breakfast at a restaurant across the road. I read 2 Corinthians 8 in my Bible looking for the verse that had come into my mind while I was getting dressed that morning - *"If a man is willing, it is accepted according to what he has, not what he doesn't have"*. I had been wondering how much I was actually prepared to give up to honour my vow to God. But, as so often happened lately, it was another verse nearby that struck me: *"complete what you began a year ago"*. It was just a year ago that I had put together the first version of "Uncovering the Pattern", and wondering what to do with it ever since.

Also, in the first chapter of 2 Corinthians, I noticed that Paul had described the affliction he and his colleagues suffered when they were travelling in Asia. He told the Corinthians that he *"despaired even of life"*. I could relate to that. The purpose was *"that we might not trust in ourselves but in God"*. I could relate to that also. Then he said that all their prayers helped save him, and this then resulted in <u>many</u> people thanking God, which is how God receives glory. Now that's leverage, I thought - a few suffer, many pray and then express their thanks, and God gets much glory. Plus, they would get credit for their faithful prayers at the future coming of Christ. Everyone benefited. I thought to myself "maybe that's what's going on here".

This was another period when there seemed to be so many of those "coincidences". Two stories from "Chicken Soup" especially caught my attention. The first was about a school teacher whose effectiveness was based not only on the fact that she loved her subject, but that she loved her students. I am so glad I know what my gifts and calling are from God - teaching and pastoring, so I can get on with my work; but it's my relationship with the people that makes it work. That story shows why teaching and pastoring have to go together. The second one was about a visitor to Mexico walking along the beach early one morning and seeing that thousands of starfish had been washed ashore where they would die. And then he saw a Mexican coming towards him, occasionally picking up a starfish and throwing it back in the water. When they met, the visitor asked him why he was doing it; there were so many, he couldn't possibly make a difference. The other man just smiled, tossed another one back in and said "made a difference to that one". I don't have to change the whole world, I realized, just make an impact where I am.

But the clincher was a list of "What are you waiting for?". 101 things were listed but #67 stopped me; it was "A signal from heaven?". I thought: "Perhaps that's what I've been waiting for, some dramatic indication, and that's not the way it necessarily works". I must be prepared to trust God in the ordinary ways He works. In reading Deuteronomy in the Bible, I had come across this: "I am setting before you life and death...choose life". It was all a matter of my choosing to obey, I realized. "God", I prayed, "I choose life. I pledge obedience, but I need to know exactly <u>what</u> to do." And then I remembered that "The Eternal Purpose" had been the culmination of an exercize I'd had over many years - and God had used it. So was "Uncovering the Pattern", but it hadn't been used yet. What might that develop into? I thought about other dreams I'd had. Years before I had thought about starting a live-in college in our home for a few young men and women at a time - such as for four-month semesters. They'd learn to study, pray, visit people, learn a skill and develop their spiritual gift in a specific ministry - "field work". I knew that the churches of God were intended to be a place which encourages individual exercize and gifts and ministries, and harmonizes them all. (Adele's counselling skills were a case in point.). But what could I do about any of these, chained to this hospital bed?

In August 1995 Sandra and I fit in a short visit to Vancouver to visit Adele and her husband Bruce in their home. People were startled to see me, when just one week before I had been high on their critical prayer list. And here I was three thousand miles from home and my doctor. I was totally amazed myself at how I kept bouncing back.

I returned to work with the doctor's permission after Labour Day 1995, but it turned out to be premature - for an unexpected reason. On August 29th Sandra and I had gone to Princess Margaret Hospital for an interview with a Dr. Jeff Lipton to see if they might accept me for an allogenic bone marrow transplant. ("Allogenic" means donated by another person, as distinct from "autologous" where the patient's own marrow is harvested, purified and then re-transplanted.) It was a lengthy meeting and very informative. The staff showed us a video and gave us books. Dr. Lipton explained that there were primarily three criteria: I must be presently responding to chemotherapy; I must have a donor; and I must be otherwise in good health (which they would check out in detail closer to the time). The age limit was now 55 rather than 40, which had ruled me out back in 1988.

He went into considerable detail about the procedures and the risks. He explained that the whole thing would be intended to try to completely wipe out my bone marrow - and therefore my immune system and my ability to generate blood cells - and then replace it with new bone marrow in the hope that it would begin to work in its place. The combination of destroying as much as possible of my own marrow, and the positive immune capabilities of the good marrow, once it became established, would be designed to eradicate my leukemia cells over time. "That", he said, "is what we are trying to do."

In my case he estimated there was a 10% to 15% percent short-term, plus a 10% to 15% long-term, mortality risk - in other words a 20% to 30% risk I would die in the attempt. The major risks were serious infections and pneumonia, through having little or no immune system for quite some period of time, and a serious case of "graft-versus-host disease" where the donated marrow would reject me. Both could cause serious complications, including fatality, which of course the doctors would do what they could to overcome, but there was no guarantee. And even after that, there was some substantial possibility that the leukemia might remain, at some level, which they wouldn't be able to assess very conclusively for up to a year or more afterwards. Other possible complications included pancytopenia (deficient marrow), VOD (a serious complication where the liver stops working), mucositis (a tooth and gum disease), chronic graft-versus-host, infertility, cataracts, and secondary malignancies. He seemed to go on and one, painting a very bleak picture. The transplant was certainly not a "slam dunk", but considering what my alternatives were.....

He said that Dr. Brandwein had been "pulling rabbits out of the hat" for me with my treatments for some time. Then he came back in and told us that I was accepted, but subject to a couple of things: firstly, I must have my spleen removed, then I must have two more heavy chemotherapies, to further reduce the level of leukemia in my marrow. And he was in a hurry; the longer I waited, the greater the chance my condition would deteriorate and I would be disqualified. What did I want to do?

What an agonizing decision to have to make. I had heard and read enough to know that it was a gruelling experience and very high risk. If I did it and I died, I would in effect have killed myself. And if I survived, I might still have the leukemia. But if I didn't do it, the next time I needed chemo (and one of these times the doctors would have to finally give up), I would then have given anything to have tried the transplant. But I had to decide now, and right now I was feeling quite well. And back and forth it went in our heads.

It was almost easier on those occasions when decisions were taken out of our hands because there were no alternatives. Imagine how our children must have felt. "I could have my dad around, likely for several months, or he could go into this procedure and be dead two months from now. And he wants to know what I think he should do!" This wasn't a theoretical exercize; it wasn't giving advice to somebody else. *This was literally life and death. And the doctors were making it very clear: this was my decision. They wouldn't tell me "the right answer".*

We discussed it several times as a family (Adele included, by phone), and Jennifer and Andrew came with Sandra and me to discuss it with Dr. Brandwein on September 7th. Andrew said to us: "some chance is better than no chance". They all agreed that we should go ahead; I would have hated to have had to try to talk one of them into it.

For over twenty years I'd had a reported allergy to penicillin, but Dr. Lipton wanted to have me retested and, if only mildly positive, be desensitized to it. It would open up a whole powerful family of antibiotics to their use if I could take them. Some people told me that allergies were for life, but Dr. Brandwein managed to get me into Sunnybrook Hospital quite quickly, and I tested negative. It would turn out that this would become very valuable in future battles against infections.

I hadn't realized how rare bone marrow transplants were for C.L.L. patients. At that time only about a hundred had been done world-wide, and just five at Princess Margaret, mainly because most patients were too old. The procedures were largely the same as for other leukemias but they had fewer prior cases to go on to anticipate the body's reaction. However we knew of Princess Margaret's excellent reputation. They were very careful who they accepted, had the best of medical professionals and facilities, and had an excellent record. And, to add icing to the cake, later that year they would be moving to brand new premises on University Avenue, with special facilities for bone marrow transplants on the 14th floor. I felt as though it were being done especially for me.

Afterwards Sandra and I both felt sure this was God opening the way. The text on our calendar that morning had been 1 Corinthians 16:9: "*a great and effective door has been opened to me*". So many things coming together - Hilary's marrow being a six-out-of-six match with mine, my otherwise good health, the "unusual" (according to Dr. Lipton) response to the May and July chemo's. I asked him what my chances were medically of surviving twelve months without this transplant; he just held up his fingers and made a zero! When I mentioned that to Dr. Brandwein, he agreed. That made the decision easier - at least in our heads.

I went in for the splenectomy on September 26th. I was apprehensive, as I'd never had major surgery before. My spleen was 20 cm. long, six times its normal size (like a watermelon, the surgeon said) and my platelet count was pretty low, which made it highly risky for me to be bleeding through an operation. But Dr. Brandwein had arranged for me to get a top surgeon, Dr. Koo, which I was able to confirm through a family friend, Bill Tucker, who was a neurologist at St. Mike's. They scheduled me for last in the day to give themselves as much time as necessary, which left Sandra in the waiting room until about 5:30 p.m. anxiously wondering what was going on. She had been told it would take under two hours; instead it took four and a half hours until she was notified I was alright. For the second time, I found out later, she turned her thoughts to what funeral arrangements might have to be made.

The operation itself took three hours, and they transfused platelets into me during it. Afterwards I was told that Dr. Koo had performed "almost a bloodless operation". It's amazing what they can do. They took me to my room about 8:30 p.m. and Sandra and Shirley came in, but I was pretty groggy. But the next day when Sandra arrived, she was surprised to see me sitting up in bed. Dr. Koo told me that, immediately after the operation, my platelet count jumped from 28 to 90; soon after it soared to about 200 - well in the normal range. My spleen had been absorbing and destroying a lot of my platelets which had kept the count so low.

I was in hospital for a week, then back in for a day when I got severe pains. Later Sandra and I were able to spend some time up at the condo and had some important conversations about what lay ahead.

One day up there we were having trouble talking to each other about the transplant. Eventually it all came out. We talked at length about all our conflicting emotions - our very real apprehension, yet our guarded optimism; how glad we were for the opportunity, but how in suspense we felt because of the uncertain outcome. I knew that my illness had reached the point where I was almost out of runway - something was going to happen pretty soon. As I increasingly opened up to Sandra about it, it hit me just how scared I was. I was about to launch myself into this big black hole, and there would be no pulling back. My body recoiled at the prospect. "You don't have to do this, you know", she said through tears, "if you decide you don't want to". Without thinking, it just came out: "I have to do this - for you and the children and for me". My eyes welled up and my whole body shook as I said it. My fear had burst into a deep resolve and I was determined to go through with it.

It was a very compelling moment. As I had allowed myself to feel just how terrified I was, and had not tried to avoid it, it had brought out of me from that same depth a source of strength. Now, not only Sandra, but I myself knew for sure how I felt about what lay ahead. As I look back now, that was a defining moment for me. I was scared, but I was in no doubt what I must do.

For ten weeks after the operation I had severe diarrhea. They put me through every test known to mankind, all of which came back negative, and finally attributed it to stress. It didn't stop until I went on an antibiotic for an infection I got after the next chemo in mid-November. All of this put me away behind schedule, which the people at Princess Margaret were not aware of. We got a call one day from them to say my transplant was scheduled for December 21st - just before Christmas. I would be admitted on December 12th for the pre-chemo. But I knew I was in no condition to begin then, and I hadn't even had the second treatment. However Dr. Brandwein called them and cleared it up, but they were obviously in a hurry.

Meanwhile I was having more tests - a bone marrow biopsy and aspiration, and a catscan. We met with Dr. Brandwein later and he reported that the November chemo (again the "DHAP" regimen, attempting to "debulk" the leukemia in my marrow) had not worked sufficiently. And so I had two alternatives: I could forego the transplant or go for one last chemo attempt - a "salvage regimen" (that term didn't conjure up positive thoughts) - which would be the heaviest they could give me. He told me to think about it over Christmas, but I phoned him back two days later and told him I'd go ahead. I'd never have known whether it would have worked had I not tried. The family again agonized over it and again, to my relief, they were in agreement.

Despite what lay ahead we had a very pleasant family Christmas, after not knowing if we'd have one together. I had written special letters over the previous few weeks to Sandra and each of the children, and I gave them to them that day. It allowed me to say a lot of things that I wanted to express to each of them.

It would have been better, I suppose, to have done this in person, but it allowed me to set out in detail many things I wanted to convey. The original suggestion came from Sandra's counsellor and I took about three months to ponder what I wanted to say, making notes, and getting the words and the tone just right. I needed each of them to know how I felt about them individually, what it meant to me to be their father or husband, what I wanted for them, and what I thought about what lay ahead. And I wanted them to have it in a form they could keep. Later Adele told me she was quite upset by it because she thought it was a "goodbye" letter.

And so in early January I went back into St. Michael's for the big treatment - and was there for twenty-six days, the longest stint yet. I felt like I was in prison ("cell block 767" I called it). I couldn't face the hospital food and every one of those days Sandra went out and got me some supper that I thought I could stomach. We discovered "Ensure Plus", a high energy nutrition drink in various flavours that I was able to take and that was available through the hospitals and also in drug stores. I tolerated the chemo reasonably well, but of course my blood counts plummeted again and I got a fairly serious mouth infection. Adele and Bruce had come in from Vancouver beforehand and so were able to visit me in hospital for the first time. Every other time we had seen them I had been at home, or occasionally visiting them. Later Adele said it was remarkable how our family automatically switched to "hospital mode" when I was in.

In late February, remarkably, I felt well enough that Sandra and I thought we could take a vacation. We flew to Arizona (with permission) and spent time in Scottsdale and the Grand

Canyon. We took a balloon ride over the Sonora Desert at dawn one day. It was something I'd always wanted to do and it was exhilarating - until I felt the wind almost blow my hair piece off. Which actually would have been hilarious, as well as totally embarrassing. At the Canyon we took a flight on a single-engine plane across and back (I think Sandra had her eyes closed most of the time). It was a great trip and I felt progressively stronger throughout it. But the day after we returned was to be our big consultation with Dr. Brandwein to find out if I would be able to have the transplant or not. I was trying to block that out so not to spoil this glorious holiday.

When the day came, we seemed to wait outside his office for ever. Then he came out to go to the lab to get my information. He saw us, but didn't say anything. He looked very sombre. (Nurses and resident doctors come and go all the time, but when my own doctor comes to see me he has my total attention. I read meaning into every word that is said and not said, and every raised eyebrow.) Sandra said quietly "I think this is going to be bad news". When we went in, I could see him psyching himself up to tell us. It must be so hard for these doctors to have to do that.

Sure enough, he had to tell us that the treatment hadn't made any difference at all, that my test results were virtually identical to the time before. The transplant was off! And Dr. Lipton had agreed. Not just off temporarily, they said, because they could not foresee me ever getting back to where I would need to be. I had stopped responding to treatment.

In the hall outside as we were leaving I said to Sandra: "what did you think of that?". We both had tears in our eyes. All our hopes had been resting on this transplant; we had been so sure everything was working together to make it happen. This was clearly God's solution to my problem. And now - slam!

As we drove home quietly, a brighter side began to emerge - a sense of relief that I was not about to undergo this terrible process. My immediate condition was quite good and I was getting stronger. My counts were doing well and I might well be able to enjoy a few good months. But that relentless leukemia would be back, and then what? They had nothing to offer at that stage (although he said Fludarabine, which I'd had back in 1992, might help a little when the time came, since my platelets were no longer being inhibited by my spleen). He asked me if I planned to go back to work and the question took me by surprise; I had been expecting instead to begin a long transplant procedure.

Sandra and I were so very perplexed by this outcome. We had been so sure that the transplant was the Lord's answer to this whole problem; everything had pointed to it. And now the door seemed to be permanently closed. But we had to continue to leave it in the Lord's hands. He doesn't make mistakes. I had trusted Him when I thought I was going to have it; would I trust Him when I couldn't have it?

7. Experiences with God

Throughout this book I have not attempted to avoid referring to the very real spiritual and scriptural aspects of my experience. In my life they are integral to everything else. This does not mean at all that I went from spiritual high to spiritual high throughout the period of my illness. Far from it. It's really quite amazing. I've been praying for most of my life, but I still find myself very inconsistent about it; too often it's the last resort, and I forget. Also, I know full well, and have often taught others, the scriptural truth that we don't rely on our own strength and effort for spiritual energy; it has to be drawn from God. And yet I constantly find myself regressing to doing just that. It's quite frustrating. Old habits die hard, and new habits take a long time to become engrained. So this whole period was very much one of ups and downs. I was in school with God; and school isn't always easy.

If anyone were to get the impression that I am some sort of spiritual superman who has this all figured out and just goes from strength to strength, I would be very upset. Because it's just not true.

Frequently I was muddled and perplexed. If I had an unshakeable confidence in God throughout, then that's His doing, not mine. There were many times when I felt myself at a distance from Him, and I didn't like it at all. There were many times I was ashamed at the thoughts that came into my head. But other people generally didn't see that - because it was all going on inside.

However, there is no question that I also experienced some unparalleled times with God, that fed me spiritually and enriched my understanding and appreciation of Him and His Son. (That second part is important - Jesus said in John 14: "*You believe in God, believe also in Me*". Many people have a belief in God, but not necessarily in Jesus Christ.) I think the forced confinement had a lot to do with it. As Psalm 46 says: "*Be still and know that I am God*". I would make a point of reading my Bible in hospital (which provoked a few interesting reactions from nurses and visitors, and even the chaplain). But sometimes I would just lie there and contemplate. Sometimes an hour or two would go by and I would have really enjoyed it, without actually reading a word. I liked to focus on the greatness of who Christ is and the enormity of His work of salvation for us, and the awesome majesty of God. It was great spiritual medicine. And I found on those occasions when I was able to attend the services of the church of God of which I am a part, it enhanced my worship and prayer contributions.

The Bible has always been a unique book to me. I truly believe it is, alone, the directly written word of Almighty God. I know there have been lots of attempts to prove and disprove that over the years, but to me the fact is - it works! I constantly marvel, the deeper I get into it, how it all fits together in an incredible pattern. It not only informs, inspires and stimulates, like a lot of other books do, but it can touch me time and time again in the real experiences of life. That doesn't happen every time, of course, but it does happen frequently, and so I keep putting it into my mind, mainly avoiding substitutes, and trying to read what it really says, what it really means, while trying to push aside preconceived notions. It's powerful stuff. And so to me it contains not just pious sayings or sentiments or truisms, but personal living messages from God attuned to my needs.

Over the years many, many people have said or written to me that they are praying for me. I'm not always sure exactly what they mean, but I appreciate it anyway. Are we all praying to the same God or "higher power"? Are they formal, religious prayers in church or personal, intimate prayers at home, and so on? It would be interesting to ask them all. For myself, I have been learning more about the reality of prayer. It's certainly more than a wish list from a benevolent dictator, like catalogue shopping; it's entering into true communication with the unfathomable God of heaven through the intermediation of His Son, and of His Holy Spirit who takes up residence in believing Christians. So often when I would begin to pray because I felt in need, what would flood into my mind would be all the things I had to be grateful for and so, but not because I planned it that way, the greater part of the time would be spent in giving thanks. And I learned gradually the variety of ways and people through whom God gives answers. They weren't always immediate and not always direct, but in retrospect it was amazing how often an answer had come.

It was through my sister Shirley in August 1948 that I first came to know the Lord. The steps leading up to my conversion are an interesting story. Here is how she tells it...

"During World War II, several German airmen were shot down over Scotland and became prisoners of war at a camp in Ayr, on the south-west coast. Jack Ferguson, my uncle, went to visit them to tell them about the gospel, as a result of which several of them were born again. The camp gave them permission to visit those who had befriended them and to attend church with them. One Sunday evening two of them, Erhardt Nessler and Fritz Ruhf, were visiting Jack and Olga Ferguson, as was I; I was eight years old at the time. The five of them squeezed into a four-seater Vauxhall car, with me sitting on Herr Nessler's lap in the front seat with a big doll, when he asked me if I knew the Lord Jesus as my Saviour. I was embarrassed and replied "well, sort of". And so he explained it all clearly to me. I was fascinated by his accent. He asked me if I understood, and I said "yes". "Well?", he continued. I shrugged. "Let's ask the Lord Jesus into your heart now" he said. And so we quietly prayed together, and it was done. The others in the car were chatting and didn't know about it until later. But I knew at that point that it was real. I am amazed that a man raised in Germany, trained to fight the British, was brought to the Lord by one of the "enemy", and in turn led one of the littlest of the enemy to the Lord. It was then important to me to make it just as clear to my little brother. And so I explained it all to him, at five years of age, and eventually he got it."

I can remember so clearly kneeling down beside my bed in our house on Southannan Road in Fairlie (just a few miles north of Ayr) praying and taking the Lord Jesus into my heart, with Shirley coming in every few minutes to ask "have you done it yet?".

I am so grateful that I was shown the true gospel early in my life. The simplicity of God's message that I am by nature sinful, and therefore inevitably alienated from Him, and need to be "saved", can so easily become obscured as we grow older. I was shown clearly that *the only way to God is by putting full reliance on Christ's death for me on Calvary, by which He totally satisfied all God's requirements. I put my simple but complete faith in that, and I was forgiven, cleansed, and received. I learned that a true relationship with God (both for this life and for ever) can only start with this "new birth". It's not complicated, but it's hard to get rid of the notion that it somehow depends on me. I am so glad that I was able to allow God to show me in His own way and time the reality of what He says about Himself in the Bible.*

There is no question that I was given a great legacy in my youth by my parents and others. I was taught and shown well about the Lord from an early age and, while I questioned and challenged it several times thereafter, it has been the mainstay of my life. The older I get and the more I see of life in the world, the stronger that conviction becomes. I find that it encompasses all aspects of my experience - family and other relationships, my job, and everything else. It is, simply, my way of life. As a result I have a longing that so many others of my acquaintances would experience this too, in growing degree. As the Bible puts it (in 1 Samuel 17:46, John 17:3 and Philippians 3:10), firstly...

*"that the world might **know** that there is a God..."*

then...

*"that they may **know** the only true God, and Jesus Christ whom You have sent",*

then...

*"that I may **know** Him and the power of His resurrection, and the fellowship of His suffering...",*

which is what I am currently increasingly learning about. This knowledge is of course a lot more than facts or words; it's knowing by personal first-hand experience.

A very important part of my spiritual life is the community of Christians with whom I worship. It's "the churches of God" in the Fellowship of the Son of God (the expression comes from 1 Corinthians 1:9). It's not large, although it does extend to many countries in the world. I have had a growing conviction over the years, based on a lot of searching of scripture, that they are the equivalent of the churches of God in which disciples were gathered in New Testament times, which is what we are trying to emulate. I had been learning increasingly that my relationship with God was more than an individual thing. For it to be complete, I knew it must involve my association with others - and in the way that God Himself has prescribed. Because I had been learning that there is only a certain kind of service to Him that He says is acceptable. And as that conviction grew, it became increasingly important to me to take advantage of whatever opportunities I had to share it with others. One of the frustrations that I had to deal with during prolonged periods of inactivity was my lack of opportunity to do that. But I came to realize that periods of seclusion and reflection are vitally important also. And in my case they were being forced on me.

8. An Eventful Year

(March to December 1996)

The period from March to early December 1996 was almost "normal" and I enjoyed most of it enormously, although I kept my eye on my constantly-increasing white cell count. I knew the good times wouldn't last for ever. My strength gradually increased, my appetite and weight returned, and people said I was looking great. It was so good to get up in the morning and feel well. I'd lie in bed, thank God for health and strength for another day, and then get up. The stress on the family was becoming noticeably less.

I returned to work, and it felt good. However there was no way I could resume the full slate of responsibilities that I'd previously had. I had several conversations with Matt Barrett and he agreed that I should relinquish many of my responsibilities, while picking up some special project work as I was able. That was a big relief, although as the months went by I found it increasingly unsatisfying just being on the fringe. I had to be involved and contributing; I knew this was only a temporary solution. I would have liked to have done some teaching at the Bank's Institute for Learning, but I was in no position to make fixed scheduled commitments.

The uncertainty was so frustrating. I was used to feeling in control of my life, and I just wasn't in control right now. But I kept all this to myself. What could anyone else do about it? But I didn't like it at all. And so my thoughts bounced back and forth like a ping-pong ball.

One of the very positive by-products of being back in contact with my business colleagues, however, was a number of personal conversations I had. Because I was more open about talking about my own experiences now, I found that others opened up more easily to me. This was a bit of a revelation, although it seemed so obvious once I had discovered it. Apparently some of them had the idea that I didn't like to talk about my leukemia. That wasn't the case at all, but obviously I had been giving that impression. I discovered several colleagues whose spouses had cancer and were wondering how best to support them. I tried to help, although I could only talk from my own experience.

I was surprised how much it seemed to help them, and it felt good to do it. I talked about some of the things that I had found to be most useful, such as getting acknowledgement (not advice) when I was feeling badly, how empty it sounded when someone superficially told me not to worry because everything would turn out all right, and how encouraging to my own will to live it was for someone to just be there with me so I didn't feel alone.

On June 20th Sandra and I had the pleasure of sitting in Convocation Hall at the University of Toronto, watching Jennifer receive her hard-earned Bachelor of Commerce degree. I reminisced about the time twenty-two years previously when

I had sat in the same place and received a similar degree, but I almost think it means more as a parent. Well done, Jennifer.

At the end of June we all (Bruce and Adele from Vancouver included) headed over to Britain to attend a youth rally. We then had a family holiday on the island of Guernsey in the Channel Islands. We walked along the high cliffs, a great place for deep contemplation. We threw around a little football we bought, something I had missed doing with Andrew for a few years. Following that holiday, we visited relatives and friends in Britain. This included a visit to Mr. Jimmy Black, a farmer in his eighties in Kilmacolm, Scotland, who was one of many who were praying for me every day. The whole trip was a series of good and uplifting experiences. These respites between the storms were so vital and I found that it was amazing how my body could recuperate so quickly after all it had been through. As the scripture says: "*we are fearfully and wonderfully made*". In Guernsey Andrew kept pointing out all the Mazda Miata (M-5) convertibles; he knew I had a weakness for them and he would soon have his own driver's license. When I came home, I indulged myself and bought one, rationalizing that we really did need another car with four drivers at home.

By now my hair had returned sufficiently (except for one permanent bald round spot on the right side that I still have - damage from the chemotherapy) so that I was able to dispense with my hair piece. That was a great relief. It felt and looked so much better. I hated wearing it, but I just hadn't been able to stand the sight of myself without it.

In September Sandra and I went to Boston for Board meetings with the Barbados directors, then followed it with a nice holiday in Plymouth, Cape Cod and Newport, Rhode Island. We enjoyed it thoroughly. We walked miles, as a result of which I developed a very painful case of "plantar fasciitis" after I got home - in my left foot. By now I was learning to take more responsibility for my health and so I decided to actually do something about it. Was it related at all to my leukemia? I couldn't help wondering. I went to the doctor and had it diagnosed, went regularly for physical therapy, bought special shoes for work and had orthotic supports made. Not surprisingly, before long it went totally away. I think I learned a lesson there; previously I would have been more inclined to tough it out and hope for the best.

I guess "looking after myself" requires me to actually do things, I realized - pay attention to symptoms, get the best advice, check out my options, avail myself of remedies that make sense, follow the prescribed routine, and stop doing things that make it worse! I had stumbled on to another blindingly obvious reality.

That Thanksgiving we were again able to enjoy our annual holiday weekend at Grandview with our good friends Laurie and Brenda Williams and Bruce and Bev Archibald. It has become a bit of an institution over the years, even before we had our own place, and we always look forward to it. Laurie and I had been somewhat partners in illness for a while as he had been suffering for a few years from a very curious and debilitating case of brucellosis. We often spoke of our common experiences in having so many people praying for us and what that meant. But this weekend he seemed so much better. And the weather and the colours were spectacular, and the fellowship very precious. Times with good friends mean so much in interludes like this.

True friendship is such a precious thing, and I have been learning the value of telling people what they mean to me. Bruce and I share several interests, one of which is music, and I enjoy his company and friendship. Laurie and I also go back many years. He and I are different in many ways, we have different backgrounds and different skills. But we share the same values and the same faith. Laurie is someone I can relax with. We are both competitive by nature but we don't compete with each other. He is well aware of my shortcomings but they don't get in the way of our friendship, which is something I value very much.

Around that time I "happened" to see a T.V. documentary on Barbara Frum, the newscaster who had died from leukemia a few years before. Her young daughter had written a book about her and was being interviewed. A couple of things in particular struck me about it. One was how radiant her daughter looked. She seemed to be doing very well despite her mother's death; her mother was very much alive and important in her mind. And so I thought "my kids will be fine, no matter what happens", and that encouraged me. Also, although Barbara had had the disease for eighteen years, all that time the doctors had told her that her life expectancy was one to two years. Over those eighteen years, she would often say "that's the last time I'll ever do that" or "that's the last time I'll ever be there", which is exactly what I had often found myself thinking. But often of course it wasn't the last time. She had been an avid gardener and the family said they would never be able to sell that house because all around them were constant reminders of her life. I was glad I had seen the program.

Also about that time I quite suddenly began thinking of two situations where my relationship with another person needed mending, due to misunderstandings in the past. I was quite struck by how "out of the blue" they came into my mind. But, once they did, I felt a real need to clear them up, and so I began to look for opportunities to make contact to do that. I felt grateful to be alerted to the need to deal with them, and I knew they wouldn't go from my thoughts until I did. And so I undertook to do what I could to resolve them - both with very positive outcomes. I think that was something else that needed to happen at this point in my journey.

In November, on a whim, I decided I wanted to go out to Vancouver and visit Bruce and Adele, and so Andrew and I flew out on November 24th. It was the last evening that turned out to be the reason for the trip. Adele and I got into a very long conversation, probably the longest we've ever had. We talked candidly about the few years when she was a teenager when our relationship had been a bit strained. Neither of us had really understood why or wanted it that way. When she would do things that upset me as her father (none of which were very serious in retrospect, but I was inexperienced), I would tend to go silent and withdraw. I knew that this was because I often felt incapable of knowing just what to do or say, whereas she tended to interpret it as alienation, which made matters worse. She told me she found my silence and my "looks" at those times quite intimidating, which I found surprising. I never dreamed I could intimidate anyone. It was quite a revelation. She encouraged me to be more open and expressive; she said I could be very verbally communicative when I chose to be. This would help me in my relationship with her and, she suspected, with others as well. I told her I thought I was getting a bit better at expressing my innermost thoughts but the "setting" had to be right. It could only be with people who could understand, I needed their undivided attention and it had to be in privacy.

She did me a great favour that night, and she seemed helped also. It was a long, intense and loving conversation. I assured her of my deep and unconditional love and approval of her, my admiration for her accomplishments, and of my deep interest in everything she did. It definitely drew us closer together. She has her Master of Social Work degree and is, as far as I can tell, a very good social worker, and I am fascinated by the work she does. She is really quite a young woman. Then I knew why I had "happened" to think of making that trip. It was another important step in my learning.

Over the years many of my friends have offered remedies or other suggestions that they believed would help me, and sometimes (such as in the case of my friend Don Bowles) they had gone to quite a lot of effort for me. Late in 1995 I was offered something quite unconventional but that made sense to me. I recalled Dr. Brandwein giving me an explanation as to why my malignant blood cells developed resistance to chemotherapy drugs, and this suggestion seemed to relate to that. Could this work for me? Should I try it? There was some risk, but there was a lot of risk in even the conventional things I was doing these days.

I used it for two weeks. I have no idea if it did any good. But at this point I was prepared to try almost anything that made sense to me. All I know is that when I had chemotherapy the next month my astronomical leukemic cell count plummeted. Part of the preparatory regimen had been to come off all toxic substances and caffeine for a month beforehand. I was a heavy coffee drinker, and so I switched to decaffeinated (and have never gone back). Perhaps that in fact was the benefit of my little experiment.

Around that same time, I discovered that I had several outbreaks of skin cancer. They had been there for a while, sores that hadn't healed, but I hadn't had them diagnosed. Dr. Jakubovic, a dermatologist at St. Michael's, was able to treat them fairly successfully by repeated spraying with liquid nitrogen, as they were only skin-deep. The spray burns off the top layer of skin, allowing new skin to grow underneath. And then I started to put the pieces together.

Back in the 1970's I'd had itchy feet at night for many years (starting with my left foot). I used to stop it by running scalding water over it, until I discovered a cream that worked. Then I developed a case of skin hives that lasted for a while, and then for several months I got pronounced swelling in my extremities - fingers, toes or tongue, usually. Looking back, it was as though something inside was trying to get out through my skin. Was there a pattern here? It was shortly after that time that they discovered I had leukemia. Was the whole thing the result of accumulated unresolved stress? I had to admit that many aspects of my life over the years had tended to be in the high-stress category. But I had always prided myself that I could handle stress well and it didn't show. What if, instead, I had been wrong and I had just been suppressing it and it had been building up and building up until it made me seriously ill? Certainly the mid-eighties had been a very stressful time for me in my new job at the Bank. If stress was at the root of this, I needed to get to work to identify the sources of stress in my life, and see what I could do to reduce them.

9. I Meet Another Doctor

(August 1996 to March 1997)

When I returned to work in March 1996, I was visited by a consultant, Dr. Bryan Smith, whom I had used extensively in helping us shape and communicate the "Corporate Services Vision". He had previously taken an interest in my health problems and had suggested one or two things for my consideration. Bryan suggested I might consider a visit to a doctor that he knew who had some useful alternative approaches - not instead of my hematologist, but as well as - to consider broadening my options. I asked what kind of alternatives, but Bryan didn't elaborate; he just gave me the phone number. In retrospect, perhaps this was one of the reasons why I got involved with the Corporate Services Vision and Bryan Smith in the first place.

I did nothing with this information, and the phone number sat on my credenza until August. Finally I called Dr. Larry Nusbaum. He just suggested I come and see him, but to allow two hours! That seemed excessive for me to just check him out. He worked out of his home near Broadview and Danforth. I knocked at his front door and a relatively young man in jeans answered. I said "Hi, Larry, I'm Keith" and he welcomed me in. We went upstairs to a small room with two chairs facing each other. It reminded me of my initial meeting with Dr. Brandwein - nothing pretentious, relatively young men, with me wondering what happens next. I soon came to have profound respect for both men.

We talked for the two hours. He is an M.D. but a few years ago found it increasingly difficult to limit himself to conventional forms of medical treatment. He described himself as a student of people, especially of cancer patients who get well, and he wanted to understand more about that process because, he told me, you can only teach others what you've learned yourself; anything else is just out of a book.

He told me how I may hear a lot of different stories of people claiming what worked for them - and they're often true; but it doesn't mean it will necessarily work for me. I have to learn to select carefully from other peoples' experiences, and I can learn how to do that instinctively. I have to be like a scientist - to be open to new possibilities, without being gullible - and then to check things out.

Actually, I did most of the talking. I described what was going on in my life, what was important to me, and I found it very easy to be open with him, including about my strong views on God and my spirituality. He watched me intensely as I spoke, picking up on my body language; when he spoke, he did so carefully, often pausing to think first. When he illustrated a point, it was based on something I had already said - he seemed to remember everything. I was as intrigued by his process as I was by the content.

I felt pretty good when he said that I was clearly having a profound effect on a lot of other people, through my illness. But was I focussed enough on my own well-being? I had always regarded myself as someone who took my responsibilities seriously, but didn't take myself too seriously. But Larry pointed out that I wouldn't be much use to others if I didn't take care of myself.

He asked me to elaborate on how I pray. I thought briefly and then said "I guess I do it in three different ways". Occasionally quite systematically I will get down on my knees and spend some time talking with God about a variety of things. Often I pray "on the fly", based on what's happening at the moment - a brief silent thank you or request for help. But sometimes, when I've been in real distress, I've called out "Lord, help me!" With respect to the second, he was impressed that I would deliberately set aside more conventional sources of power that people tend to rely on under pressure (such as position, wealth, and personality) to allow the power of God to be used through me (such as before going into a business meeting, even before coming in to see him that day).

He said I seemed to be a person who was seeking for knowledge and was prepared to some degree to be open to new things. I gave him some examples of answers to requests - such as my crisis assurance of the reality of God in my late teens, and how I started going out with Sandra at age twenty-one, and my decision to leave the accounting partnership at age forty and join the Bank of Montreal...

I can remember distinctly the night I stopped praying. I was in my late teens and in university. To someone who had been brought up to believe a conventional Christian faith, that was an alien environment in the early 1960's. Everything I had taken for

*granted seemed to be being challenged, and I often found myself on
the defensive, and I didn't like it. Eventually the inner conflict got
to be too much for me. I was in the habit of getting down on my
knees each night beside my bed and praying. But this one night, I
remember it so well, I just stopped in the middle and I said out loud:
"Who do I think I'm kidding? Nobody can hear me. This isn't going
beyond the ceiling.". And for the next several weeks I went through
a real crisis of my faith. Finally one night in desperation I got back
down on my knees again and I said: "God, I need to know - one way
or another. I need to be sure whether you're real or not, and I need to
know, for sure, whether what I've always thought I believed is true
or not. So show me, without any doubt, because I've got to know,
whether I can convince anybody else of it or not.". And I got up and
went to bed. Nothing happened right away, so I just waited. But
over the next two or three months a whole series of things occurred
that, cumulatively, bred in me an unshakeable conviction of the
reality of the person of God and of the absolute truth of His Word. I
can't explain how it happened - but it happened. I had asked, and
the answer had come.*

*The story about Sandra is actually quite funny. I was twenty
years old when I suddenly decided the time had come for me to have
a steady girlfriend. I had dated a little but not much. So, I decided
to tell God what I wanted, to give Him the specifications so He could
go to work on it. I laugh when I think about it now. She had to be
a good person, a believing Christian, very good looking of course,
not taller than me, and crazy about me. I didn't think that was
too demanding. Marriage was not in my thoughts at that point,
but if I was going to get involved with someone, it might as well be
right. Not long after, I was at a young peoples' weekend in London,
Ontario when I "noticed" Sandra. I had met her before but didn't
know her well. Not long after, in February 1964, I had a twenty-*

first birthday party and of course made sure she was invited. As everyone was leaving after midnight, the car she was to go in (back to a friend's house in London) developed a fire in the back seat! Sandra said "There's no way I'm going in that car". I immediately said "I'll take you to London", and ran into the house to ask my mother for the use of her car to go the 100 miles to London. "London, tonight?", she said. Gerry Armstrong (now Gerry Gillespie), who had figured out what was going on, helped convince her this was a good idea, and so we set off, with Sandra (of course) in the front seat beside me. By the time we were passing the airport on Highway 401, I had got up the nerve to gently take her hand (Sandra: "he grabbed it and squeezed"). That was the start. By Easter I was madly in love. Three and a half years later we were married. God had come through - again.

As I thought about these events so long ago at Larry's that day, there was a pattern there with respect to major events in my life. Larry talked about patiently waiting for an answer and being ready for it to come in unfamiliar ways. He compared it with planting a vegetable seed in the garden. It only takes a few seconds, but it launches a profound process. I can't go back every day and dig it up to see it growing. But if I pay attention to it, one day something will show up above the ground. I may not be able to recognize what it is right away but eventually it will mature. If it were broccoli, for example, if I've only ever seen broccoli in a plastic bag and rubber band in the grocery store, I might not recognize it growing in my garden. But it's the answer to my planting. It was a useful metaphor, and it's been amazing how often I've seen that process work - both in big decisions and in smaller events as well.

At that first visit he asked me to draw my disease and so, to my surprise, I found myself with a box of crayons and a blank sheet of paper. But what came out was quite revealing. I tend to think about things in visual images and diagrams anyway (I'm a "visualizer"). I drew my body (not very artistically) and my circulatory system. Then I zeroed in on my left upper arm and showed the bone and inside it the bone marrow. I drew a gate, left open wide, and a "gatekeeper" flat on his back, either dead or disabled, and all the underdeveloped lymphocyte cells being released unconstrained into the blood stream. No one was in control! I drew the blood vessels in disrepair as a result of accumulated stresses and strains, and lack of maintenance, which had allowed some intruder in through a crack - and he had "done in" the gatekeeper.

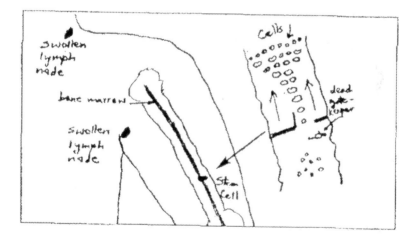

Did I have an over-vivid imagination, or was this my subconscious picture of what had been going wrong? Larry asked me to describe what I had drawn, why I had used the colours I had, and to label and characterize all the parts. Pay attention to the details, he said.

I also drew a crowd scene at the midway at the Canadian National Exhibition. The good, mature cells were dutifully trying to go about their business - delivering oxygen, attacking alien infectors, etc. But they were being crowded out by this huge and increasing crowd of unruly kids. He got me to write out a dialogue between one of the mature cells and one of the kids (another way of accessing what's in my subconscious thoughts, because we write differently than we speak). The good cells were very frustrated. The kids didn't care; they were just having a blast. Not a good situation.

As well as visualizing my disease, I drew what healing would look like, and it featured the arrival of a new gatekeeper. This gatekeeper, even though I didn't know what it would be or where it would come from, became a central theme and Larry would often encourage me to relate to it whatever exercizes I did. How significant this would become I never imagined at the time. Other exercizes included:

- "planting" (posing a question very precisely - either in my mind or on paper - such as to my gatekeeper, and seeing what response came back);

- "harvesting" (becoming aware of, and articulating, what had occurred in my life in relation to previous planting that I had done; it wasn't enough for the broccoli to grow - I had to eat it - it helped to keep me alive);

- dialogues with parts of my body (such as my foot when I had the plantar fasciitis, and my skin sores) - which seemed a very weird thing to do at first; and

- listing "things I know"

I did a planting exercize one day after I had caught on to this notion of stress as a causal factor. I was able to identify five clear sources of present stress in my life at that juncture, and I was surprised how I was able to come up with things that would alleviate them, once they were identified. It helped me to figure out if they were real or just in my head, and to deal with them one at a time.

It was quite revealing what came out from these exercizes. I certainly wasn't deliberately making it up, but I knew that what came out on the paper as I wrote was coming from within me. The day I found out about my skin cancers (November 28th, 1996), I wrote out this dialogue with them to ask them whether these sores were related back to that previous problem I'd had for many years, the very itchy feet at night, hives and swelling on my skin. It went like this:

Me: Is there any connection between all these things over the years that would help me to understand my disease?

Skin-sores: There's something going on. It looks like something's been trying to get out through your skin.

Me: Did scalding my feet each night to make the itch stop do any damage?

S/s: You wouldn't do that to a child if something was wrong, would you? You treated your feet like they weren't human.

Me: Oops. I'm sorry. I guess the cream was better. It certainly seemed to work better. My feet have started to itch again a bit.

S/s: Maybe things are trying to get out again, instead of into your bloodstream. That could be good news, would it not?

Me: Yes, if it means that they're attacking my blood cells less. Is it stress-related? I need to understand better the bodily effects of excessive stress build-up.

S/s: Why?

Me: So I can learn more about how to release it so it won't build up.

S/s: So finding out about your skin cancer today was good news?

Me: Perhaps. I didn't feel badly when I heard. I was glad it was diagnosed and could be treated. But maybe it's a clue - another connection.

S/s: So how would you expect to see that this is working better?

Me: I see you're asking the questions now. Well maybe my feet will itch more for a while - at least that's a more noticeable sign of stress build-up. But the goal is to learn how to release it all so that not even my feet will itch.

Larry encouraged me to express everything in the first person instead of generalizing. Instead of saying "you feel this", it was more helpful to say "I feel this". The tendency to lapse into the second person was a clue that it was quite personal. By using the first person, I found it affected me more deeply when I said it.

At the end of the second session I had a very emotional experience. Larry asked me to focus clearly and in detail in my mind on what being healed would be like Then he asked me to focus on how much I wanted it. I looked away and began to see it happening in my mind. Suddenly tears came to my eyes and I blurted out "more than anything in the world". Quietly he said to me: "Then ask for it, the way you've asked for other things, in any way you want". And so I did, never more fervently. Then he told me to leave it there and just wait patiently and alertly for the answer.

I had never as deeply felt throughout my whole being just how much having this cursed illness taken away mattered to me. I could almost tangibly feel what it would be like and it gripped me. And I felt at great peace that I had transferred my unbearable burden into the hands of the One who could lift it from me. I just sat there, limp.

These exercizes that I experimented with over the next few visits were ways to strengthen communication to and from otherwise inaccessible parts of me. I initially found them difficult and unnatural, but so is any new skill. But without fail something would emerge that gave me some insight into my situation and what my response should be.

I found that the greatest advantage of my visits was that I was able to integrate what was going through my mind. Typically I would arrive with all kinds of thoughts, ideas, questions, and difficulties about my illness, my treatments, and the effect of it all on my life and my family. Through the processes that Larry asked me to apply, I was often able to fit things together, discover answers, see patterns. For example, I discovered that I always tended to think of the root of my disease as being in my left side (particularly my left upper arm); the left side of my body is of course controlled by the right side of my brain - the emotional side.

Hmm, I thought, that's interesting. That makes sense, from what I'm discovering. And when something makes sense to me, I'm much more likely to act on it. Another little piece of the puzzle had fallen into place.

Never did Larry direct my answers; they came from me. Never did he challenge my faith or my relationship with the God of the Bible. He just asked me to elaborate and to link it in. I found the sessions invigorating and looked forward to going, although I needed prodding to do my "homework" in between. I seemed to need the discipline of the sessions to apply it properly, especially in the earlier days. It was only after several sessions that I realized I was in therapy; Larry never mentioned the word. If I had known what Bryan Smith was recommending, I probably would have been one of those men who want nothing to do with counselling sessions or therapy. Take it from me, with a skilled and compatible counsellor, it can do a world of good. And it's actually fun. My advice is: don't rule it out without giving it a chance. Don't limit your options; I almost did.

Another thing Bryan Smith did was to give me a copy of a book by Bernie Siegel entitled "Peace, Love and Healing". Bob and Donna Wells (Bob is the Bank's Chief Financial Officer) had given it to me two years previously, but I had just scanned it and put it down. But timing is everything; I had made a lot of progress since then. This time as I re-read it I became fascinated by it and even typed out a summary. I found it highly relevant. A few of the points that hit the mark as I attempted to apply them personally were as follows:

- Modern medicine and self-healing are not mutually exclusive; I need to examine all my options

- I should use my adversity as a gift for personal change; it takes courage for me to confront my own mortality; the illness should cause me to ask myself what I'm doing that's out of harmony with what I should be doing - my particular business on this earth

- Survival statistics don't apply to me; I am an individual

- I need to decide to live until I happen to die; not living is worse than dying

- My feelings are a chemical in my body that can kill or cure me; they are the primary way I send messages to my body; I shouldn't say "I'm fine" when I'm not; it sends a message that being sick is normal

- When I change my state of mind, I open myself to the possibility of healing; it's my body that heals, not the medicine

- I need a fighting spirit, not just stoic acceptance; I need to take responsibility for my own health, not just simply rely on the doctors; I need to assert "I want to live!"

- I can't control the events in my life, but I can control my reactions to them; I shouldn't judge apparently negative events too quickly; they may be insights or important developments

- I can't ignore my own needs and just focus on others' needs (or vice versa); I can't ignore myself and be useful to the world

- Cancer can often be the outcome of repressed emotions, of a controlled life, or pressure to perform (ouch!)

- I need to stop the constant busyness, and take time-outs to reflect within myself

- I shouldn't refuse offers of help or stay aloof; when I show my vulnerability and humour, and am prepared to cry, people can't wait to show their love; when I share my pain, it makes it easier for others to share theirs

- What example am I leaving my children in how I deal with this?; would I want them to get sick later in life because they followed my example?; (as Adele wrote to me once "Dad, thank you for not giving up on yourself; we never have").

10. My "Model"

In September 1996 I was invited to give a series of addresses to the Brantford church. I chose to speak on a topic that I had been studying from the Bible for years and only recently pulled together, and also one which I was personally experiencing in real time. I called it "Our Spiritual Journey". In effect, it attempted to provide answers to the question: what does it mean to live spiritually in the real world? It featured the Bible's model of us as humans - spirit, soul and body - three very different but highly inter-related parts. What functions did each part perform? How did they affect each other? Which ones were more or less developed in me? I had recently been doing quite a bit of research into the physical aspects of my leukemia, and increasingly finding out useful information about the body-mind connection. Many of them made some references to the spiritual aspect but they were highly subjective. I lived my life by the Bible, as I was able to understand and apply it, and I needed to relate what else I was learning to that. The word of God must be the ultimate test of everything, and the ultimate authority for the spiritual realm. I needed specifics.

I gave the four talks in October. It was very personal and emotional for me. Sandra said I was "different" than when I usually made presentations (which I enjoy doing) - more energetic and expressive. A friend in the audience told me she thought to herself "That isn't Keith; I'm seeing the Holy Spirit at work in front of my eyes". While I was doing the second one, explaining something from a chart I was using, I had an insight into my own situation. It hit me that if my new gatekeeper was going to come from God the Holy Spirit within me, He could only "get at" my body (where my leukemia was) through my own spirit and my soul, not by by-passing them. They work in a series. It had to start with God (His direction and His power), be received by my spirit as I continued to be in active and submissive contact with Him, have it guide my thoughts, and then make decisions accordingly.

This prompted me to begin drawing my own internal "map" of how I work. I have a uniquely-created spirit (which is how I, and others, can receive knowledge and guidance from God, commune with Him, and have my conscience enlightened). Then I have a soul (the actual "me" - my mind, my emotions, and my will), and thirdly my body (which I find useful to classify as: my intake senses, my outward communicating devices, and my internal systems). Nine parts in all. I now had a Bible-based, if simplistic, overall framework for beginning to piece together all I was learning about each part and the inter-relationships. The diagram on the next page shows how I drew it; the order of the components is significant.

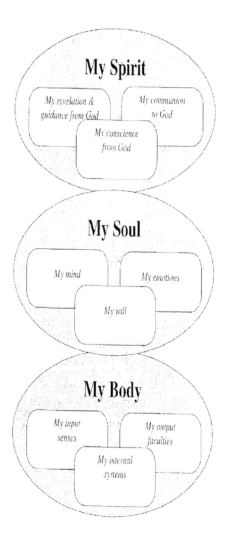

I don't pretend that this is theoretically correct or precise, but it is highly useful to me. There are a myriad of details that I have since been filling in, and I suppose I'll never finish doing that as I learn more about how I operate.

As this gradually became more complete, it occurred to me that what I needed to do was a personal assessment. Nothing too complicated, just identifying which ones were relatively stronger than the others (and therefore which ones I tended to rely on more, as being in my "comfort zone"), and which were relatively weaker and needed work. In effect I was looking for "wholeness" (another Bible term for health), since in my condition I couldn't afford to have any weak links in the chain. It was quite interesting what I learned.

I gave myself passing (not perfect) marks on:

- revelation and guidance (e.g. reading and learning from scripture and listening to guidance from God in my daily life);

- my conscience (knowing right and wrong as God sees it, regardless of society's variable standards);

- my mind (my analytical abilities);

- my will (my resolve and determination); and

- my 5 senses (my ability to sense my environment).

I also gave myself a tentative O.K. on my internal systems - my general health and bodily functions, with the major exception being my bad blood, but that's what I was trying to find the answer to. I viewed it as an effect and not a root weakness.

The others did not come out so well:

- my communion with God (while I prayed frequently, sometimes the quality and fervency was not what they should be; all too often prayer was a last resort);

- my emotional expression (I was often reluctant or unable to express my feelings or else I was too blunt; I once said to Larry Nusbaum "I think I have a weak emotional side"; he replied "I disagree; you have a very deep and passionate emotional side; it's just not public"); and

- my talking and other communications (too often I created the wrong impression, or didn't speak clearly, or clammed up; and I didn't smile enough).

There was obviously a pattern here - the elements on the right side (as I had pictured them) were the weaker, corresponding to the left side of my body. It was amazing how many of my ailments over the years had begun on my left side. This was so helpful. But what I needed was a plan - there was no point in being muscular on one side and underdeveloped on the other.

Larry Nusbaum was quite intrigued by my "model" and thought I would find it highly useful. In one of my sessions with him, I did a "harvesting" exercize in writing in which I queried my new gatekeeper (which I defined as the power of God within me) as to what I should be learning from what had been occurring to me since I had first asked so fervently to be healed - what would help me to receive His power to overcome my illness. Here is some of what I received that day:

"Keith, the learning from this is that there are opportunities there for you - for Me to work through you - anxiety gets in the way - peace of mind is a gift from Me - it requires that you not try to be in control of everything - it won't get out of control - and I love you and know what's best - let Me look after it - I'm quite able to...

Keith, having a loving relationship with someone involves more than understanding them and their needs; it involves understanding how they see you and react to you and the impressions you give - including by your body language and what you don't say. This is something I want you to learn. You're a conduit for Me to reach other people - and this can inadvertently get in the way...

Keith, the learning from this is that you don't have to do it all - I have many others also. I won't overburden you, so if you're overburdened you're doing it to yourself - maybe for the wrong reason - perhaps personal gratification? Check it out. Remember what it's all about - I get the credit, not you (remember your vow - it applies to more than your illness)."

Even reading these words over now, months later, affects me.

In one of my sessions with Larry he asked me to write out the essence of what I "knew" about God, in my own words. Here is what I wrote:

"God is all-powerful, all-intelligent, all-loving energy - personified. He has plans for His and my good. He has revealed Himself in terms of our humanity in Christ, who has eliminated the barrier to my union with Him. He has a pre-ordained path for me which I can realize only as I fully align myself with Him. This full alignment is my only hope for healing; medically my chances are zero."

In one of my later sessions Larry got me to draw another picture - this time of the present situation as I saw it. I drew a big dark cloud, which I was in, but I was moving through it to sunshine and health. Was I near the end or not? Only when the necessary changes were established would I emerge from the cloud, I felt. What would I be like when I was in the sunshine with the cloud behind me? I described it in three dimensions, corresponding to my three areas of development (and then realized they rhymed):

- *"a man of prayer"* - more consistently and fervently, and at deepening levels, as the source of my power;

- *"a man who shares"* - his thoughts and feelings with others, and so encourages others to do the same, to strengthen relationships, without which I can't make a difference; and

- *"a man who cares"* - who ministers what he has learned to other people, largely on a one-to-one basis, as opportunity presents itself - as my mission in life.

Obviously I couldn't become any of those unless I did all three; they were clearly related - which I took as good news. And it wasn't like I was devoid of these aspects, but God needed me to move to a higher level because of His plans for me. I might be satisfied with mediocrity, but He's not. And He needed this affliction to get my attention, and it sure had taken long enough for me to catch on. I was being shaped by the divine potter, and He wasn't going to give up.

And so my goal became clear - but it was at a macro level, too general. I needed a micro level plan - a set of routines to move me forward, and a personal discipline to stick with it. Without this I would never ingrain the habits that I needed to develop. Larry suggested I write down what those routines might be. Actually when I tried, I found it quite easy to do. They were things that previously I had been rather hit-and-miss about. I called it "my prescription":

- take a 15 minute brisk walk with Sandra three times a week after supper

- take my 5 selected vitamins and tonics at 10 p.m. every day

- talk openly with my family about my feelings, such as at mealtimes, especially after these sessions with Larry

- spend time in deep systematic prayer 3 times per week at 10 p.m. (after the vitamins)

- stop all intense mental activity at 9 p.m. every night (earlier if headaches, fatigue or other symptoms indicate)

- each Friday evening spend half an hour in quiet visioning, internal communication and journaling, identifying present sources of stress and remedies

- make personal contact (by visit, by phone or by note) each Monday evening with at least one person that I have committed to help

- continue to avoid toxic and unsafe foods (mainly just a potential problem when we eat out).

He observed that my prescription was specific and didn't appear too onerous; it seemed very legitimate to him. Then he asked me what he could do to help. I said "I've never been very good at daily routines; I need an authority figure to tell me to do this, and to hold me accountable until I have developed the disciplines to the point that I don't need that any more." He looked right at me and said "Keith, I want you to write out a weekly program of these 8 things, check off when you have done each of them, and then come and see me each week and show me what you've done!" I'd asked for it, but it was what I needed at that point.

11. Working with Young People

While I've been active all my adult life in church work, my special passion has been the teaching and nurturing of young people. I taught Sunday School from age 16, was a counsellor at our Mount Forest children's camps for 14 years and camp leader at children's and teen camps for 6 more. For twenty-odd years I've held young men's Bible study groups in my home on a regular basis, and I don't think anything in that area gives me more pleasure than to see some young person catch on and take hold spiritually.

I came across an anonymous poem one day that seemed to capture this thought. It goes like this:

> "He came to the crossroads all alone
> With the sunrise in his face.
> He had no fear for the path unknown;
> He was set for an ambitious race.
> The road stretched east and the road stretched west,

So the boy turned wrong and went on down,

And lost the race and the victor's crown,

And fell at last in an ugly snare,

Because no-one stood at the crossroads there.

Another boy on another day

At the self-same crossroads stood.

He paused a moment to choose the way

Which would lead to the greater good.

The road stretched east and the road stretched west,

But I was there to show him the best.

And the boy turned right and went on and on,

He won the race and the victor's crown

And came at last to the mansions fair,

Because I stood at the crossroads there.

Since then I have raised a daily prayer

That I be kept faithfully standing there,

To help the runners as they run,

And save my own and another's son."

Many of the young people whose lives I have been privileged to touch are parents themselves now, with growing families of their own, but the bond is still there. I played ball with them, I hung out with them in our home and elsewhere many times, and I tried to teach them to live by the scriptures - both by word and by example. Young people need positive role models and mentors. In my teaching I avoided using a lot of secondary sources. My motto was the Lord's words in John chapter 17 when He was explaining to His Father how He had equipped His disciples to carry on in His absence - simply *"I have given them your Word"*.

Dr. Nusbaum asked me one day who my own role models were. Immediately two people came to mind, both of whom are now dead (and both coincidentally were chartered accountants in business). One was my Dad, who died of emphysema in 1977 after terrible suffering. My Dad always put his family first; he left a very good business position in the United Kingdom because he felt that Canada was the land of opportunity for his three children. It was indeed, but he paid the price for it personally. I didn't fully appreciate his sacrifice until much later in life. He had a deep, if fairly private, faith in God; he didn't talk a lot about it but it was totally reflected in the way he lived his life. He didn't have a large number of close friends, but those he had were very loyal. He was a man of strong principles and he taught those clearly to me. He firmly believed I needed to develop a strong sense of responsibility. For example, I remember I had to pay every penny of my university fees and expenses, and my recollection of those days was of living in student poverty (of course that was clearly overstating it). He was stoic in suffering, never complaining. If I could talk to him today, here is what I would like to say to him...

"Dad, I was at your bedside when you passed away. I had been sitting there for hours, watching you struggle for breath, waiting for the moment. When it happened, I don't know if I would have tried to bring you back if I could have, because you had been suffering so much. But a wave of panic came over me. My father was gone. Things would never be quite the same.

I wish you could have lived longer, in good health. Mom sure has been lonely without you, and we can't fill that void. I really wish *you could have known <u>my</u> son, your grandson Andrew, and seen your two grand-daughters grow up.*

The older I get, and the more experienced a father I become, the more I realize just how good a father you were to me. I understand much better now why you always expected me to do my very best, and why you gave me what you did and withheld what you did. It was always for <u>my</u> good.

It's been almost twenty-one years now since I saw you, but your memory and your influence on me are as strong as ever. I love you, and I miss you a lot."

The other person was my uncle - Jack Ferguson. Because he lived in Barrhead, Scotland, we didn't see each other too often after I emigrated with the family at age 11, although my frequent business trips to London over the years allowed me to make many weekend visits. Uncle Jack was a man who affected many lives. I always knew he cared for me. He and my Aunt Olga had no children of their own and she admitted to me that I was like the son they never had. He was a systematic Bible teacher, a great public speaker, and a builder-up of small congregations. He was man of wisdom and he always had an agenda - the spiritual well-being of the people of God, especially young men. He called himself "a man's man".

I recall one time they were visiting us in Ontario and we spent the day at Black Creek Pioneer Village. Getting ready to leave, I went to pick up our picnic equipment. As Uncle Jack saw me go off by myself, he ran to catch up to help me. The first thing he said was "Now about this matter of worship, Keith" and he proceeded to tell me what he wanted to pass on and had probably been looking for the opportunity to do all day. He always had something on his mind. At the end of their trip, there was a gathering for their many friends to say goodbye. It was rather hectic for them but eventually we got them in the car to go home before their flight the next day. He sat down in the front passenger seat and turned to me. "I got it all done", he said with relief. To others it had just been a pleasant social occasion; to Uncle Jack there were six particular people he had needed to talk to about various things before his work was finished, and he had got it all done despite the distractions. He was always thinking about individuals - always with a purpose, a word of encouragement. I miss him too, and still think about him frequently.

He died suddenly and peacefully at age 80 in 1989. When we got the call I just knew I had to go over for the funeral. As expected the turnout was huge; they were there from all over. It was held in a school auditorium, which was packed, except for the front row which was reserved just for family. On that row there were just three of us - Aunt Olga, her sister Sheila, and me. I was so glad I'd gone.

Attending funerals since then has become more meaningful to me. No matter who the person is, it is important that we acknowledge their life and not forget them or just let them pass on un-noticed. I think I'm doing some transference to myself here, as I have become more conscious of my own mortality.

I sometimes couldn't help wondering: "What will they say about me? Will a few people attend because it's the right thing to do, a few positives from my life will be carefully selected and highlighted, and then people will go on about their business? And that will be that." That would be awful - as though my life didn't matter. Well, doesn't theirs matter just as much? And if these people are important in my life, shouldn't I tell them so, while they're still able to hear it?

And so I had some important role models myself as I was growing up and even now I find myself almost unconsciously emulating my father and my uncle.

In 1983 I had taken out a license to perform marriages, and since that time have married twenty couples in the church. In almost every case I had known them well for some time, and I counted it an honour to be standing a few feet away from them when they looked into each other's eyes and said their vows to each other. And so I feel I have a stake in their marriages. It got Sandra and me into pre-marital counselling with them, because we felt obligated to offer that assistance. Seldom were we turned down. It even resulted in us publishing a book on it, called "Getting Married".

But the crowning touch was on December 30th, 1993 at The Manor at Carrying Place, north of Toronto, on a lovely winter evening, when I married my oldest daughter Adele to Bruce Robinson of Vancouver. That was special, and it felt good that my daughter, whom I had cared for to the best of my ability for 23 years, would in turn care for and be cared for by a very fine young man, who has become such an important member of our family. At the reception, Adele stood up and gave a memorable speech addressed to us as her parents. She thanked us for being an example of a strong, loving marriage. She referred in particular to her mother's sense of caring, her sensitivities to others' needs, and to her example as a mother. Then she thanked me for showing her about leadership, that it's OK to fail as long as you try, about striving for excellence, not just getting by, and for setting proper priorities. There no feeling quite like your own child spontaneously saying things like that to you.

Adele had rather an eventful birth. She was born six weeks prematurely and we had to make a whirlwind two hour drive from our holiday at Miner's Bay in Haliburton early in the morning of July 29th, 1970. What with roads under construction, being almost out of gas, and rush hour traffic on the Don Valley Parkway, we only arrived at St. Michael's Hospital three hours before her arrival. I fell asleep in the waiting room, but I well remember being wakened by the doctor's words "come and see your new daughter". We were parents.

She wasn't very old when she got whooping cough - from me. She ended up in critical condition in Brantford General Hospital. It was so hard for Sandra and me to leave that tiny, sick infant behind in the hospital.

Adele always seemed to have a purpose in her life. She determined quite early on that she wanted to become a social worker, and she set her sights on it. She worked hard and obtained her Bachelor of Arts and Social Work degrees from McMaster University in Hamilton, and then (after her marriage and relocation to Vancouver) her Master of Social Work from University of British Columbia (where she was first in her class). She has that combination of intelligence, determination and insight that makes her a success in whatever she does. (And I don't think there's too much fatherly bias in that statement.) She is our firstborn; we are very proud of her and love her very much.

In the spring of 1996 I had the opportunity to hold a series of three classes in Hamilton for about 50 young people, outlining the Bible teaching on the churches of God and why we do what we do - a vital subject. It is so important that they get a good grasp of it. I was especially pleased that Jennifer and Andrew, my own children, were there. The sessions were well received and I felt that I had accomplished an important mission. These young people are so precious to God and to us, and they need to be well taught. As "Chicken Soup" said: it's so important for a teacher to love the student as much as they do the subject.

In June 1992 we had attended a large Youth Rally in Wales. It was a great event. I had given the opening theme talk and met dozens of young people from many countries whom I had never met before. At the closing talk, a decision was made to do it again four years later. As I sat there in the audience, I was thinking "That's a great idea, but I won't be there". Given the medical prognosis of my disease at the time, it was probable I wouldn't be there.

But in June 1996, I <u>was</u> there, with all five other family members. As I drove through the gates of the old mansion of Kinmel Hall, I silently offered myself for the weekend to God. I had no assigned responsibilities. But two things happened; I had planted, and the answers came. On the third day I was approached by one of the organizing committee to see if I would give them a little devotional talk at one of their meetings; they had been so busy, they hadn't been able to get any spiritual benefit from the event themselves. I spoke to them about the apostle Paul's testimony in Acts 22 - how he described himself as well taught and well brought up and very zealous for God. All of those things were true of the young people I was looking at in that committee room that afternoon. But it wasn't enough - not for Paul, and not for them. Paul had to be humbled until he had no agenda of his own and was not relying on his own ability at all. Only then could he begin to be used to make a real difference in other people's lives. Apparently the message struck home. Later one of them wrote to me and said it was a turning point in the weekend for them. That's God at work.

They asked if I would stand up and address the big Sunday night meeting and tell people my current health situation. I was a bit reluctant to draw attention to myself like that, but they pressed me on it and I remembered my vow of a few days before. And so, in front of 600 people the next night, many of whom had been praying for me for years, I was able to tell them what was happening to me.

As I told them about my thoughts at the end of the previous rally, I pointed and looked down to where I had been sitting four years before. There, looking right up at me was my daughter Jennifer - in the exact spot. I quickly tried to regain my composure.

I told them that the previous August two doctors had said that without a bone marrow transplant my chances of surviving twelve months were zero. But I hadn't been able to have the transplant and here I was ten months later as large as life. I put the question to them "does God answer prayer?". The answer was obvious. It was a very moving experience for me and allowed me to fulfil an on-going desire - to testify to people of the greatness of the Lord's work in my life, to His glory and credit.

12. The Worst Crisis Yet

(December 1996 to April 1997)

Bruce and Adele came out for Christmas 1996 and again we had a very good time as a family. These times were very precious to me. I was feeling good and looking better than I had in a long time although I knew that the new year held more treatments in store. "Happy New Year" now had a big question mark after it. The year ahead was a big blank in my mind. I could only think or plan a short time ahead.

We had a family portrait taken. On Christmas afternoon I came down with an ear congestion which stubbornly wouldn't go away. I had been invited to make a short trip to Scotland at New Year's to speak at a conference, but the "Ear, Nose and Throat" doctor at the hospital told me I shouldn't fly. And so I had to cancel the trip. I was really disappointed, but it was the right decision. It was the cold and flu season and that would have been running unnecessary risks. Sandra was very relieved because she knew I wasn't well enough to go.

As with so many of the decisions I was constantly having to make, there were always the two sides - what I wanted and what was smart; what might provide a break-through and what was safe. Sandra and I would chew them all over. In the case of this speaking engagement, I had felt honoured to be asked and somewhat obligated to fulfil it if I could, although they had a backup speaker. It would also have allowed me to say thank-you to a lot of people in person, and I wanted the opportunity to do that. There weren't a lot of things in my life these days that I could look forward to. But - it obviously was not to be. Maybe one of these years I'll make it, I thought.

And so on January 13th, 1997 I went back into St. Mike's for the first of at least three chemotherapy sessions. Dr. Brandwein had decided to try a combination of Fludarabine and Cyclophosphamide, based on some success in clinical trials at the M.D. Anderson Cancer Center in Houston. Although I'd had both of those drugs before separately, the combination had worked fairly well in cases like mine which were resistant to other protocols. At this point my white blood count was 540! I could hardly imagine all those leukemic lymphocyte cells in my blood vessels, when the normal level was 4 to 11. How did the good cells manage to move around through all that?

Although Dr. Brandwein didn't seem overly concerned about the white cell count itself, I wondered: "How high can they go? They're multiplying at an alarming rate. How will they ever come down? Will the treatment work?"

I never got used to chemotherapy. I would look at that bag of what looked like water on the I.V. pole and I could almost taste the bitterness. I knew that each successive round of treatments was stronger than the time before and was cumulatively damaging my body. I imagined my blood cells saying "here it comes again", and trying to hide to avoid being wiped out. But it was the lesser of two evils. The procedure was so familiar, but it still made me recoil. I just waited - knowing that the effects would eventually hit me and I would again start sliding uncontrollably down the slippery slope.

After the chemo my ear problem returned and Dr. Brandwein again put me on the neutrophil growth factor "GCSF" for a few days to stimulate my immune system. After the infection I didn't really improve too much and my energy level remained low. But soon it was time for the second treatment. In the meantime I decided to order a new hair piece, as the original one was getting a little "tired". It's quite a procedure to have the template prepared to exactly fit, but I preferred wearing a wig when I was at work or out in public. But it takes several weeks to make after it is ordered. However I didn't lose a lot of hair this time; instead over several weeks my hair just became thinner and more lifeless. Blah!

Meanwhile I was trying to go into work when I could, but it was rather hit and miss. I felt like my name should be "Bob", because I kept bobbing up and down, never sure from one day to the next how I would feel and how much energy I would have.

For several years I have had a very good executive assistant at the office, Susan Hodges, and through my many absences she has kept the administrative things going, never quite sure when I would be away or for how long, and when I would suddenly turn up with a flurry of work. I am indebted to her for that.

At this time I was also taking injections of Eprex on a clinical trial, designed to boost my hemoglobin, and they worked quite well. But I still didn't feel that well. I wasn't bouncing back after these treatments the way I usually did. However the chemo did wonders for my white blood count. From an all-time high of 540 they dropped to below one! Yes - 540 down to 1. That was a lot of cells being killed and flushed through my system.

On a spiritual level, I was also not enjoying the peace and strength from God that I so much needed. I thought I knew how to draw on that but with me feeling physically as weak as I did, I obviously had more to learn. It can't just work in the good times, I thought. I resolved to make that a priority when I headed into the third treatment at the end of March. Little did I know what a momentous event that would turn out to be.

When I was due to have my third chemo, I reported to Dr. Brandwein that I was very short of breath and quite nauseous. I wasn't eating. A chest X-ray revealed I had a large build up of fluid around my left lung - a "pleural effusion". The pleural cavity was about three quarters full on that side. He drained off about one and a half litres of it, again by inserting a needle in my back, through my rib cage, and siphoning it into a container. The fluid then went off to the lab for analysis. That postponed the chemo for a week - to the following Monday, at which time the fluid was still there but no worse. The treatment lasted for three days. But the nausea and vomiting were the worst yet; I was hardly eating anything, and what was getting down didn't stay down. By the Saturday we knew I needed medical care and so back again we went to Emergency. Sandra was out of the house at the time and Jennifer found me lying on the couch in the family room shivering (with the fire going) and having difficulty breathing, and she took over. I felt too badly to even think of taking my temperature or phoning the hospital or even telling her I needed help.

Whenever I was in a state of suffering I always tended to "shut down", to withdraw within myself, which made it hard for others to know what to do to help me. All my energy was being focussed on coping with the moment, and I wouldn't be thinking clearly about what I ought to be doing about it. The greater my discomfort, the shorter my time horizon got. In extreme suffering, all that matters is "now".

Here we go again, I thought. I was getting so tired of being admitted to hospital, with all it entailed - being cooped up in a room for a week or more, constantly being poked for blood tests and to insert I.V. needles (and by now I had very few veins left that hadn't seized up), unplugging and trailing my I.V. pole into the bathroom every time I had to go there (which was often, with all the fluid being pumped through me), measuring and recording all my output, constantly having my blood pressure, oxygen saturation and temperature taken, swallowing all kinds of pills (which I've never been good at) and being injected with antibiotics - all the sights and sounds and smells repulsed me. And there was also seeing the strain on Sandra when she came to visit me - every day without fail for several hours, no matter how she felt and whether she had been at work that day or not. But I was sick and I needed to be there.

In Emergency they ran all the usual tests, including an X-ray. (By now every time a thermometer was stuck in my ear I would pray like mad that it would be below 39.) The blood test showed my neutrophil count to be below 500, which I knew was the magic number. I wouldn't be sleeping in my own bed that night. That brought the usual deflated feeling. They drained off some more fluid through my back, and then admitted me to room 768, the same as last time. (The John 3:16 text given to me by Gordon Miller that I had left on the wall was still there.)

As the week progressed I got worse. Despite being on four different antibiotics, I had a high fever. They kept draining more fluid (quite an invasive procedure) and taking more X-rays. The effusion had now spread to my right side as well. I had to lie on my back if I wanted to be able to breath. They put me on oxygen - initially just the prongs in the nose, then a mask, and finally "the whiskers" ("horns" I called them) - extra side-pieces added to the mask. I looked like a space alien. Plus I had to have ventolin treatments with the oxygen, which were unpleasant and left a horrible taste in my mouth. I was still vomiting with no warning, but it was just wrenching as I'd had nothing in my stomach for ten days.

Dr. Brandwein was looking worried. If he was worried, I should be worried; but I had enough to do. On Thursday morning he phoned Sandra to tell her that he was calling in two top specialists - one for lungs (Dr. Epstein) and one for infectious diseases (Dr. Fong). He told her he was very concerned about the fluid and I'd had a very bad night. They ran numerous tests, tried growing cultures, and even checked me for tuberculosis. Everything came back negative, yet the fluid got worse. Late on Thursday the three of them had a major consultation and then informed me that the next day I would be having a bronchoscopy and a pleuroscopy and then be on a respirator (a breathing machine) in Intensive Care. A bronchoscopy is an exploratory scope down in the lung; a pleuroscopy is the same sort of thing in the pleural cavity around the lung, and is more invasive because they have to go in from outside instead of through the mouth. The young doctor who brought us the news just dropped it all on us like a bombshell. Sandra said to him "Could he die from this?" and he rather casually replied "Well there's some chance of that, but he should be O.K.". I was so angry I felt like jumping out of the bed and throwing him out of the room for giving my wife an irresponsible answer like that. Instead, I asked him very directly if Dr. Brandwein was aware of this plan; he replied that his team was. I told him I wanted him to tell Dr. Brandwein personally and then ask Dr. Brandwein to talk directly to us.

It was important to me to know what Dr. Brandwein thought. I have a great respect for good professionals, and am prepared to rely heavily on them. Perhaps it's because of my own professional training. Initially I relied too heavily, and didn't do enough investigating on my own. But Sandra always made up for that, and by this time I was fully into knowing and understanding what was going on. A top professional and a fully informed client are a good combination.

Sandra phoned Dr. Brandwein at home to tell him herself. He hadn't been aware of the plan for the pleuroscopy. He said he would talk to Dr. Epstein and call her back. A few minutes later, Dr. Epstein himself came in and he was very good. He'd just spoken with Dr. Brandwein. He stayed a long time and answered all our questions. He really inspired our confidence. Later Dr. Brandwein called back and discussed it fully with Sandra. He agreed with the plan. That was good enough for me. But Sandra told me later that she'd also asked him what the end would be like. While I didn't think it was the end, at one point I whispered to her: "I don't want to die in a hospital".

By now Sandra was staying overnight on a cot in my hospital room, which I found very comforting (although she didn't find it very comfortable, and didn't sleep much). She was going on sheer adrenalin, and for a third time began thinking about the need to plan for a funeral. I wasn't eating at all, and not sleeping much either due to being interrupted every fifteen minutes by a doctor or nurse. I felt like a pin cushion. You know you're really sick when you get that much attention; it's a good sign when they leave you alone. Sandra phoned Adele in Vancouver to bring her up to date; they had been wondering whether to come. When I heard the procedures I was going to be having the next day, I knew I wanted her there. We called her back, but she and Bruce had already decided to come. (She had phoned Dr. Brandwein herself from Vancouver.) I learned later that they had previously booked a week's holiday in Cancun for that week! Through the efforts of our friend Glenn Smith who works for Canadian Airlines, they managed to get two seats on that night's "red eye" overnight flight. They had an hour to go home from work, pack and get to the airport. I found out later that Adele had packed for a funeral.

On Friday morning early they arrived at the hospital, directly from the airport. Adele got quite a shock; she'd never seen me nearly that sick before and with all those tubes in me. I was in distress. I hadn't been allowed to swallow any liquid or solid since the previous midnight, because of the surgery I was going to be having. My blood pressure was low (80 over 40), and I had to take some foul-tasting gravel-like potassium. Adele sat down beside my bed and held my hand. I was so glad to see her. I just poured out my heart to her. I told her I had never been so sick and I was struggling so hard. She said I was so strong, but I said I felt anything but strong - so absolutely weak and helpless. She asked me if I was scared. I told her I wasn't scared about the surgery that day, but I was scared they wouldn't be able to find out what was wrong and give me relief, and I wouldn't get better.

Then Jennifer and Andrew arrived. They were both obviously very upset and it troubled me greatly to see them that way. Jennifer had tears in her eyes; I hugged her and said "It's O.K.

to be emotional; I certainly am". I hugged Andrew and asked him to help me fight this thing (we've always had a little motto between us: "We're on the same team"). Looking at my family standing around the bed - Sandra, Adele, Jennifer, Andrew and Bruce - gave me the will to keep going.

Before long Sandra's sister Jessie arrived. Then our friends Greg & Liz Neely came; they weren't sure if they should, but they came anyway, and I was glad they were there. No-one knew what to say. It was like a morgue. I tried to relieve the pressure with some "gallows humour". To me it was like a dream or an "out-of-body" experience; none of this was really happening. My mouth was so dry. Adele asked me what I was thinking. I pointed to my Bible. She gave it to me and I turned up Psalm 22 and pointed to verse 15, which refers prospectively to Christ on the cross: "*my tongue sticks to the roof of my mouth; you have brought me to the dust of death*". She read it and said "Is that what you're thinking about?" I said "Yes, but He suffered a lot more than me".

A couple of days earlier a friend of ours, Anne Taylor, had sent me a card with that famous little story "Footprints" by Margaret Fishback Powers. (It's her story of a dream of someone walking along the beach - her life's journey; the Lord was with her, and so there were two sets of footprints. But there was only one set of footprints at the lowest and saddest times of her life, and she couldn't understand why He had deserted her when she needed Him most and so she asked Him. He replied that it was then that He was carrying her.) I'd read it many times but this time it really moved me. Frequently I would look at it on the wall and call out to the Lord "carry me now". The Lord's presence felt very close right then. In my previous stay in hospital I had been bothered by the fact that when I felt at my worst, I didn't seem to be feeling the strength from God that I needed. I seemed to be struggling when I needed it the most. And so this time I had decided I needed to experience it when I was weakest. When I was able to read my Bible for five minutes, I did. When I was able to whisper a brief prayer, I did. I was drawing nearer to God, and I knew He would then draw very near to me. I remembered that when Christ calmed the storm on Galilee for His disciples, He hadn't done it from the safety of the shore; He had been right in the boat with them.

Then they put me on a gurney and began a platelet transfusion because of the bleeding that would occur in the surgery. But there was a long delay. Sandra tells the story:

"The anaesthetist came into the room, talked with Keith and then told me: "There's going to be a delay. There's a problem. We have two people booked for surgery who need an Intensive Care room afterwards, and there's only one Intensive Care room available. So we have to decide." I said to him: "So, how do you decide?". He said: "I'm just going right now to talk to the two doctors involved, and we'll decide who needs it the most". I turned to him and said: "He has to have it. He can't wait." The anaesthetist said: "I'll be back". I said: "How long?" "Within the hour" he replied and left. (Meanwhile Keith was still having his platelet transfusion, waiting for the operation.) He was back in five minutes. "He's on", he said, "we'll be taking him down very soon.""

And so, after what seemed for ever, the call came and it was time to go As I was wheeled out of the room I saw two nurses I knew in the hallway - both believing Christians. I called them both over and asked them to pray for me. One of them, a Trinidadian named Stalin, offered to take me down to the operating room. The layout of St. Michael's Hospital is very complicated and on the way we got lost. Imagine getting lost on the way to surgery, I thought, and with all the entourage of family trailing behind. It actually made me laugh (my humour comes out at the strangest times). When we arrived, Stalin took me inside and had a short prayer with me. He told me later he's only allowed to do that if the patient asks for it. I said goodbye to each of my family; later Adele admitted that she thought that it was the final goodbye.

It's strange to be waiting for major surgery. I thought back to September 1995 and my big splenectomy. Both times I was aware I might not wake up. I wasn't scared and I had confidence in the doctors but, just to be sure, I prayed and got "saved" all over again. And then in I went.

Dr. Thomas was the surgeon, and apparently very experienced. They got me on the operating table, spread-eagled me, strapped me down and then gave me a general anaesthetic. At one point I apparently got into some breathing difficulty and they had to ease up on the anaesthetic. I seemed to regain partial consciousness and later I could remember actually visualizing momentarily what they were doing inside me. They had a scope with a camera and tweezers to take biopsies; I could "see" it roaming around, taking pictures and samples. Everything looked pure white. But I felt nothing.

The next thing I knew it was two hours later and I was in an isolation room in Intensive Care, somewhere in the hospital. The respirator was in my mouth and down my throat (and through my vocal chords); it was doing the breathing for me and so my oxygen mask was gone. I was wired up to a whole battery of machines behind me - like Battleship Galactica. But I could hardly hear anything. People would be talking right beside me and I couldn't make out what they were saying unless they spoke loudly directly into my ear. As I looked around I had no idea where in the hospital I was. There was a full-time nurse sitting at the end of my bed and Sandra was there, of course. What a tower of strength she was the whole time. How she kept going I don't know. As always she was anticipating my every need. I felt so dependent, but very safe.

While I was obviously very sick, I wasn't in the breathing distress that I had been earlier. There were always doctors and nurses around, paying close attention to me. The three nurses who rotated shifts - Laura, Janice and Maureen - were so competent and so caring. I felt that no matter what might happen to me, they'd know what to do. Maureen knew Donna Goldthorp, Sandra's colleague at her work. (Later, we heard through Donna that Maureen had said, in all her years of nursing, she had never seen a family like ours; we had an aura of closeness and love that could be felt.) Because I couldn't talk, they gave me a clipboard to write on, and for three days we had some interesting and funny conversations with the family and the medical people - them shouting into my ear, and me writing on the clipboard. We kept all the pages. Reading them over later, I couldn't believe some of the things I had written (or my poor spelling).

They gave me morphine to help me sleep. At all times there was a family member in the room with me - usually Sandra, Adele, Jennifer or Bruce. My sisters Shirley and Hilary also visited regularly. The nurses had allowed the family to take over one of the visitors' lounges as a headquarters. On Saturday Andrew came in. He found it very hard to visit - but he did it anyway. He told his Mom: "I just can't handle seeing Dad with all those tubes in him". He wasn't enjoying this at all - and no wonder. The last time he'd seen me had been very frightening. However when he saw me and we had some shouting/clipboard dialogue, including a few jokes, he cheered up considerably. I felt good about that.

Saturday was a rough day. Periodically they had to help me cough up mucous with a suction tube, which was painful and exhausting. I'd had my left pleural cavity drained during the operation, but now I had to be tapped again for the other side (they had now drawn out a total of 6 litres). But the worst was when they tried to insert a feeding tube through my nose down into my stomach without any sedation. It was necessary because I hadn't eaten in thirteen days and lack of protein can affect the heart. A resident doctor came in to do it, but he didn't do it very well. They held me down and kept telling me "swallow", while he rammed the tube down. He forgot to put in the insert to keep it from buckling. I was struggling to the limit of my strength and I almost blacked out. I heard him say "only six inches to go". I went into bronchial distress and Sandra almost fainted. I felt like I was falling down a black hole and couldn't stop. Finally he just pulled it out and gave up. But he had caused some hemorrhaging in the lining of my stomach. I just lay there exhausted. Sandra told them never to let that doctor touch her husband again. She registered a complaint, and received an apology. However, with that one notable exception, the care I received was outstanding.

I was still on the four antibiotics and potassium by I.V. The erythromycin and potassium burned my veins on the way in and I needed morphine for the intense pain at the I.V. site.

On Sunday morning they decided to try to wean me off the respirator. I was very nervous about that. Would I be able to breathe on my own without it? Not being able to breathe is very frightening. But if I stayed on it, they'd need to try the nasal feeding tube again. No thanks. They managed to get me off it by noon and back on oxygen (prongs only). Dr. Brandwein came by (I was always relieved to see him; I had so much confidence in him), and when he saw I was off it he gave a big grin. Initially I couldn't speak very well, only croak, but my voice came back within about a day. But I still was without about ninety percent of my hearing, and they said it might be permanent because of the antibiotics!

I started sipping a little fluid. Later that afternoon they asked me if there was anything I might like to try to eat. Adele shouted "Dad, what are your taste buds telling you?". So I thought and then wrote out: "Campbell's Cream of Tomato Soup". They all just looked at me. But Bruce took on the challenge. It was late Sunday evening in downtown Toronto, and he's from Vancouver. But almost an hour later he was back. He'd found a small grocery store open about ten blocks east, and had the soup - and milk and a can opener. Maureen, my nurse, made a big fuss of it. She put it in a bowl, micro-waved it, and then presented it to me on a tray. I ate it - my first meal in two weeks.

That evening they decided it was time for me to go back to my own room on the 7th floor. I didn't want to go. I felt safe here in Intensive Care, and the 7th floor was the scene of all my previous distress. But Bruce and Adele stayed late with me, and Sandra again spent the night. For five days and nights she hadn't been home.

Gradually during the week that followed, I began to eat better and my blood counts improved. They gradually reduced the oxygen level from four to two. I had daily chest X-rays. On Tuesday morning, Dr. Ball, the resident who had admitted me in Emergency and had been so attentive and diligent during my stay, checked my X-ray and said "this is a miracle; am I looking at the right X-ray?" The fluid was going down on its own!

I was absolutely delighted of course, but not overly surprised, I remember. I expected to get better. Wasn't that what everyone was praying for? I didn't know how or when, but this was supposed to happen. I didn't need an explanation as to how it was happening.

That afternoon I was dozing in bed. Only Bruce was there, sitting reading across the room. A nurse came in and he spoke with her quietly. It suddenly dawned on me: "I can hear what they're saying". I said to Bruce: "Say something to me in a normal voice". He did, and I could hear him perfectly. My hearing was back! We tried to pull a trick on Adele and Sandra when they returned, because they didn't know I could now hear, but it didn't quite work.

I had a lot of visitors that week. In addition to the family and my sisters, Greg and Liz came again, Geoff Hydon, Mike Bowcott, Jeff Chisholm from the office, Rachel Kennedy with the children Jordan and Jennifer, Rodney Falconer and Joel Clements, and of course my Mom. Rachel had offered to drive to Brantford and get her and then take her home again. She was so relieved to see me, although we'd kept in touch by phone. I hadn't wanted her to come when I was in Intensive Care; she was eighty-three and I was concerned it would be too much for her. Dr. Kopplin also visited from time to time and informed us what the other doctors were talking about, and he also passed word along to Matt Barrett and Tony Comper at work for me about my condition.

My driver from work, John Fawcett, kept very busy driving people to and from the hospital, as he always did when I was in. What a help he has been to me and my family through this whole illness. There's nothing he wouldn't offer to do. He worked weekends and holidays when we needed him. We are all indebted to him.

Every day I began to hear more stories about people who were calling and assuring us of their prayers, all sparked initially by just three phone calls from Sandra. For example: Marg Smith called from Bournmouth, England, where she and Ian were on holiday; from Terry Dougan from Belfast (who was a very frequent caller and always had a word from scripture for me); from Myanmar (Burma); from Nigeria; from Melbourne, Australia; from Colorado; from Kinder Mattu in Vancouver. I heard about ladies in Brantford gathering for special prayer, of midnight prayer meetings in homes in Richmond Hill and Mississauga. It truly boggled my mind. All I could say was "thank you". The whole community of the saints in the churches of God (and others besides) was my support system. Later I heard about the Chappel family (the family of Andrew's public school friend) gathering for prayer, as a result of a phone call. I got a call again from Ian Stewart, my boyhood friend in Scotland, who mentioned that their family had probably prayed for us a thousand times since I became ill! I got a lovely letter from my young friend Jon Smith, who told me what my friendship had meant to him as he was growing up.

I felt as though I had three rings of support as I lay there helpless in hospital. Firstly there were the medical people, who were so competent and working so hard for me; then there was my family, supporting me emotionally and in so many practical ways; and then this huge throng of friends. I kept thinking "the saints are praying"; it was a great comfort. And it was obviously working. Every single test came back negative and they were within minutes of putting me on tuberculosis medication for several months, by default. I told the doctors: "We don't know what caused the problem, but I know what's curing it". I think by this time they were beginning to believe me. Dr. Brandwein admitted: "You gave me a few sleepless nights". He said "The only thing I can think of, after talking to the Houston Cancer Clinic, is that you've had a very rare reaction to the Fludarabine chemotherapy, but I'm not at all sure". This wasn't a medical solution; and God should rightfully be getting the credit.

On Friday evening I was discharged, just five days after I'd been in Intensive Care. We went home and had a nice family dinner which Sandra presented beautifully. It was so good to be home again, even though I had lost so much weight and was so weak.

It was so good to be out of hospital, and almost too much to take in. I was very tired and I felt like I was in a daze, with the family moving about around me. But I felt contented. I just wanted to savour the moment and enjoy their warmth.

Bruce and Adele returned to Vancouver the next evening, very relieved I was out of hospital. What a support they each were. Bruce is very helpful, always cheerful and very thoughtful, and a good companion for Andrew. And Adele had been such a comfort to me. Like her mother she seemed to know what to do and what to say. I had written to her on the clipboard: "You are a wonderful care-giver". She just smiled. She was part mother to me that trip, and part my little girl. She had always felt out of the loop being so far away in Vancouver, and it bothered her, but she was sure in the thick of it this time. When I mentioned their cancelled vacation, she said "There's no place I'd rather have been than here".

On Sunday morning I sent along a message to our church congregation. I personalized hymn 465 in our book when I wrote:

"You moved the hand that moves the world, and brought deliverance down".

What an awesome contemplation! Never had we experienced such an outpouring of prayer from so many. And never had we seen such evident response from the God of heaven. He heard and He did what no one else could have done. I thought of that verse in the Psalms (although out of context): "*This was the Lord's doing; it is marvellous in our eyes.*" As we told our story to doctors, nurses, business colleagues of Sandra's and mine, and neighbours, they didn't have an answer. Obviously something was going on here that they couldn't explain.

The crisis was over - except for two things. The following week, Sandra was exhausted. She was so physically and emotionally drained that she was almost beside herself, and I became quite concerned. I found myself trying to minister to her for a change. She gives and gives until it's over.

Also, I made a decision. I couldn't go on living like this. I wasn't sure I could undergo any more of these foul chemotherapy treatments with all their complications and the severe stress on the family. Things were getting close to the end, it seemed, and there was a limit. Something had to happen. Little did I realize what it would be.

13. The Door Begins to Re-open

(May and June 1997)

In early May 1997 Dr. Brandwein gave me another bone marrow biopsy and aspiration to assess the effect of the three chemotherapy treatments. He had to repeat it a week later as the first one wasn't conclusive. These tests aren't usually painful, just a bit uncomfortable. They gave me local freezing on the rear hip and then drilled into the bone until they reached the marrow inside. A week later Sandra and I went to see him to hear the results and his recommendations. We were very anxious. I knew I didn't want to continue with more treatments, but what other options were there? For some time he had been looking into possible clinical trials in the area of immunology research, but nothing had surfaced yet. As usual we went with our list of questions.

He told us the chemo had worked extremely well, better than he had expected. Not only were my blood counts good but the level of leukemia in my bone marrow was down again from about 80% to the 50-60% range. I could go without treatment for several months, he expected, but it would return and he had nothing presently to recommend. I reminded him he'd told me the same thing a year ago, but he said: "They're on our coat-tails and sooner or later they're going to catch up". Because of the serious pleural effusion, which he was having to conclude was from the Fludarabine treatment (or else some virus), he said he would be afraid to try that again. He had again consulted with a leading C.L.L. hematologist at the M.D. Anderson Clinic in Houston. So that was the good news and the bad news. There always seemed to be some bad news mixed in with any good news.

Then he dropped the bombshell. He had spoken again to Dr. Lipton at Princess Margaret Hospital and told him that I was again responding to treatment. Would Dr. Lipton reconsider me for a bone marrow transplant? "Send him over", he had replied. The Houston doctor had concurred that this would be by far my best option.

This was almost too much. It was the last thing we expected to hear, and what a big decision, so soon after surviving last month's crisis. And they would want to do it right away - in early July. And so, with me carrying the little vial of my bone marrow, we went up town to see Dr. Lipton.

So many thoughts crowded in. "I shouldn't get my hopes up too high. It's too soon to decide about this after what I've just been through. How could this happen when they had totally ruled it out? Do I dare start to hope? Let's just wait and see."

When he walked into the room, the first thing Dr. Lipton said was: "Am I delighted to see you. I never thought I'd see you again. When I told you a year last February that you couldn't have the transplant, I was thinking to myself 'He's got nine to twelve months to live; go and enjoy it'."

He filled us in again on the whole procedure, all the pre-tests I would have to pass, and all the risks. He said in my case there was probably up to a 20% risk of fatality, either from infection or "graft-versus-host disease" (where the donated marrow rejects me), and up to another 30% chance that after it all I would still have some degree of leukemia left. In other words, it was 50-50 whether I would be leukemia-free after it all, and they wouldn't be able to definitively assess that for at least twelve months. But 50-50 was better than my alternatives.

He told me to expect to spend six to eight weeks in hospital, much of it in isolation, and then several months at home, out of public. The first hundred days from the transplant were the most critical. I would be taking so many pills I would be sick of them. I would have to visit the clinic twice a week after I went home, probably for several months, then gradually less frequently. What did we want to do?

We gave him a tentative "yes' to get on the schedule, but told him we wanted to discuss it with the family and we were just about to go on a two-week holiday. Could we confirm it as soon as we got back? He agreed (I could take myself off the list at any time before it began, but not thereafter of course) but he said we shouldn't delay; every week my condition could get worse, and there was just a short window of opportunity.

On the way home, Sandra and I were at a loss as to what to think. Such a big decision so soon. What would the children think? Why had the door closed a year ago and now apparently re-opened? I thought back to what had transpired during that intervening year. It had been so eventful. My general health was better now than it had been in February 1996 when I had expected to have the transplant. We'd had some great holidays together - Arizona, U.K. and Guernsey, and New England. I had put on the classes for the young people and my presentations in Brantford, I had mended some relationships, I had learned so much from my sessions with Larry Nusbaum, and my illness in April had stiffened my resolve to not just keep going from one series of treatments to another (even if that were possible). Maybe the answer had always been "yes" but the time was not then but now. We had two weeks to finally decide, but I knew instinctively that I must do this. Was this to be my new "gatekeeper"?

We told Jennifer and Andrew that night and phoned Adele. Adele was very positive about it, seeing it as an unprecedented opportunity. Jennifer was in favour, but was naturally concerned about the effect on her studying for her difficult final C.A. exams. She wanted to be able to give priority to me during this time and so wondered if she should defer the exams. Once again a major episode coincided with her most stressful time. Andrew wasn't quite so sure at first. I seemed so well at the moment and he needed to be sure this was the best option. I had a talk with him, just explaining how I felt about it - how fed up I was living this way and looking this way, never knowing what was going to happen next, being "in limbo" at work, not being able to be the father and husband I wanted to be. He listened very carefully. I told him we'd talk again after our holiday. I then phoned Hilary to see if she was still willing to go ahead with the donation, and she said "of course".

And so Sandra and I set off on May 20th. We flew to Berlin for a few days, then got the train to Hamburg for a week's cruise down the river Elbe to Dresden, and then finally to Prague in the Czech Republic. It was a wonderful, relaxing and educational holiday. We walked lots, ate lots and I never felt better. We saw the remains of the old Berlin Wall, Martin Luther's Wittenburg, the highlands of Saxony, the bombed ruins of beautiful Dresden, the Nazi concentration camp at Terrazin (which was shocking), and the beautiful old city of Prague. It was a tonic.

Then it was home to reality and a family conference on June 5th about the decision. This time there was strong endorsement all around, which I was so glad about as I would have hated anyone to have felt any regrets if things hadn't turned out as we hoped. So we began communicating the decision to family and friends. Everyone was delighted for us, but we were initially a little concerned that they didn't realize there was a big down side to all this. There were considerable risks, and it would be a long and difficult ordeal for the whole family. We still needed all their support. But there were two other things to be done first.

One was for me to make another visit to Larry Nusbaum, to help me get focussed on what lay ahead. It really helped, and I came away convinced I was now ready to get well. At the end of our session, Larry reminded me of certain things which I'd previously acknowledged, such as:

- allowing my emotions to emerge has the effect of stimulating my resolve

- I should remember the power of just posing <u>any</u> question to myself and seeing what turns up; like planting, it starts a generative process

- when my answers don't seem too profound, they may actually be very significant; don't dismiss them

- when I'm not that comfortable with a process (such as harvesting or dialoguing), it may mean in fact that it's working, like any form of exercize program

- I'll sense when I'm "in the zone" and energized (when things seem to just flow effortlessly and effectively); I should "go with it"

- I need to stay in touch with my gatekeeper - it's central - and I could use my journal for this purpose

- I should keep imagining what it will be like to be healed; it may be the most powerful drug I'll take

- I am a complex system, and all my parts respond to respectful communication (just like a business).

And then he made some personal observations. He said I had changed a lot since he first met me nine months before, and I seemed much more comfortable communicating with myself and with others. And - I was having an impact on a lot of people, including him. He told me to consider him part of my team, with the doctors, family, etc., and he was available to visit me, talk by phone, whenever I wanted to. I was very grateful.

The other was an Open House, which Sandra and I had talked about having as long ago as two years before, but now seemed the right time. We wanted to thank as many people as possible for their faithful support and to fill them in on what lay ahead. Well over a hundred dropped in that Saturday evening and we had some very good conversations. Sandra has always been an excellent hostess and she was at her best, although it was very taxing for her. Adele flew out for the weekend to be part of it, which had the added bonus that the next day was Father's Day.

I was ready!

14. Here We Go

(June to August 1997)

One of the many positive outcomes of this whole experience has been to bring our extended family closer together. Sandra's father passed away in 1985 and her mother late in 1994. Sandra was very close to both of them and they adored her. And so she had her mother's passing to deal with in the midst of my serious illness. Her brother David and her sisters Betty and Jessie keep in close touch with her. Jessie frequently sends her cards and letters and has been prepared to do anything for us, including my Christmas shopping and our laundry.

On my side of the family, my two sisters and I had not spent a lot of time with each other during much of our married lives. We always got on well together but our paths didn't cross frequently. They have both been through a lot of adversity in their own lives, and it pleases me so much that they seem to be very happy these past few years. That distance has all changed in recent years, and I now realize just how much we mean to each other. I truly count that as one of God's many gifts from this situation. Just before my transplant, on June 23rd, the three of us and our spouses spent a very happy time visiting together at Shirley and James' home in Cobourg.

Shirley is the oldest one of the three, and now that she is living in Cobourg, close to Toronto, she often takes the initiative to get us together. She visits frequently, sends encouraging cards and prays with me. We have reconfirmed our love for each other. Her husband James is a lovely man. He works overseas in Malaysia some of the time, and is a gentle and loving husband who would give you the shirt off his back. I am very fond of him.

My sister Hilary, seven years younger than me, is quite an outgoing person and fun to be with. She is quite unpredictable. She and her husband Bryan, live in Oro, north of Barrie. Bryan is a very positive, upbeat person, who speaks his mind. They are a great couple. My mother told me that my father had given Hilary the middle name "Joy" because he said she would be a joy to them in their old age; if only he could have been here to see what she was about to do for me. Hilary had also visited me a lot in St. Michael's, once bringing me a "love cushion". I owe Hilary an insurmountable debt for giving me her life-giving marrow. She says it's nothing, anyone would have done it. But to me it's everything, and I know that it's been pretty significant in her mind to be able to do this for me. It's a wonderful gift from her and, when I think about it, it's from my Dad and Mom too over forty years later, which is quite a legacy considering my father has been gone these twenty-one years. Hilary and I joke a lot about me becoming like her because I now have her immune system (and Bryan keeps asking me jokingly if I'm now having trouble staying away from shopping malls), but there's no question that this has strengthened the bond between us. I love her dearly.

Here is what Hilary has to say about her experience as a bone marrow donor:

"I remember well the night my brother phoned to tell me he had leukemia. It was remarkable for two reasons. First, because of the shocking and painful message he had to tell. But second because my brother rarely called me - just as I rarely called him. We led separate lives and we usually had little to say to each other. It's not that we didn't care for each other, it's just that there was little to say and we were both busy going our own way. For over thirty years the manner in which he and I have chosen to express our values and beliefs has been very different and so our lives have been divergent.

That notwithstanding, I have always loved and respected my brother as much as is it possible to do so. Even as an adult I have looked up to him as "my big brother", knowing that he was "there" for me if I ever needed him. I have regretted that we were not closer in age, outlook and temperament to enjoy the bond that I, at least, have always felt lay deep beneath the surface of our relationship. So when that awful call came telling me he had a fatal disease about which I knew little until then, the pain of possibly losing my brother overwhelmed me. And the loss of not having enjoyed a closer relationship over all these years accentuated the grief.

After the shock and pain, my first reaction was the need to do something, to fix it. That's always been the formula in my family. When faced with an obstacle, you buckle down, think about what you want the outcome to be and work hard to fix it. And through this process, we've all achieved a good measure of success. But it seemed that my brother was already applying the formula to his problem - he and his wife, Sandra, had been actively researching alternative treatments and, while somewhat successful, had been unable to completely stop the progress of the disease. The doctors said chemotherapy was no longer sufficient.

I can't remember if Keith first suggested that a bone marrow transplant might ultimately be required or if I asked if there was anything I could do. All I knew was that if there was any way that I could help "fix" the problem and keep my brother, I would do what it took. I did not want to lose him any more than I already had all these years when we had little contact. Even if the odds were long, count me in for the fight. But Keith said that if the transplant were to be considered, it would be a long time away.

From that point on, my sister and I and our husbands kept tabs on Keith's treatment as best we could, rejoicing with Keith's family when the news was encouraging and coping in our individual ways when the news was disheartening. It became increasingly evident that more drastic treatment was imminent.

So when the day came a couple or so years later that Keith was going to be considered for a bone marrow transplant, it was more than welcome news - a beacon of hope amid the darkness of chemotherapy and drugs. When Keith advised me that my sister and I were his only potential donors, my heart sank that the odds were so poor but redoubled my resolve to do whatever I could to fix the problem.

My sister and I went for the tests. We knew that we were the only two possible candidates and that, even though we were siblings, a good match was unlikely. The doctors said that they would not even consider undertaking the procedure unless 4 out of 6 factors matched and they would prefer 6 out of 6. My sister and I applied our own brands of faith, optimism and possibly delusion, reassuring ourselves and each other that everything would turn out okay. And then we waited the few days that turned into an eternity.

Finally Keith called. It took a couple of minutes for Keith to explain that we had beaten the odds, won the lottery, that he and I were a perfect match! All my pent up hope welled out in tears of joy and I felt my heart leap with happiness - my brother could live! And I felt an odd sense of kinship with him - we were perfectly matched! A great blanket of gratitude encompassed me as the implications sank in. It had been a very close call as underscored by the results of my sister's test - an insufficient match.

I have always been close to my sister and, despite a decade's difference in age, we're the closest of friends. She's about the best sister anyone could have. When people tell me how much I look like her, I know it's true. In fact I once looked at a photograph and wondered how it came to be that my sister was wearing my graduation cap and gown - and then realized it was me! But inside myself, I have always felt an indefinable sameness with my brother. It's an odd feeling. We manifest our thoughts and feelings so differently and yet when I look at him, I see a part of me. My niece, Jennifer, has the same eyes as her father and at one family get-together, I looked into her eyes and saw myself at her age; quite frankly, it scared me. When I heard the news that we were a perfect match, that's what I thought of. We're more than brother and sister - we're connected by our very makeup and I've felt that all along. Of course, given the nature of our relationship, I had never shared this feeling with my brother.

The transplant was to take place a few months later, if Keith were in good enough shape to undergo it. The family held our collective breath but the transplant was not to be. One infection after another followed the chemotherapy treatments and news came that the last treatment had not been successful enough to anticipate a successful transplant. Keith had no option but to go home and, in essence, wait for a cure. Now we were beginning to experience in deeper measure the emotional roller coaster that Keith and Sandra and the kids had been living with for years. Their strength and patience was a standard for us all. But through it all I wondered why we were a perfect match against all odds if the transplant was not to take place. There must be more to it than what we could see.

For the next few months, the leukemia was in remission and we felt the slim thread that hung between Keith's health and the potentially fatal consequences of infection. After a while we began to believe that Keith would be okay, that life would be as normal as possible. After all, he was back at work and regular tests indicated the disease wasn't acting up. But eventually, there was news of declining test results and infections and, before we knew what had happened, in April Keith ended up in the hospital's Critical Care Unit with fluid on the lungs which had to be removed immediately. Many of the family members showed up at the hospital that Friday morning knowing that the operation was so high risk that we might never see Keith again. What a close group was there in the waiting room, strengthening our common bond of love and concern.

For several weeks I had been reading about the power of love and meditation and so actively tried to concentrate on sending messages of love to Keith in the other room. I believe we're all connected to a divine force that's within us and which joins us together. I also believe this Divine Force is Love. If it is true that we are all connected by love, then what Keith lacked in strength at this particular time, we could bolster with our strength. Amid the chaos of family anxiety that Friday morning, I felt a deep sense of peace and power that I had never felt before.

The concept of "fighting the disease" has been counterproductive for me for some time and I now felt that Keith was going to come through this ordeal if only he would stop fighting and accept the love we were sending him. And love aplenty was in the waiting room *and among his friends around the world. The sense of the power of our love helping Keith continued to build as I travelled the almost two hours home and into the next day. Finally, on Saturday night I knew I had to drive back to the hospital on the Sunday morning to give him the message - "don't fight, just feel the love". It became urgent that I do this.*

When I got to the hospital, I gave him the message. I don't know if he completely understood how important it was that I had to do so, but he told me later that he had felt as if he were being held up by bands of love - of the medical staff, of the family and of friends praying for him. What I didn't tell him at that time was that his illness was focusing me on what was important in life - love, relationships and spiritual growth. But from then on, we both started to undergo a healing process - his physical, mine of spirit. And from then on, I knew that we'd both be successful.

Well, Keith's recovery was astonishing! Within a few short weeks he was back at work and even fit in a vacation to Europe. Just like nothing had ever happened! And during his regular check-up just prior to leaving on vacation, to everyone's amazement, the doctors resurfaced the option of the bone marrow transplant. Would Keith please inform them of his decision about it upon his return from holiday - they'd like to do it two months later! Of course we were elated, if you can moderate elation with caution - we'd been disappointed before. However, this was remarkable news and I felt the story put on hold a year earlier was beginning to unfold again. I would play my part as well as I could. I would be as strong and healthy as possible so my brother would have the best chance going.

My own family learned to eat fruit three meals a day. Yoghurt became a staple in the refrigerator. No more staying up late at night. If I felt the least bit drowsy, I took a nap. I consciously avoided people with colds or the flu. I concentrated on positive thinking, actively dismissing the negativity which creeps into our minds on a regular basis. I spent more time playing with my dogs and enjoying our walks and less on the nightly news. I learned to inhale deep purifying breaths of joy and peace and exhale toxic feelings. For the first time in my life, I started to heed my husband's advice to not "sweat the small stuff". My mission was clear - get those bone marrow cells in the best shape possible so my brother's chances of full recovery are maximized. That meant good physical conditioning and good mental preparation.

By the time the day came for the procedure, my body was ready - I'd been talking to my bone marrow about its mission for a few weeks and visualizing positive outcomes (my husband was beginning to doubt my sanity)! And I was mentally ready. The love and positivity I had been dwelling on was carrying me into the operation with anticipation and joy. Even in the final minutes before the procedure, I felt it was important to breathe in joy and love, and breathe out worry and doubt. Seeing this deep breathing in the pre-op room, a couple of the nurses assumed I was very nervous and they tried to reassure me. What they didn't realize was that I had never been so calm about anything in my life - this was absolutely the right thing to do and I had no qualms about it. That marrow was primed to do its work! My lack of fear and worry let me recognize the kindness and care in the medical staff and appreciate the vital role they play in people's lives, literally, every day. I felt like we were a team working together to save my brother's life and it was such a good feeling, I just kept grinning. I guess they've seen it all in pre-op!

The procedure took place first thing on the Tuesday morning. When I arrived at Princess Margaret Hospital, I went first to see my brother who had been admitted a few days earlier because I knew he would be anxious that I had arrived safely. It was 7:00 a.m. and *he was lying in bed alone in his room. He turned his head, gave his wry smile and looking at me with love said "This is a very good day". It was indeed!*

The actual "harvesting" took about 45 minutes under general anaesthesia and when I woke up an hour and a half later, I felt really stiff and thirsty. But I immediately remembered what was happening and the peace and happiness returned. Now it was up to Keith and my migrant marrow.

I was discharged the next morning, satisfied that the actual transplant had gone well for Keith but understanding that we wouldn't know the full outcome for months to come. For the next two or three days my body felt like I'd been participating in the Calgary Stampede. The bruising on my back around the pelvic area was intense but the pain was quite bearable as long as I shifted position once in a while. It was never so intense that I had to take the recommended painkillers once I got home. Maybe euphoria was compensating for the pain - I don't know.

Gradually my mobility returned and the bruising subsided. I was able to go for longer periods of time without taking a nap and within about two weeks I was doing a full day's work without any problem. The doctors prescribed iron three times a day and said it would take 4 to 6 weeks to regain my full strength. They were right - I think it took five. And now, almost four months later as I write this, the only physical signs that remain are six little incision scars on my lower back, which get a little itchy if I get overtired.

For the few weeks before and after the transplant, many people wrote to me or told me in person they thought it was a wonderful thing I did in donating the bone marrow. They were very well meaning but completely misguided. Put yourself in my position, knowing what you now know about my relationship with my brother. Did I have any other choice? Would you not have done the same in my shoes? I was the lucky one. I was given the power to be able to do something about Keith's illness while others sat idle in frustration.

I have often wondered "why me?" This is not a selfish question. Ultimately we all direct attention to how a situation affects ourselves. I believe now that I needed Keith's illness and my role in it as a catalyst for inner exploration and spiritual awareness, just as Keith perhaps needed it for something different. I learned about love - about loving myself enough to give myself the gift of this experience. About discovering the love that others show, about the connectedness among us all.

And so when asked if I would do it again, I explain that I would do it without a moment's hesitation, not just for my brother who I started off loving, but for anyone needing a transplant of marrow I could provide. Because the gift would be to myself by giving to them. And we are all related in love.

None of us knows all the effects our experiences have on others. During this process I have learned enormously from reading about others' experiences. And I know others have learned from this experience of mine. As a result of my brother's disease, several of my friends have registered as potential bone marrow donors. And so the ripple of love that has touched my brother's and my little pond is beginning to spread outwards in ever-widening circles to a bigger and better world. I believe the story is still unfolding. I'm sure there's more to come. And no matter what the future holds, I have grown from this experience.

I may have given bone marrow to my brother but he's given me something so much more. And together we are richer for our joint experience."

What could I possibly add to that?

One of the things I wanted to do before starting this phase of my journey was to write to Dr. Brandwein. I was being transferred for several months into Dr. Lipton's care, and I thought this a good time to do it. While several times before I had mentioned to him how I appreciated all he was doing, I wanted him to know just how much. And so I wrote to him at the hospital...

Among other things, I told him that my bone marrow transplant was a frightening prospect for me, but that I saw it as is an opportunity I had never expected to have again after it was denied me last time, and so I was very grateful for it and was confident about the outcome. I told him that when someone is battling a fatal illness like mine, their doctor becomes a very important person in their life and that I had come to have a profound respect and admiration for his ability and his concern for my well-being during the ups and downs of the past six years; it was very evident the regard that the other doctors and the nursing staff had for him. I had often thanked God for him. I said that I thought I fully understood the range of possible outcomes of this transplant procedure, and that I was as prepared as possible for whatever might transpire. I was under no illusions as to the seriousness of my condition and the lack of further medical remedies. I told him that his complete honesty with Sandra and me during the many episodes of my illness had helped us immeasurably in coping with them and in making decisions. He had not concealed important information, nor had he exaggerated. I had therefore learned to have great confidence in his judgment and advice. I acknowledged that he had worked tirelessly on my behalf, and should things not turn out well, it would certainly be through no fault of his; he had done everything possible.

When I had finished writing it, and had sent it off, I was glad I had been able to express to him in words what he had meant to me to this point.

On the long July weekend, Sandra, Jennifer, Andrew and I went up to the condo for a short holiday before the transplant process began. We had a good time - golfing, boating and just being together. Then it was home to begin. On June 24th, I'd been into Princess Margaret with Hilary for tests - for her: blood tests and a bone marrow aspiration, as a final check on the quality of the marrow I would be receiving; for me: a pulmonary functions test, full dental check-up and cleaning, blood tests (they took thirteen tubes), chest X-ray, kidney test, mugascan and bone marrow aspiration and biopsy. If we heard nothing during the next week, we had a green light. On June 27th I went again and received my medications and a full explanation. Starting the next day I would be taking about 150 pills a day for several days - mostly Busulfan, a very powerful chemotherapy drug that they were using on me instead of radiation. Somehow I managed to get them all down. I wrote in my journal:

"I spent some time this morning thinking about what lies ahead. I think I'm as ready as I can be. I thought about so many people who have worked so hard for me to get well; I have to do my part. I've told my bone marrow that it's going to have to die - for the sake of its fellow-members, or else we'll all die. That's the ultimate sacrifice. It has been so heroic, continuing to produce good blood cells despite all the chemo, the infections and the incredibly high white counts, enabling me to recover my health each time. It's done so well, it needs to go out with honour. And then we all need to welcome my new bone marrow on the 8th. It will be like moving into a new home for it; it will take time to get settled and fix the place up (clean out the old leukemia cells). It's a new resident - but family.

Larry Nusbaum called to see how I am. I told him I wanted this when it was over to be a chance to minister back to so many people who had ministered to me. He said "You're doing it now to me". He said I must be on a lot of people's minds right now, including his. I began to feel stronger about getting my story into a book.

At noon today I took three Dilantin pills. The journey has begun. I've strapped myself in and here we go. An image that came into my mind was a frightening tunnel that we went through at the concentration camp in Terrazin a few weeks before - a very long, narrow, winding, dark tunnel with the only exit being at the other end, wherever that was. For those victims the other end meant the firing squad; but for me it meant sunshine and life - but only if I went all the way.

Paul Altman called from Barbados and told me some things that I found incredible. Greg Neely called to say they had set up special prayer meetings for us - elders every Sunday, the prime focus of the assembly on Wednesday evening, and gatherings at each end of the city at other times. I also spoke with Laurie Williams. He said he is very nervous as well (he's a better participant than spectator). Several others called, including from overseas. I am sure not going through this alone."

On July 2nd I got up at 5:30 a.m. for more pills and then left for the hospital with Sandra. I said goodbye to Jennifer and kissed Andrew on the cheek as he was sleeping. I was admitted to have inserted a double "Hickman" central venous catheter into the main vein near my heart, which would stay in for several months. It would preclude the need for constant poking of my veins. It had to be flushed three times a week, the dressing changed weekly, and the caps changed at least monthly. Quickly Sandra learned how to do all this.

Calls, cards and news about more arrangements for special gatherings for prayer arrived. Bill Beck, a Christian friend, phoned and said I was again being highlighted for prayer with their congregation of about two hundred. And eighteen months beforehand, in preparation for when we thought I was going to have a transplant, Marg Neely had prepared a special journal for Sandra to write in, complete with a cartoon and also a scripture text for each day. Now as Sandra began to use it, the first day (timed to be the day I was first admitted) was *the things which are impossible with man are possible with God*.

That night I was allowed home, but next morning, July 3rd, we set off for the hospital again. I wasn't absolutely sure I'd ever be home again - I knew the risks. Waiting for me on the hall table as I left were two letters - one from Jennifer and one from Andrew, expressing their love for me and their support for what I was about to do. That meant so much.

Jennifer was gearing up for her very difficult Chartered Accountancy exams two months later. But she made a conscious choice to spend a lot of time in the hospital with me, and to do whatever she could to support me over the following few months, recognizing that she might be jeopardizing her own chances to get these exams.

The Bone Marrow Transplant Unit on the 14th floor of Princess Margaret Hospital, now still less than two years' old, has fourteen patient rooms. I was assigned to Room 208, not large, but attractive and bright, with a large window facing west. To the south I could see Lake Ontario, and the sailing boats in the evening, to the north the central campus of the University of

Toronto. On entering the room there was a special corridor and, while I was in isolation, everyone (doctors, nurses, family and any visitors) first had to wash their hands outside and then stand in that corridor for fifteen seconds with the air fan turned high. That drew out the air and re-circulated the room with fresh air several times, which negated the need for masks.

Once in hospital there arrived the inevitable intravenous pole and pump (my "dancing partner" Dr. Callum called it). However it was connected to my Hickman lines which was not painful or intrusive. They immediately started me on the second chemo regimen, Cyclophosphamide, the same as I'd had in April, but ten times stronger.

I felt very vulnerable. I was committed now. My body could not survive after these two chemos, and yet Hilary and my new bone marrow were still fifty miles away. I'd have felt safer if she'd been safely locked away in the room next to me.

Dr. Lipton was my senior doctor and my primary resident was Dr. Jeannie Callum, who turned out to be the daughter of John Callum who was a C.A. colleague of mine several years ago. I had seen her once before at St. Michael's, but not gotten to know her. She came to see us at least once a day, to conduct examinations, ask me questions, and give us results of tests. She was just great - so informative and so upbeat. Every day I would receive a printout of all my blood results for that day and every question received a full and understandable reply. Occasionally Dr. Lipton or another doctor would come in and he also could not have been more helpful. My overwhelming impression was of a team of highly capable and caring doctors, not leaving anything to chance. I could visualize them meeting in their consultation room, pouring over my information and deciding what adjustments to make to my medications or other decisions to take.

Finally the big day came - July 8th - Transplant Day - "Day Zero" (everything would be counted from this day). I prayed Hilary and Bryan would have a safe trip down from Oro (there had been a bad accident on Highway 400 the day before).

Hilary must have known how I'd be feeling, because she popped in to see me at soon as she arrived at the hospital at 7 a.m. She said "I'm here". Whew! It was an emotional moment for us both. I said: "I've got nowhere to go without that bone marrow". And she replied: "Well, it's ready".

She was admitted to the 18th floor early that morning and, mid-morning, they harvested her marrow. She had agreed previously to be on a trial of GCSF, the same neutrophil growth factor I had previously been on several times, because it was thought to enrich the marrow and help it to engraft. For her it was a double dose and for several days before the harvesting she could feel the effect in her bones. Dr. Meharchand and Dr. Callum did the extraction, which is similar to having a few bone marrow aspirations at the same time. It inevitably left Hilary with a very sore hip for a few days. That afternoon Sandra went up to see her and presented her with a framed engraving she'd had prepared of a lovely poem to Hilary that she had composed herself:

> *"The gift you have given your brother today*
> *No silver nor gold can ever repay.*
> *It is willingly given, displays so much love,*
> *Bound with God's perfect plan from above.*
> *Hilary, you were chosen when you were born,*

This most precious gift in your body being formed.

However could we know, so many years ago,

That life-giving marrow to your brother would flow.

You are now bound by blood-ties in more ways than one.

Perhaps some day soon your brother will run

With this gift of life he has visioned so long.

His heart will abound with much laughter and song.

So, Hilary, our hearts are full of much grace.

As for you, we can't show enough of our praise.

Our children, our families, with hearts overflow,

Must thank you again for the life that we owe."

About 3 o'clock in the afternoon the nurse arrived in my room with a large bag of 800 ml. of what just looked like blood. "Happy birthday", she said, "today you receive your new bone marrow", and "as of this minute you are now in isolation". It took a couple of hours to transfuse the marrow and blood into me; physically it was really no different than any other transfusion except that the nurse monitored my reactions every fifteen minutes. But after it was over, and I got up and went into the washroom, it hit me what had just happened after all these years. I put my head against the wall and just cried. Maybe my long ordeal was almost over. Maybe I was almost out from the cloud and into the sunlight; I could see the silver lining at its edge. I told this to Jennifer when I came back into the room and she pointed out of the window. It had been a gloomy day outside, but the bright sun had just broken through!

Most of the time that I was in hospital I felt pretty miserable and I wasn't good company for Sandra or the three children when they visited. Adele had taken two weeks off work and arranged to fly down to be with me for the potentially worst period - the last two weeks of July. I had extreme nausea practically the whole time I was there, in all its forms, despite the various remedies I was given, and for the last few weeks I was also hyper-salivating. A few times I had to go on oxygen briefly. For those few weeks I completely lost my sense of humour and couldn't force a smile.

Sandra was there every afternoon and evening of course (she had taken a two and a half month leave from work) and it bothered her that we couldn't communicate more so that she could do more to help me. Also the room was very warm, on purpose as I was usually chilly, and the sun through the western window in the afternoon added to it, which aggravated her headaches. My whole hospital stay was very hard on her; she was so tired and of course anxious. Most of the time I didn't feel like reading, listening to music, writing and certainly not talking. I watched TV very occasionally. I felt very tired. Jennifer and Andrew, and Adele during her stay, were also very faithful in visiting, although it couldn't have been much fun for them.

Life in that room consisted of routines and drudgery. All my medications and all my nutrition were being given to me intravenously; I didn't eat or drink by mouth for several weeks. But I generally kept my weight. I had to measure every drop of output, from every source, and keep it to have samples taken if it was unusual. I had my vital signs (temperature, pulse, oxygen saturation, blood pressure lying, blood pressure sitting, and weight) monitored every few hours. I had to use a special mouthwash every two hours and use a "flow machine" device to stimulate deep breathing. There was an exercize bike in my corridor which I was to use when I could (I eventually got up to 250 turns of the pedals at one sitting - from there to College

Street, I estimated). I made a point of not lying around in my pyjamas all day, as apparently most of the patients did; I got up each morning, showered and dressed. It made me feel better despite the effort. I had a real advantage in that I was one of the few patients from the Toronto area and so family were with me every day and able to bring me clean clothes and other things I needed. But time dragged by. After the first couple of days I wondered how I was ever going to make it for several weeks. So I decided I needed to stop thinking that far ahead and focus on twenty-four hours at a time.

Despite my discomfort, medically I was doing very well. My blood counts began to come up to a reasonable level quite quickly (I only needed one blood transfusion and two platelet transfusions during my stay), and my neutrophil count quickly reached 500, which allowed the isolation restriction to be lifted on Day 18. I now had an immune system. My eyes were sometimes jaundiced and sometimes some of my blood chemical levels were a little off, but I developed no serious infections at all. I did develop a case of mucositis and thrush in my mouth with several cankers, as they had predicted, but it was a lot less than it could have been and was treated with mouth care and medication. They were especially careful to check the fluid level around my left lung as I still had a residual pleural effusion from April; I was taking in a lot of saline and other fluids through the I.V. and fluid tended to congregate there. But the chest X-rays showed everything to be under control.

Here are some excerpts from a few days of my journal during my hospital stay:

Day 16: Yesterday was not a happy day. I was very nauseous and vomited several times through the night and daytime. So they gave me Decadron and Maxeran but they conked me out. Nothing stops the nausea... I'm on oxygen this morning despite doing my breathing exercizes and my bike, but no temperature so far! Dr. Callum says I might see my white counts coming up next week - not too quickly hopefully, as that might be an indication of leukemia cells that have survived...

Day 17: Vomited when I got up. Dr. Callum came in and gave me the good news that my white count was up to 1.4 with .7 neutrophils, so I am no longer technically nutripenic! They want to wait one more day to be sure before they take me out of isolation. Still no infections, which is very rare (less than ten percent of the cases). Thank you Lord...

Day 18: Out of isolation!! No more blowers required. I went for a walk with my pole and met Sandra arriving from the elevator. Was she surprised...I now had an immune system of sorts; I wasn't totally vulnerable. Thank you again, Hilary...

Day 21: Last evening Sandra left here quite upset. It's really getting to her. The room is so hot, she's got migraines, and I don't talk or smile while she sits there hour by hour. After she left I just called out: "Lord, help us". Sometimes the answer comes by suddenly realizing what I can do to make things better. I decided that when she arrived today I would be at my best, with God's strength, so I could communicate with her and we could go and sit somewhere else in the hospital for a change. It worked. As a bonus, I had a good report to give her from the doctor...

Day 22: The nausea continues unabated, plus vomiting, wrenching, diahrrea, hyper-salivating, etc. Dr. Callum says my stomach lining and asophagus are pretty irritated. They put me on pills today to try to get things moving but I can't keep them down. I've been trying to eat dry toast, crackers, and apple sauce and drink ginger ale - but only tiny amounts. Dr. Callum says I can't control the vomitting (the brain does that) and I can't make myself want to eat; it's like trying to will my white count up... I can go out of my room for walks now, but it's chilly out there. I can never get warm and Sandra says it's stifling in here...I don't have any kidney or liver problems and still no fevers. I'm still tending to accumulate fluid, including a little in what's left of the pleural effusion from April, but not seriously. They keep giving me Latex to make me go. Dr. Callum says I'm sailing through; I should see some of the other patients...

Several times Dr. Lipton said he was surprised how well I was doing, especially in view of how much chemotherapy I'd had in the past - twenty-one cycles in all. Perhaps this was going to be the answer to the question I'd pondered a few years before. If my recovery was routine, perhaps the doctors and the medicine would have received all the credit. While they were playing a vital part, this was looking more and more like a typical characteristic of God's handiwork. I thought of references in the gospels such as Matthew 9:8: "*Now when the multitudes saw it, they marvelled and glorified God*". And He always finishes what He starts.

Occasionally I would reflect on what was going on within my body. My old bone marrow was disappearing. My stomach was having a terrible time of it. I tried to imagine what was going on inside. It must have been like the boiler room on the Titanic when the water started to flood in. Everybody going crazy, working furiously, while the first-class passengers on the top deck (my head) were oblivious to it.

From time to time, as I was able, I would read (or be read to) a few verses from the Bible. I always looked for just one thought from the Lord - and I never failed to get one. Each day I prayed about just the next twenty-four hours - for each member of my family; I was in no position to look after them. And frequently I would whisper a thank-you for how well I was doing. It wasn't intense but I knew I had the presence of God with me all the time. And I rested on that.

It wasn't too long before my hair started to fall out quite quickly because of the chemotherapy, and so a nurse offered to shave my head. She tried to make me feel better by making light of it, but I was in no mood for that. It bothered me, even though it was pretty insignificant compared with all that was going on. I waited a couple of days until it was rather obvious to me I needed to have it shaved off, and again it took all of a few seconds for me to become completely bald. I knew I would be that way now for several months.

Almost every day at least one card or letter arrived and we put them up on the notice board, which was quickly covered. Fred Marks from Brantford wrote to me saying that 100 days is a long time and so he was going to break it into ten day chunks and write to me each time. A few times I got a card from the Neely family (usually humorous, which was good because I didn't feel like smiling a lot), with a note inside from each of them - Dave and Marg, and the teenagers Michael, Kathy and Sara. It was good to hear some news; we were so shut off from the world. Previously Hilary had suggested I get myself on the Internet E-Mail and I had done so, and every few days Sandra would access it for messages from James and Shirley or Bryan and Hilary, and keep them posted on my progress. Mom was up north and not easily accessible by phone, and so she arranged to phone us every Sunday. I also used the computer to access remotely the Bank's internal E-Mail system to keep in touch with a number of people there. Visitors other than family were not generally encouraged but I did have a few, including Tony Comper, the President of the Bank, and a couple of times from Dr. Bruce Rowatt of Toronto Hospital who, like Peter Kopplin, acts as a medical advisor to Bank executives. He revealed that he too is a Christian and we had some interesting chats, although I found it hard to hold up my end of the conversations because of how I was feeling. As I said, I wasn't exactly stimulating company.

Soon after I was out of isolation, I began to see the effects of a case of "graft-versus-host" disease. I was already taking medication to prevent me from rejecting my new marrow, but this is potentially more serious, where the new marrow rejects its new environment - me. It tends to be more prevalent with unrelated donors and where the marrows aren't totally matched, neither of which applied in my case. On the other hand, it seldom occurs when the donor is an identical twin, which is in itself a potential difficulty. The optimum is to have a low grade form of the disease, since the new marrow then recognizes and attacks any remaining leukemia cells, since even all that chemotherapy can't be relied on to get them all. With Hilary being a related, totally-matched donor, I was in the optimal situation. God doesn't work by half-measures.

A low-grade case was what I had, and I came out in a rash and a few other side effects, which they immediately began to treat with Prednisone and Cyclosporin. I was checked constantly.

By this time (Day 23) the medical staff were talking about working to get me ready to go home. It would take a while because I was totally dependent on the intravenous. I was going to have to learn to eat and drink again and take lots of pills, and with my constant nausea and vomiting that wouldn't be easy. It was quite gradual, with a few setbacks along the way. I was given a guide to "safe-eating" for when I was home and Sandra set out to have the whole house spring-cleaned and the curtains and drapes all cleaned. There could be no pets (we don't have any) or plants in the house. We even had a new furnace and air-cleaner installed; we needed one anyway and so this was the ideal time to do it, although Sandra had to manage all this herself in just a few days. Finally on Day 29, August 6th, the medical team came by and asked if I'd like to go home on a pass overnight.

Would I? If all went well I could be discharged the next day. I would make sure everything went well. I could hardly believe it. Again I set a record packing my case. It reminded me of the time at St. Mike's when I was walking about packing to go home while still receiving a blood transfusion. But I'd learned that being told and actually getting to leave are not the same thing. There are forms for doctors to sign, prescriptions to be written out, and sometimes tubes to be pulled. But if all I had to do was wait a few hours, I could handle that.

Although I would be seeing Dr. Lipton frequently in my clinic visits, I asked him if this was a good time to say a big thank you to them all, and Dr. Lipton replied "it's always a good time". So I did. I was so grateful to them all, and to my God for how things had gone. Sandra had little gifts for the staff and something special for Dr. Callum, who had been so helpful and attentive. The last thing was to have my medication prescriptions filled. It was a large shopping bag full - an average of about two dozen pills a day. When I got home I typed up a medication schedule on the computer, as it would be constantly adjusted in the weeks ahead, and posted it on the fridge door. I was on a portable pump that we attached each day for an hour to my Hickman line to receive a Vancomycin antibiotic, and a Home Care nurse was arranged for a few days to give me saline to supplement my fluid intake until I could drink enough.

And so on Thursday, August 7th (Day 30) I was discharged. I had been in hospital thirty-six days, which is about the average. It was a nice room, but there's no place like home.

15. The Recovery Continues

(August 1997 to January 1998)

For the first three weeks I was at home I did very well. I soon ate well, slept well and was able to be up and around and reasonably active around the house. During this time I spent quite a bit of time working on this book. Often throughout the years the comment had been made to me "you could write a book", occasionally "you should write a book". But my standard response usually was "Yes, but who would read it?" Only when several people said "*I* certainly would", did I seriously start considering the possibility. I had no idea how difficult it would be, or how rewarding an experience it would be for me. It helped me to know that someone else might benefit from my experience.

I also avoided the outdoors during the daytime (it was August and I was not to be exposed to direct sunlight - it aggravates the graft-versus-host disease - "GVH"). Anytime I did go out, I covered up and used sun-block. One day I treated myself to a short ride to a nearby plaza in my sports car with the top down.

But generally I restricted myself to walks in the cool of the evening.

My main challenge was to take the daily dosage of pills and fluid. My schedule on the fridge door began at breakfast and finished at 10 in the evening - initially 26 pills per day of several types. The fluid challenge was to consume 3500 ml. to keep my blood chemical level (creatinine) in balance. This meant starting first thing in the morning and always having a drink beside me. Unless I reached about 3000 by supper-time, I felt very bloated by bedtime. Regardless, I obviously wasn't able to sleep uninterrupted for very long at a time.

Once or twice each week Sandra and I visited the hospital clinic for my blood tests and examination, and adjustment of the medications. While we had expected to be on a twice-a-week schedule for several weeks, it wasn't very long until they reduced it to once a week. This allowed us to make one visit up north to the condo for a few days in late August, which was a great break. We even managed to get a short ride on the lake in our boat, which was a bonus. While up north, Mom managed to pay us a short visit from Miners' Bay Lodge in Haliburton, which is about an hour away. Linda Seath had kindly offered to bring her. It was the first time Mom had seen me since before the transplant and she was clearly relieved to see me in person for herself and to see how well I was doing. It reminded me of how much she too has suffered, as it is her son who has been so ill. Once again, she brought us news about so many people at the Lodge who were praying for us - part of our invisible network. We sent a note of thanks back, to be put on their bulletin board. I would like the opportunity for us to go there one day and thank them personally.

It was during this initial three-week period that Sandra and I started to talk again about our future. This may seem to have been a bit premature, but it was indicative of our reduced stress level and sense of optimism. We talked about her chronic migraine headaches, which she has suffered for many years. While there are clearly physiological causes for these, stress unquestionably makes them worse, and they had been especially bad these past few weeks - for obvious reasons. Because my health had become such an all-consuming priority, she had discontinued taking the measures that she had been taking previously that had given her some relief. And so she began to again make plans to find a good chiropractor and acupuncturist, and she joined a fitness club. She also began to think again about finding a suitable counsellor to visit.

On Day 34 I had my scheduled bronchoscopy, where a probe was inserted down my throat into my lung, and a biopsy taken, to detect any CMV pneumonia. This can be a very serious condition and it had previously been the cause of a number of fatalities during bone marrow transplants. But this procedure, which had been adopted fairly recently, greatly enhanced their ability to diagnose it early and so treat it effectively. To my relief my result came back negative. As a continuing precaution, my regular blood tests began including CMV tests periodically.

Day 50 arrived (Wednesday, August 27th). This was halfway to the 100 days that the doctors had previously described as the high-risk period, and all seemed to be going well. Hilary must have given me good marrow. I recalled with sadness being told that, of the fourteen of us in the Bone Marrow Transplant Unit when I was there, three didn't survive. Why was I doing so well, I couldn't help wondering.

Then things started to happen. I began to get recurrent fevers. I would notice them initially because I would feel chilly.

Sometimes they would be relatively mild (temperature below 39), sometimes stronger. I had standing instructions to phone the hospital whenever my temperature reached 38.5 or higher (normal is 37). This happened first on Day 52 and, in Sandra's absence, Jennifer drove me downtown to the hospital. Jennifer always made herself available to help me if Sandra wasn't there. I was put on a couple of antibiotics and admitted - this was just the place I did not want to be. My temperature came down quite quickly but the next day my blood counts had dropped a lot. My hemoglobin was down from the 90's to 75 (normal is 130) and so I was given two units of blood. My white count was down from 6.7 to 3.9, just below the normal range. And my platelets had fallen from 76 to 41 (normal is 150 and higher), and then kept falling, eventually to 15 a week later. Obviously we wanted to know what was going on. Was my new bone marrow ceasing to function properly? Even imagining that possibility made me go cold.

Eventually we managed to see Dr. Meharchand, but she was in a rush, and we weren't able to make full sense of her explanation. She thought it was probably all being caused by whatever infection was giving me the fever. However the Septra medication I was taking may also have been contributing, she thought, and so she took me off it and replaced it with a monthly inhalation program of Pentamidine. She also put me on Folic acid pills to help my platelets. However none of the blood cultures grew organisms and so they were unable to identify the cause of the fever. I was released on the Monday (Labour Day).

One week later I had a fever again and was again admitted on antibiotics. My blood counts were still down. By this time they had concluded that the infection must be in my central venous "Hickman" line, which apparently is quite common, and so they decided to take it out. On the Monday I first had to have my Day 60 scheduled dental review, which was no problem, then have a temporary catheter inserted in my arm, and then have the Hickman line removed. It was a busy and tiring day. The I.V. nurse had difficulty inserting the catheter line in my left arm. It bled profusely. They gave me a platelet transfusion through it and after a few minutes it began to be excruciatingly painful. It turned out that the line had pierced the wall of the vein and the platelets were going into my arm tissue and muscle. She had to come back and take it out and replace it in my right arm. My arm continued to hurt for several days. I found myself getting upset at the nurse, who admitted it wasn't her finest piece of work, but later we became good friends.

We were very hopeful that having the Hickman line out would be the answer to these constant worrying fevers. But two days later at home my temperature was 37.8. I spent the day trying to stay warm and doing whatever I could to keep it from going higher. Sandra was very concerned about it. Later that day she figured out that it must be the graft-versus-host that was causing the fevers and depressing my counts. She said they had started when they reduced my daily intake of Prednisone to below 65 mg. So she put a call in to Dr. Lipton. He listened to her idea and said she might well be right and said he wanted to see me the next day to check it out. So back we went again to see him (it was Day 65), and he agreed to increase the Prednisone to see if that would put a stop to the temperatures. It turned out I had only a mild case of graft-versus-host but it still could be the culprit.

He also gave us the results of the bone marrow test from the week before and said he was encouraged by the result - definite improvement from before the transplant, good cell production, but still of course quite a bit of evidence of old leukemia cells, which he had told us to expect. It can take two or more years for them to disappear, which is not a problem as long as they are not multiplying. Overall Dr. Lipton said he was happy with my progress. That put our minds at ease. If he was happy, I was happy.

Later that day Dr. Lipton phoned us at home. One of the blood tests from that morning had come back positive. I had the CMV virus after all! A week before, the test had been negative. He wanted to see me first thing the next morning to start treatment. "So we have an answer", he said.

It was a shock. I knew how serious it could be. Before they had learned how to treat this effectively, which had been in the last year or so, there was a 90% fatality rate from this. Dr. Lipton had explained this to us back in May. "Now", he had said, "if we detect it early enough, we can treat it effectively, and it's largely been eliminated as a problem". Although I was comforted that the risk was minimal, I stayed depressed for quite a while. But if I needed another reason why the transplant hadn't taken place back in early 1996, I had it.

Early detection was the key. If Sandra hadn't figured out that perhaps GVH was causing these fevers, we wouldn't have gone to hospital that Thursday and I wouldn't have had my blood tested that day (which included the test for CMV). It would have been at least the following Monday before it would have been detected. Another "coincidence"? If...if...if... God was definitely looking after us.

The treatment for the virus was Ganciclovir, a fluid injected into the line in my arm. For two weeks, it was injected at home twice a day for an hour; then for eight more weeks it was five days a week, once an hour. Sandra (or occasionally Jennifer) had to flush my line before and after the drug each time, to keep the line open. This meant I had to have these injections whenever she was available. Over the ten weeks I had to have the line moved to five different locations, as the sites became inoperative. The treatment for the CMV pneumonia was Gammaglobulin, which was administered intravenously in Day Care in the hospital. I received it five days a week for two weeks, then once a week for four weeks. Meanwhile my blood was being checked weekly to see how I was responding to these treatments. To our relief these tests showed that the medications were being effective in dealing with the virus. The final treatment was on November 21st. The following Monday I had the line removed from my arm.

Meanwhile I continued my weekly checkups at Clinic H on the 14th floor of Princess Margaret. Based on my blood results that day and on the doctor's examination of me, they kept reducing the amount of Prednisone I was on - from a high of 75 mg. per day when I first came out of hospital, to a low of 2-1/2 mg. per day. I finally stopped taking any on November 24th. Had they reduced the dosage too quickly, they said, my graft-versus-host disease could have flared up, and so I was always conscious of any evidence that this was happening, such as skin rash, pinkness in skin colour, or itchiness. As the daily dose got down to 7-1/2 mg. and below, I experienced total loss of appetite and a decline in my energy level. 7-1/2 is the level at which my body had to start producing some on its own again, and it had been relying on outside sources for a long time. It needed to be woken up.

Every day at home I was required to take all my medications and to drink a lot in order to avoid kidney and liver problems. Initially I was required to drink 3-1/2 litres per day; later it was reduced to between 2-1/2 and 3 litres per day. If my Creatinine level got too high, I was told "Drink more!" I generally found that grapefruit juice and milk were the two things that I was able to take the most. One of the medications was large magnesium pills - up to eleven a day at one point. Initially I had to crush them and pour them on food to get them down, but eventually I mastered swallowing them. While they were necessary because of the Cyclosporin I was taking, they also caused diahrrea, which persisted for a few months - longer than I care to remember.

Back on September 23rd I had been fitted for my new hair piece at home. My own new hair was just beginning to show, but it would be several months before it was long enough. This hair piece was more comfortable than previous ones and I began wearing it every day, even around the house. Although the family had become used to seeing me with no hair, there was no question in my mind that I looked better and healthier with hair, even if it wasn't my own. Also, it was getting cooler outside, and having no hair is chilly. While I wasn't trying to pretend to anyone that this was my own hair, it was interesting to notice people's reactions when they saw me with it on for the first time. But nobody ever said anything, except Dr. Lipton at the hospital. He did a double-take and said: "Is that your own hair?" I said "Of course not". He just laughed and said: "I thought it was too soon".

Thursday, October 16th was a memorable day - Day 100 since my transplant on July 8th. While nothing dramatic happened health-wise that day, it represented an important milestone. The highest risk period was past. Many of our friends had been counting the days with us, and on day 100 they celebrated with us. For example, I received phone calls from Marilyn Chuli and Des Clements, a fax from Andy McIlree and Brian Tugwell in Myanmar, another from Greg Neely and his family, a card from Heidi Hart (Andrew's friend at school), and flowers from Cam and Marg Ramage in Caledonia. I also got a call from Dave and Marg Neely and their three teenage children in Brantford, singing "Happy 100th day to You" over the phone!

After that I thought it was safe to start going out in public a bit. I began attending the gatherings of my church again, after an absence of almost four months.

I was pleased to be able to contribute again. In our worship meetings there was so much that had built up over the months in my appreciation of the Lord, and thankfully sometimes I was able to get it out and express it. And now I was also able to join in prayer with many of the people who had been praying so faithfully for us. But re-entry after a long absence isn't easy, and I found the experience emotionally exhausting.

Sandra and I thought this would be a good time to send out letters to a lot of people to bring them up to date on my status. People frequently reminded us that it was so helpful to know my current situation so that they could pray more specifically. And so, on Thanksgiving weekend, up at our condo in Huntsville, we prepared and mailed over ninety letters - to all the churches of God around the world. We expressed our gratitude for all their care and prayers to this point, and the assurance we had that God was answering their prayers. We asked them to continue - but with a different focus. Now that the immediate risks from the transplant itself were subsiding, our attention was turning more to praying that the leukemia would not return, since there was no guarantee of this.

As I continued to grow stronger, I found myself experiencing conflicting emotions. I was so grateful for my health and progress, and the mere thought of a relapse or having to go back into hospital filled me with dread. But on the other hand I was beginning to feel restless and "in the doldrums". I knew I wasn't ready physically to return to work (my body hadn't caught up to my mind, which was always on the go) but I lacked the stamina. I had the feeling of being "in limbo", at loose ends. I was able to keep myself busy, but I was gloomy, and it showed. I wanted our home to return to being a happy place for each member of our family, and for so long it had been like a war zone. Sandra and I talked often about this, and she was experiencing a lot of the same feelings. She was much busier than I was. She was back working at the Institute for Sports Medicine two days a week, and she was busy with chiropractor and acupuncture appointments, helping her niece Cheryl look after her new-born twins, and running the home. But with both of us, something was missing.

We began to realize that we were both recovering from the trauma of the events of the past year. Now that there was less of a crisis, and we weren't running on sheer adrenalin, there was an inevitable letdown. The future was anything but clear and we weren't completely sure what we wanted to do when we were able to. I talked with Larry Nusbaum about it and he compared it to veterans returning from war. "They aren't the people they were before", he said, "and they're not yet the people they will be; life has gone on in their absence, while they've been out of circulation." I knew I didn't want to just rush back into doing all the things I used to do - either at work or in my personal life. But I wasn't really sure what I wanted to do, or whether I would be able to do it. One type of uncertainty had been replaced by another. And yet one thing was for sure; I did not want to go back to being ill. The very thought of the leukemia coming back and what that would entail made me shudder. I did not know what I would do if that happened.

I have found that, for me, a large part of coping is understanding what is happening to me and why. It was entirely reasonable that I would be feeling as I was, given what I had been through and the medications I was on. That didn't take the feelings away but, as I acknowledged them, I slowly began to be able to focus again on what I was doing and what I wanted to do.

While I was no longer in hospital, it was still a period of forced confinement, and again my thoughts often turned to the changes that had been taking place in me. They were still frustratingly incomplete and inconsistent, but they were very real. I fervently hoped they would continue and become part of me. I tried to identify them...

I had become more open to new experiences than I had been before, and more flexible about what should happen in the future; I didn't feel as much the need to control my life and force events; God had proved Himself to be a much better "engineer" than me... I had a fuller appreciation of the value of relationships with other people, and the impact on them of how they perceived me in different situations...I was definitely more sensitive to others, especially when I sensed they were having difficulties, and more tolerant of their idiosyncrasies (realizing how subjective and silly such an assessment was)...I was more aware of when I was being used by God in a situation, as a conduit for His work, rather than just trying my best on my own...I was much more conscious of my own weaknesses and more willing to ask for and accept help...I was much more apt (and a bit better able) to express my real feelings to others, to tell them what they meant to me and to communicate the passion that I felt about certain things; my emotions were always much closer to the surface, and tears came to my eyes much more easily...I was more attentive to the details of my life (because God is often in the details), and more appreciative of the simple, good things here and now... I was more alert to opportunities to help and contribute, without feeling as much of a personal responsibility to "fix" everything myself...and I was more inclined to take "time-outs" to reflect and recharge, rather than have to be "doing" all the time.

It was a fairly overwhelming list. They were just small steps in many cases, but all in the right direction. God had clearly been changing me, which of course had been His plan. He knows what He wants, but I have to learn it little by little, often the hard way.

My relationship with many people who were important in my life, family and others, had deepened and strengthened, and I realized just how valuable that was. My view of God's direct intervention, as He worked tirelessly and often imperceptibly in people's lives, had been from a front-row seat and it was wonderful to watch.

Late in October I started getting intermittent headaches - always in the same spot, in the back right side, just above my neck. They were quite severe, and I took Tylenol 3 to try to get rid of them. I couldn't figure out what the cause was, and neither could the doctors, because I had no other symptoms. Some weeks I would get one almost every day; other times they were not so frequent. I now think they were the cumulative result of all the drugs.

We had a lovely surprise on the evening of November 8th, when Bruce and Adele arrived from Vancouver unannounced. They had booked a week's holiday and arranged with Jennifer to come and spend it with us, without telling us. We spent about four days of it with them up at Grandview. It was the first time they had seen me for a long time when I wasn't ill. I had another good long talk with Adele while going for a walk on a chilly day, and that also helped me to sort out my thoughts and feelings. We miss not having them nearby - it would be great to just drop in on them from time to time.

On November 20th I went back to St. Michael's Hospital to visit Dr. Jakubovic, the dermatologist. Five skin sores had broken out again, due to my suppressed immunity, and Dr. Lipton wanted them to be treated. After having them sprayed to burn them off (which stung), I dropped in to see Dr. Brandwein and the nursing staff in Day Care. It was the first time I had seen them since June and I got a great reception. They were very pleased to see me and to hear of my progress. They deal with so many sad cases, it must be encouraging to see some good news.

On Friday evening, November 21st, Sandra and I had the pleasure of hosting a dinner for our family and a few friends. We wanted to acknowledge how much their support had meant to us so far and it seemed like a good time to do it. Everyone seemed to really enjoy themselves and to appreciate being there. We all had a common focus, and it served as a time of collective appreciation of what God had being doing.

On December 1st, at my regular clinic visit, I talked with Dr. Lipton. I was now no longer on Prednisone, Ganciclovir or Gamma globulin. That day he also cut out my Zantac, reduced my Cyclosporin dosage, and reduced my Magnesium pills from seven a day to four. He told me I could go back to work when I felt strong enough to do it, and even told me I was free to go on a trip if I wanted to - "as long as you go somewhere nice". He didn't need to see me for another two weeks. I looked at him and said: "All that sounds to me like good news". He just smiled and shook my hand.

However I found out there is a down-side to coming off all the medications. Having been on Prednisone and the other drugs for so long, some of my body's natural stimuli had been dulled. Reducing the dependence on them fairly quickly requires the body to go through quite a withdrawal adjustment and for a few weeks in November and December I was lethargic and nauseous. I slept a lot and had little appetite. On one occasion I fell backwards to the floor and almost blacked out, while vomiting suddenly at the kitchen sink. I hate that feeling of having no energy, which had been all too common in recent years.

The doctor said that this was quite normal. Some people have a terrible time getting off Prednisone. Every Monday, when I was in clinic, I would see many of the other patients who were going through the same trip as me. I got to know one of them quite well. He was David Stoliker, from Peterborough. He told me he'd had three transplants. Three! I couldn't imagine going through even a second one. The first one was a couple of years before but his leukemia came back a few months later. So he had a second one around the same time I did. But it didn't take. So they had to go back to his brother Al, who was the donor, and extract some stem cells from his marrow and transplant those. David was doing fairly well, but still had a very sore mouth and was having difficulty eating. Everybody was having their own different problems getting through this. I also saw other patients I had met that had caught the CMV virus too. I recognized the treatments they were getting.

As December arrived, my pace of activity started to pick up. I got heavily involved in a couple of projects I was interested in. One was the production of a teaching videotape on "Uncovering the Pattern" for the churches of God, which I'd been asked to do - it was the unfolding of what I'd worked on two years before. I also did my own Christmas shopping for the first time in three years. (Marilyn Chuli and Jessie Drewitt had kindly done it for me previously.) And I resumed seeing Dr. Larry Nusbaum. At one session with him, I wrote the following dialogue with my new gatekeeper (which in this case I defined as my new bone marrow):

Me: It's a while since we talked, and I've never written to you before. How are you finding things? Does it feel like home yet?

Gatekeeper: It's certainly different than at Hilary's, but it's much like she told me it would be. And I feel like I'm really doing some good - controlling those old malignant lymphocytes.

Me: Dr. Callum told me the trouble with them is they don't know how to die (like old behaviour patterns, I guess), which is why they stay around so long. The chemo did as much as it could to eliminate them but I'm relying on you to do the rest. Are you up to that, do you think?

G: Yes, I think so. They're under control at present. None of us knows what the future holds. The other cells are healthy. Your counts have come up and stayed up very well, despite all the immuno-suppressive drugs you've been on.

Me: Does it help you for us to communicate like this from time to time?

G: Yes - I need to know how you're feeling, and that what I'm doing is important to you. I don't need to hear it a lot, just once in a while.

Me: I want you to know that I think you are doing really well. You were my only hope - and I'm so grateful that you've come and fitted in so well. I shudder to think of what the alternative was. I want so much for you to keep doing what you're doing, and I want to know when there's something I can do to help you. I don't ever take it for granted.

G: Thanks. You can count on me.

On December 13th we made a showing at Matt Barrett's annual Christmas black-tie dinner for senior executives of the Bank and their spouses. I was glad I felt well enough to go, to see again for the first time in many months many of my close colleagues. I was overwhelmed by the welcome I got, and I had many very good conversations with some of them. When we were getting ready to leave as dessert was being served (it was past my bedtime), Matt got up and made some very nice remarks about me to the group. The whole evening reassured me that I had not been forgotten and that, when I was able to return, there would be a place for me.

It's quite remarkable how quickly I began to feel out of things, whenever I was not able to work. It had started to undermine my confidence in my ability. It made me question what kind of work I was really capable of doing. But with those feelings there also came a gradual reassurance that I had been on the right career track after all and doing what I was good at. I hadn't made a mistake. And I increasingly began to feel that, when the time came, I would be given something to do that I would find fulfilling, and in which I could make a substantial contribution to the organization that had been so good to me. That was a very reassuring conclusion. And so I decided that, God willing, and subject to the doctors' assessment of my bone marrow at the six month mark in January, I would target going back to work (part-time at first) in early February 1998.

The morning after the dinner, when I got up, I had a rash from head to toe, and didn't feel well at all. The next day, when I went to the hospital for my weekly visit, it was even worse. They took one look at me and said "the GVH is back". It was the result of the rapid reduction of my anti-rejection medications. They replaced my Cyclosporin with Imuran pills, and put me back on 60 mg. of Prednisone daily. The plan was to reduce it by 10 mg. a week. Sure enough, the rash and other effects went away in three or four days. It reminded me that this graft-versus-host disease was never very far away.

If I was going back to work in February, I had better get busy. There was a lot to get done by then, and this gave me a focus that I had been lacking. I had been so used to operating with a very immediate time horizon - 1 month, or 1 day, or even 5 minutes (during chemo) - that to start thinking and planning for a couple of months ahead seemed strange.

Christmas was a delightful time with the family. I appreciate it more every year. And for the first time in years I didn't have chemotherapy scheduled for immediately after the New Year. There were just the four of us at home on Christmas morning and again I enjoyed so much watching each member of my family opening their gifts. That afternoon we went to Brantford and had a great time at Tom and Jessie Drewitt's with Sandra's side of the family. The next evening Adele and Bruce arrived from Vancouver and on the Saturday we went up to Bryan and Hilary's for another lovely time with my side of the family. We were so much closer now, after what we had all been through. Mom said it was almost too much for her to take in - Hilary at one end of the table and me at the other, with the whole family around. We went straight up from there to the condo until New Year's Eve. Then we celebrated New Year's Eve with our friends the Archibalds and Williams, who had offered to host the evening in our home. Bruce and Adele also had a few young couples over.

As we reflected back that night over the year that had just been completed, it seemed too much to take in. What a year! Hardly a day's respite. I'm glad we didn't know it all in advance. Every day had its trauma, its decisions, its uncertainty, its unpleasantness. How good it felt to arrive alive and well in 1998. In four months it would be ten years since this all began - that's a large portion of my life. We had seen at close quarters so much of the Lord at work. I just felt so contented and optimistic, and I savoured the moment. So did the others it seemed, because nobody wanted to leave. So I left them and went to bed, telling them I was out of gas. My body is doing remarkably well, but I am much more aware of when it has reached its limit.

I signed up for a fitness program to start getting some strength back in my body. It had spent so long being quite idle. The only real exercize I had been getting had been walking, which was very important but not enough. I was much more attuned now to the need to take sensible preventative precautions with respect to exercize, diet and rest. My hair was coming back in, although quite grey this time, and so I got up the nerve to stop wearing my hair piece, which felt a lot better. Again my family helped me to know when it was ready for public.

On January 5th I had my six-month bone marrow aspiration and biopsy. I wouldn't hear the results until my next visit in two weeks - "unless there's a problem", they said. January 8th would mark six months from my transplant. Dr. Al-Zharani, who did the marrow test and my check-up that day, told me he couldn't see or feel any problems - no swelling of lymph nodes, no lung problems, no rash. But the next day I got a phone call at home. It was the nurse at the hospital. I froze! However she was calling about something else, but it was remarkable how instantly that feeling of fright had come back.

On January 15th, I went back to St. Michael's to the dermatologist again. But on the way out I decided to drop in and see Maureen in Intensive Care, Yvonne in Day Care and

Dr. Brandwein. I wanted in particular to talk to him about my book, since he was such a large part of it. He told me he would look forward to reading it because it's hard for doctors to put themselves in the position of their patients. I told him there were often times I wondered what he really thought; he said he sometimes wondered what I was thinking. I said to him: "Off the record, was there ever a time when you thought it was all over for me?". He said: "No, even when you were very ill, I always thought you'd pull through. Someone was obviously looking out for you.". Someone indeed.

And so, on the 19th, Sandra and I went back to the clinic for my check-up and to hear the results of the bone marrow test. We were both very keyed up. This was an important check point. Dr. Lipton came into the room, checked me over and gave me my blood counts. They were virtually normal - hemoglobin 122 (just below the normal level of 130), platelets 180 (well above the minimum of 150), and my white count was 6.3 (well below the maximum of 11 - and <u>down</u> 3.1 from the time before). He said he didn't need to see me for four weeks. Then he told us that my marrow test showed improvement from the time before, which is what we wanted to hear. So I asked him: "Is there any indication of a resurgence of the leukemia so far?". He said "not at all", and sounded very optimistic. It was so good to hear him say that; we could tell he felt good about it too, even though he could give us no guarantee about the future. What a huge sense of relief we both felt. We decided to go down the hall to the Transplant Unit to tell the doctors and nurses there. One of the nurses couldn't get over how much I was smiling, compared with the way I'd been last July.

"It's amazing", I thought, as I recalled those early days of July, when I had been lying in bed so uncomfortable, "what good news to

begin a new year, and at another major milestone in my journey". I walked out of the clinic with a lightness in my step, feeling that the future was just opening up to me - the beginning of the rest of my life. I could almost see the sunshine at the end of that long tunnel I had been in.

16. Love is the Greatest Gift

For many people, one of their favourite chapters in the New Testament is 1 Corinthians 13, the chapter about love. It is often quoted at weddings. The previous chapter lists a variety of gifts that are given to Christians, some temporary, some more permanent, to be used for the benefit of others. But chapter 13 ends this way: *"now remain faith, hope, love, these three; but the greatest of these is love"*. Without hope I never would have had the will to go on, and faith was the conviction I had that my hope would in fact be realized. These were both vital and wonderful gifts from God, but love is the greatest of all.

The love that's being referred to is not just a sentiment, not just affection or attraction (different words are used for those). It's the love that originates with God, and is always unconditional and always giving - it's "caring in action". It's the kind of love I have received in so many different ways from so many different people, although I for one am sometimes embarrassed to label it that way. It's the kind of love without which I wouldn't have made it nearly this far...

It's the love shown to me every day by my wife Sandra as she has devoted her own life to doing everything in her power to making things easier for me and getting me better, often at the cost of her own well-being...

It's the love shown to me by Adele, Jennifer, Andrew, Bruce and my extended family who have encouraged me, supported my every decision, and always done what they could for me...

It's the love shown to me by my sister Hilary who so willingly gave me what no one else could; she literally gave of herself what to me has meant life rather than death...

It's the love shown to me by medical experts such as Dr. Brandwein and Dr. Lipton by their unparalleled medical ability and attention...

It's the love shown to me by another professional, Dr. Larry Nusbaum, by his skill and dedication in helping me figure things out...

It's the love shown to me by very dear friends such as Laurie Williams and Greg Neely and others who took the initiative to keep in close touch and showed great empathy in whatever I was going through...

It's the love shown to Sandra and me by friends of hers like Marg Smith and Marg Neely and Jessie Drewitt and Katie Hydon, among others, who understood the need to "be there" for her, emotionally and practically...

It's the love shown to me by countless friends and colleagues and acquaintances from near and far who always took the trouble to enquire after my well-being, communicate with me, and faithfully pray for me. I could see it in their eyes. People really came through for me when I let them know I needed them.

I've learned as never before that caring makes such a difference - at least it has to me. None of them could cure me, but they sure cared for me, and God was using that while He was curing me. It's wonderful to be loved.

I've tried to keep all the letters and cards I've received. I can't be sure I have them all, but I have hundreds of them. That's a whole lot. And reading them over brings back memories of all the kindness and the encouragement I have received. What was always remarkable to me was the timing. They didn't come in bunches, but during the tougher times, seldom a day would go by without at least one - as though it were all arranged.

I sat down one day to try to compile a list of all the people in recent years who had called, sent us cards or messages, or written us letters about our situation. The number was staggering. Many were from the same people, constantly keeping in touch. Some were funny (and it really helps to have a good laugh) and some were very touching. So many had assurances and specific commitments of on-going prayer for us (sometimes of more than once a day). Some included short scriptures which had meant something special to the sender and now, as I read them, they affected me too. Many of these people I knew had gone through, or were presently going through, difficulties of their own, but they reached out to us anyway. I realized again what a huge and beneficial ministry this communication is. I've never been much of a card or letter sender (Sandra sends a lot of cards), but I sure know now what they can do. I want to sincerely acknowledge and to honour every one of those people who took the thought, trouble and expense to minister to us in that way.

Because of my frequent immune-suppressed condition, I was seldom allowed to have many visitors, either in hospital or at home. Even when I was out in public I was discouraged from making much contact by hand-shaking, hugging or kissing (although I violated it several times). And so I invented "the virtual hug"; "consider yourself hugged" I would say. When I first started going out after the 100th day after my transplant, I wore a golf glove on my right hand so I could shake people's hands. Most infections apparently come from our own hands through what we touch. And people were very considerate in staying away from me if they had a cold or their children had come down with something.

It's very interesting the various things people said to me over the years when they saw me chronically ill, and it's made me more conscious of what I say to others going through serious illness or other affliction. My typical response to "How are you today?" used to be "fine", which wasn't very informative, often wasn't true, and didn't tend to further the conversation. And so sometimes, jokingly, I would say something like "on a scale of 1 to 10, a 4", or "C+". If that provoked any further questions, I would begin to elaborate while gauging the response. Sometimes the other person showed real interest and listened attentively; that was what I found most helpful. Some people want to know the particulars, some just wanted to wish me well, and some weren't quite sure what to say - they changed the subject or started relating their own experiences. Different people set their own limits on how much they wanted to know and that was OK. After all, there's a lot more to a good conversation than the details of my health. And I didn't always make it easy for people when I wasn't very open with them. What I found least helpful was cliché answers and advice, and simple assurances that they were sure everything would be fine. Maybe it wouldn't be.

I say these things to try to be helpful. I needed to learn for myself the effect on people when I try to comfort them. I need to take the time to let them tell me what's really going on and to show genuine interest in it. Everyone responds in their own way, and whoever it was and whatever they said, I always took the will for the deed and really appreciated their concern.

Some folks have said that I deserved to do well and deserved that God would heal me. I don't buy that. I know myself. And if that were the case, others would be equally or more deserving. But that's not how God works. Healing is not a reward for my goodness - and am I thankful for that! God's whole approach is to work out his purposes through willing persons, all according to His grace - His undeserved favour. That's what I appeal to - not to what He owes me (He owes me nothing), not for justice, but for His grace and mercy. I want His purpose to be fully realized in my life. I'm no hero; I'm just trying to survive.

Some people have said that I'm a miracle. I hope what they mean is that I'm the result of a miracle. Because I am. So many people have told me that my illness has had a profound effect on a lot of other people - that it has reinforced their faith. If that's so, then that's wonderful. But I always find that a little mind-boggling, and it's not my doing. And it has certainly brought our families even closer together. It has clearly deepened and unified the prayer of the Christians in the churches of God, as several have testified. It has clearly spoken to a number of people who otherwise might be sceptical about the reality of the personal intervention of Almighty God in our lives and the relevance and power of His Word. It has brought us into meaningful contact with the wider Christian community in a way which would probably not have been possible otherwise.

I sense that people tended to observe closely what happened to me. Was my faith genuine, or would it collapse under pressure? Would I become self-absorbed? Did I consider myself victimized? I didn't know the answers; I had to find out also. And when people said: "It's your faith that's making the difference", I hastened to correct them that my faith is only as valid as the God I have faith in. There's no point being on a telephone line unless there's a person on the other end. My God is real and personal and specific. I know Him and I trust Him implicitly. That's what makes my faith relevant. It's much more than just a positive attitude.

17. Reflections

As we as a family make the transition from the trauma of the past few years to whatever lies ahead, we all have our thoughts and feelings about it all. It helps to bring closure to express these and to acknowledge what has occurred. My family can speak best for themselves...

From Sandra:

"How can you put your thoughts and feelings over ten years into a page or two? However, I will try to give something of my perspective during Keith's illness. I will never forget the day my life changed drastically within minutes; I actually felt my heart miss a beat and my legs felt like jelly - how could this be happening? I distinctly remember thinking that Keith had made his family a top priority during his life and we had created many precious memories over the years. Family holidays were a "must" and Keith always took the time to play with his children and to be at the "special days" at school. How eternally thankful I was for this. A dear friend once said to me in the early days of our marriage "Sandra, if an opportunity comes

for you to spend more time with your husband and/or children, take it!" I took this advice and how grateful I was that I had done this. You can't go back and make these memories after the fact. In this there were no regrets.

As I looked at my children over the years I was broken-hearted for them. How long would they have their Dad, whom they loved so much? How could I help them through this trial that went on and on? You spend the early years of your children's lives trying to protect them from any harm and suddenly you can't do this any more and a hug and a kiss does not take away the pain; in fact we were the reason for this. From the very beginning I had a struggle with what I thought God was telling me and what my human nature was telling me. It may seem strange that on the one hand I felt God was going to heal Keith in His own way and in His own time and yet there were other times when seeing Keith go through the suffering he had to and hearing what the doctors were telling me, I thought 'my husband is dying before my very eyes and I can do nothing about it!'. It was a horrible and devastating feeling. Would I be a widow at an early age? How can you go on when you have become "one" and then you lose half of yourself? I imagined it as having half of my body amputated - a very scary and frightening prospect, and yet I had experienced along life's way that life does go on and the world continues to go on regardless of my circumstance and that God would surely see me through this as well.

While I ached for my children - Adele, who when Keith became considerably sicker had married and moved to Vancouver - how I missed her, my daughter and my friend. Jennifer, who always seemed to be writing exams, etc. in the middle of a crisis, and still took the time to listen to me and comfort me. She became very aware of how her Dad was feeling and became very capable of assessing the situation and taking charge. Andrew, who was struggling with all that the teenage years entail and finding it hard to concentrate, particularly at school, found the time to give me a big hug at the appropriate moment! So many times his thoughtfulness shone through, as he would see things that normally Keith would have done but couldn't do, and he took over and did them for me or for his Dad. How I thanked God daily for my precious children whom I love so much and to whom I owe so much, for they helped me keep my sanity when at times I thought I could not handle it any more. There were many times when I was not the easiest person to be around and yet they accepted how I was and we were there to support each other.

There were many times I so much wished my Dad & Mom were still alive. Particularly in the two major events of 1997. I felt like I wanted to be a "little girl" again and have my Dad & Mom look after me - which they had done numerous times. Perhaps more than at any other time I missed my Mom and realized that not only could she have helped me, she would have been wonderful with my children. We had been so dependent on her prayers. At her funeral in late 1994, I mentioned to a friend that I wondered who would pray for my children in her place. She replied "I will". My parents left me a great legacy in a number of ways and I often found myself thinking "what would my Mom have done in this situation?" Maybe she was helping me!

Our son-in-law Bruce Robinson, who landed in this situation when he married Adele four years ago, has contributed greatly on several occasions since then. He's an upbeat person; and he sees what needs to be done and does it. I particularly think of what a difference he made in the crisis days last April. He helped us in so many practical ways, and he was especially good as a "big brother" to Andrew, making sure that he wasn't left alone at home. I'm glad he's part of our family.

I treasure the times when I was so exhausted mentally and physically, and God came in and gave me the "peace that passes understanding". How I wish you could hang onto this forever. I felt Satan was really attacking me at times and hated when I had this peace. There were several instances when I truly felt Satan was standing right beside me - what a frightening experience. I could only call upon God and command him to get behind me in the name of the Lord Jesus.

The last nine and a half years have been a roller coaster ride for me - emotionally and physically, and yet through the good and bad I have had complete confidence that God was in control and that He had a plan and somehow He would help us all through whatever it was. No it wasn't going to be easy, and it wasn't what I would have asked for, but it was what was reality in my life. I thank God that during this time He has made me more aware of other peoples' problems and concerns and has taught me to reach out to others, even during my own trials. Sometimes this was harder than others but it was always in the back of my mind. God has also shown me the immense value of heartfelt prayer and of needing others in my life. My brother David and my sisters Betty and Jessie have constantly been there for me and I feel so privileged to have them as my family. The friends that showed me they cared, they have no idea how the kind words, cards and flowers I received time after time boosted my spirits. I am humbled by the kindness and love of so many. Indeed no man is an island unto himself.

Keith has been through an experience in his life that I would have done anything to not have him go through. He is my best friend, the father of my children, and my husband whom I adore, and yet we have had some very precious times and there is no doubt that his illness has brought us closer than ever - always something to give God thanks for even in the middle of a crisis. Each doctor's visit, and every day I went to be with him in hospital my feelings would be up and down depending on how Keith was. Is he a bit better today or is he worse? There were times when we were just silent and it was okay, there were times we had great chats and there were times when I was frustrated because I needed to talk to him and he was in his own little world just trying to cope with the day. Sometimes I felt I disappointed him by not being in "top form" and yet you can't help but just react to difficult times. I tried to keep life as normal as possible for all of us and at times this was not easy - what is normal anyway?

When we were told that Keith could be a candidate for a bone marrow transplant for the second time in May 1997, there was part of me that was shocked and thought "oh no, I can't go through this again", and part of me that knew this was going to happen all along. Something inside of me would not let me get rid of the feeling that Keith would have a transplant, even when the doctors said it would not happen. I'm convinced that this was from God and it always came into my mind in the midst of the most trying times and often didn't make any sense. Sometimes it is so hard to decipher what is of God and what is just what we would like to see happen, and yet when God was telling me something, nothing could totally destroy it - not even the doctors' grim prognosis. Hilary gave her brother a second chance at life and for this I will be always extremely thankful - many anonymous donors had already kept Keith alive by the giving of their blood. Hilary gave her bone marrow so willingly and there is no question that this has brought her and her family much closer to our family. The fact is that this whole experience has brought both our families into a stronger bond with each other and we all need to take the time to show and tell each other just how important they are in our lives.

It has been extremely hard living with this day after day, minute after minute, for so many years. There have been many instances when I was spending hours and hours at the hospital and trying to think of the children at home and accomplish what was needing to be done in the house (and out of the house) that I felt "I just can't do this any more"! However, another day goes by and you find yourself doing what has to be done and yet sometimes not even remembering how it got done. There is no doubt in my mind that I made it through with the help and strength of God because my strength was completely gone - how do people who have no belief in God do it?

Are we at the end of the story? Only God knows this but I am truly thankful for God hearing and answering the prayers of so many people on Keith's behalf and our family's behalf. Keith has passed six months post-transplant - another milestone and yet he has many still to go. To all of you, my precious family, my dear friends and to some of you that I didn't even know personally, thank you from the bottom of my heart. I owe you all more than I can say.

To my husband - may God show us what He has for us to do together to bring Him glory and honour. God has been moulding me (and He still has a lot of work to do) and I await His guidance."

From Adele (age 27):

"As I look back over the past few years with respect to my father's illness, my overwhelming reaction, I think, is fear. It dominated most of my waking hours to the point where it was so strong that I numbed myself to its effects. It was fear that he wouldn't survive and, even worse, that he would have a painful death; it was more than my 'psyche' could bear. I worried a lot - that he might die without me being there, that it would be painful, that our family would never again be the same, that dad wouldn't get to be a grandpa to my children, and that mom would be alone. I worried that my *husband Bruce and I would have to pack up and head back east at a moment's notice and start our lives over should he die. And I worried constantly that, in the meantime, I should be spending this valuable time with family and not 3000 miles away. I also worried about mom's stress level and her migraines. I wondered how long she could keep this up before being in hospital with dad. I currently worry that she may slip into a depression without the adrenalin on such a constant basis.*

I have vivid recollections of dad taking me to dinner in 1992 and knowing in my 'gut' that something was wrong. From my memory, I was never told directly that he had leukemia; in fact I kept thinking everything would get back to normal soon. I felt that there were many "secrets" around his illness and that a lot of walking on egg shells was necessary in order for us all to protect each other's feelings. Looking back, I would have appreciated more open, direct communication because my imagination is often far worse than the truth. Not knowing was one of the hardest things for me and the silence around his "situation" (as everyone liked to call it) drove me up the wall. Sure, the facts were always clear and neatly packaged - but the more difficult part was how each of us was so reluctant to communicate our pain to the other. I definitely feel this is changing now, and I think the closeness my dad and I have shared in the past year can be attributed partly to this change. It's only when people can reveal their vulnerability and feel safe to do this, that true connection happens. I think we as a family have all come a long way...and have a way to go. Only recently have Jennifer and Andrew and I spoken about this. I think we're getting closer and I look forward to more of this.

I feel quite strongly that people should have been told about dad's diagnosis much sooner than was the case. (This is not a criticism because I'm well aware that dad and mom had their reasons for the timing, including the fact that they felt it best that Andrew not be told until he was a little older.) I just found that, for me, "not telling" was an added stress, and often I felt I had to distance myself from people important to me in order to deal with the stress. My preference would have been to share this and not feel so bound by silence. As a result, I remember feeling very alone. I think people deal with this stuff in different ways. My thought is we should have been free to share this sooner with one or two important people in our lives, perhaps even more. The internalized stress felt like a time-bomb waiting to explode.

It's difficult to say what lasting effects all this has had or will have on our family; however, for me personally, there have been both positive and negative effects. My relationship with dad has improved dramatically, for which I am utterly thankful. I think seeing him in such a vulnerable condition enabled me to see <u>him</u> underneath all those layers. In turn, I shed some of my intimidating qualities and as a result a lot of baggage was unloaded. This I wouldn't trade, and yet there are many effects that will take some time to undo. I think I numbed myself so much to the pain I was feeling around this that it extended into other parts of my life. I'm so programmed to not let my guard down and just enjoy life for a while that I now find it very tough to laugh and have fun. I feel like I became an even more intense person which again left me quite isolated from the people with whom I needed to have connection. It's like I need to learn to 'feel' again, because it's been too hard to feel over the past year. I would only end up hurting more. I think as a family we have learned to appreciate time more, as well as each other. We have been allowed to see the "bigger picture", and priorities, I imagine, have been shifted for the better. Also, instead of just thinking how we feel about each other, I think we now speak those feelings more, which I believe has served to strengthen us all.

Knowing what I know about trauma (from my social work), I truly believe when I saw dad fighting for his life in April 1997 I immediately went into a 'critical incident'. Ever since (although it's getting less), I have had nightmares and vivid flashbacks of walking in the room and seeing him fade away before my eyes. Also, when he was having fluid drained and going into respiratory distress, I have never experienced such an intense reaction. I think my experience was somewhat different from the others, given that, living in Vancouver, I'd had much more of a telephone experience of his worst moments rather than actually witnessing them before my very eyes. Therefore, when I did see it, my whole body went into shock.

Bruce was the person I probably opened up to the most but, to be honest, even he got the edited version. My advice to others would be that they find a place or person whereby they can express what's inside. However people deal with grief in such different ways and it's important they're not pushed before they're ready. People need to feel safe - that they can trust who they're talking to. It's helpful when friends or family check in just to see how you're doing. Other avenues are also important such as journaling, writing, art, etc.

For the most part my friends were very supportive during the whole period. Looking back, I think I didn't make it as easy for them to offer support as I could have, as I shut myself off so often. Cards and phone calls were certainly helpful, but just spending time together for a break was one of the more helpful things - reminding me I have other parts to my life. It was important for me that in my time spent with friends, and conversations with them, that they acknowledged what was going on. Once that happened I felt we could move into other areas and leave the hard stuff for a while. Again I think the biggest barrier to the support was myself, because letting people in meant being vulnerable - something I don't do overly well.

I'm not pleased to say that this experience has probably had a negative effect on my spiritual development in many ways. I was often angry and exhausted. I felt my mind was so filled with busyness that I couldn't or didn't take time to be with God, because that would have meant having to deal with all the emotional turmoil - which was easier to keep in storage. Praying was so hard, although I did try to pray consistently for dad, but not much else.

Finally, what can I say about Hilary? She gave my dad life, and for that I will be forever grateful. I wrote her a card shortly after she had donated her bone marrow expressing my thanks and how moving the whole experience had been."

From Jennifer (age 23):

"When Dad first suggested that I may want to contribute something to this book, I though it would be a reasonably easy exercize. But as I actually sat down to write, all these memories - sights, sounds, smells, thoughts, and feelings, both good and bad - came flooding over me. I realized that to express these things in an understandable and meaningful way was going to be a very difficult task. I have a very hard time opening up and sharing things that affect me deeply (a characteristic I think my whole family suffers from). As a family, and as an individual, there have been many experiences faced over the last nine years that have profoundly affected me. So my contribution here is simply a tiny glimpse of some of my thoughts and experiences throughout those years in an attempt to perhaps help others who are dealing with similar situations, or to help those who want to help them.

I first found out that my Dad had leukemia when I was fourteen - just starting high school. I still remember that day. I was sitting on my bed, with Dad and Mom sitting across from me, and they told me that Dad had CLL, which is a blood disorder. I didn't really get the CLL part, so in my mind it was a blood disorder. I didn't fully understand the implications of what they were telling me, but I knew that it was fairly serious. I also knew that although it probably wouldn't affect my day to day life at the moment, sooner or later things would change. I didn't know when, and I had no idea what those changes would be, and that really scared me. Fear of the unknown was to be a common emotion I experienced over the next few years, and still feel, sometimes so intense it is numbing. However, at that point I was usually able to keep Dad's illness in the back of my mind as he looked fine. But when he visited the doctor, and at other unexpected intervals, I would find myself thinking about it and my thoughts would be off and running, imagining everything that could possibly happen. I was still fairly young, and didn't understand everything that was going on around me, and I found it all very overwhelming.

Eventually things got worse and Dad was looking more and more ill every day. When it was decided that we should let others know, it started to hit me really hard. I had to face it everyday, I couldn't escape it any longer, and my emotions were so volatile and so near the surface that I had a very difficult time. I often felt angry - at God, at people, even at nothing in particular - and felt it was so unfair. I wished for a normal life, and felt so frustrated and helpless.

Life has been a roller coaster ride for a long time now, and as many of you know, I've never had a real affinity for roller coasters. The range of emotions I have felt, some completely unexplainable and irrational, has been unbelievable. You learn to close off certain areas of your life and shut out feelings in order to cope. Unfortunately, once learned, it's hard to break the habit. I have often found myself constantly searching for answers, to make sense of it all, and I ended up grasping at anything I could. It seemed to me that every time I had an exam to write, or any time my birthday came around, it *coincided with a major crisis in Dad's illness. Two days before my 21st birthday we were told that the doctors had run out of options, and could do no more to help my Dad; it was just a matter of time. Thankfully it is God who is in control, and not the doctors. But I couldn't help but feel that if I could just live quietly, and the events in my life could go unnoticed, maybe things would be okay. I also felt angry that as my life continued I had to fight against so much and nothing was without a struggle. You might think this association between the events of my life and Dad's illness a bit ridiculous, but anxiety sometimes clouds your thinking.*

I often felt very isolated throughout these past nine years, and very lonely. I know that I kept myself very protected, but I often felt that no one understood me or the intensity of the feelings I was dealing with. I sometimes felt like the weight of emotion was so heavy that I was going to explode at any time. Yet I felt like no one noticed, especially when Dad was doing okay at that time, so I should be doing okay too. Unfortunately it doesn't work that way. During the crises your instincts take over, and it's only after the fact that you have to face and deal with all you've experienced. And that takes time. It's very difficult to express these things to people, as feelings cannot always be pinpointed with a cause and effect. I would often turn to God at these times and pour out my fears and hurt to Him unreservedly, because although I got angry at times and questioned the fairness and reason of it all, I knew He had it in control and could give me comfort.

As I mentioned, fear was an overwhelming feeling throughout, as was frustration, and hurt. I felt it hard to concentrate on things, and got distracted very easily. I longed for a sense of normalcy, and peace, but couldn't always find it. I trusted God, and prayed for my father and my family every day, but I found it hard to pray for myself, for the help I knew I needed in order to cope with day to day life. I wanted to protect my family, to help my Mom, to be happy and not depress people when they were in my company. I should have turned to the Lord, but found it difficult to face up to everything I was thinking and feeling - the what if's especially - and so often times neglected my spiritual life. The scriptures didn't always provide the comfort I felt I needed. While I believed it all and knew that it was true, I needed to see it, to have something tangible to hold on to.

In April of 1997 Dad went into hospital with fluid around his lungs. I visited on Wednesday night and things seemed to be all right. But as we have constantly been aware of, things can change very quickly. When I got a phone call at work the next day from Mom saying Bruce and Adele had been called to come here, my heart stopped and I felt sick to my stomach. I rushed to the hospital and spent the whole weekend in a state of shock and disbelief. During that weekend I made a phone call to some dear friends overseas to let them know what was happening. The conversation I had that night, the sincerity and the message given, meant so much to me. By the grace of God, Dad survived that weekend, and even the doctors had to admit that it was a miracle.

July was the beginning of another long journey. Watching Dad go through the bone marrow transplant, and watching him suffer so much physically and emotionally was extremely hard. Especially when there was nothing I could do to help him. I still have nightmares and flashbacks of things I watched and felt during this past year, and each time they are very vivid and painful. As Dad started to get better, and was doing very well, all things considered, in the back of my head I could not forget what happened to a friend of mine. Just a year and a half earlier, around the time Dad was to have the transplant the first time, my friend's sister had one. She was doing very well, and was released from hospital thinking she was well on the way to recovery. Within 3 months of the transplant she was dead. This terrified me. I am very thankful for the support I received from people - prayers, cards, and friends who took me out for coffee just to get a break from everything. It really means so much, and I cannot repay it. Your kindness has made me more aware of difficulties others might be facing, and how I can help them. One thing I've learned is that it is very important to the person experiencing the difficulty to have people acknowledge the fact that it is hard on them. You need to hear people say that. Acknowledgement does not mean understanding what that person is going through, but understanding that they are going through a difficult time and that it affects their whole life, and is hard to cope with.

I have often reflected back on thoughts I have had and experiences I faced, to see how all of this has affected me. I don't think it has so much changed me (because of my age when this all started) as much as shaped me. Obviously, not every experience I'd had a positive impact on my life, but many have. Our family has grown closer, and shares more with one another. I fondly remember the lunch hours I spent with Dad while he was in hospital. I'd go over on my lunch break and we'd talk all about my new job and my studies, etc. and things he'd been thinking about and hoped to do one day. Even though he was in hospital, it was nice to spend that time with him and focus on something other than his illness. We took every advantage to spend time together as a family because we never knew how much time we had, and that time we spent was great. I still haven't figured out exactly why God let all this happen, and even though I'm generally okay with that, my human nature still longs for an answer at times. I still also go through the feelings of fear and hurt and frustration, and am trying to deal with 9 years of intense emotional trauma. I know it is going to take time, but I am *thankful for the support of friends and family, and the knowledge that God is in control."*

From Andrew (age 17):

"I found out when I was twelve. My family had kept it a secret for four years. The doctor felt it would be best because I was so young. My oldest sister Adele didn't totally agree with the idea but went along with it anyway. Last year my dad told me that, when he first told me the news, I had told him that everything would be alright. That seems like a routine thing to say, but it was more than that; I actually truly believed that. It took a while for it to really sink in; I guess I had to get over the initial shock. When I was about fourteen, it started to play tricks with my mind. I found it hard to concentrate on things, and that was added on to the pressures of starting a new school - high school no less! Things were getting worse, my dad was going through more treatments, and feeling more and more sick. Fortunately, in my grade nine year, I made many great friends who, little did I know, I would rely on in the coming years. But no one helped me more than my close friend Heidi. Until the summer after grade 11, she and I were just best friends. I was starting to have more bad days, but she was <u>always</u> there for me. She kept me from losing it; she kept my faith strong. Heidi never tried to fix anything, she just cared for me and listened whenever I needed her, which was often. She cared so much, and that's better than anything I could have hoped for in a friend.

In mid-April of 1997 things went wrong. My dad had a lot of fluid on his lungs, and severe complications came from that. It happened so suddenly, and before I knew it he had to go in for surgery, and not a routine surgery. Heidi was in Florida at this time, and I have to say I really wished she was here. I can talk to others, but not the same way I can talk with her. That week I really missed her! My dad had to be in intensive care and he had a tube down his throat so he couldn't talk; he had to write everything down. That was really hard to cope with. That weekend I kept everything bottled up. I didn't know where to turn. Fortunately everything turned out O.K., thanks to prayer.

This summer he had to go through a bone marrow transplant. I expected this to be the worst summer of my life. Fortunately, thanks to the thousands of prayers going up for my dad, he made it through the critical period with no complications, and things went awesomely with Heidi and me. I'm kind of scared to see what's to come, but I put my trust in God."

Andrew's friend Heidi added this:

"I don't know Mr. and Mrs. Dorricott very well, but I know they are tremendous people. I know this from Andrew. He speaks so well of his super parents. When Andrew's parents come up while I'm talking to Andrew, I always sense a great love for both of them. I have especially seen this with his dad. Andrew has high respect for his father, one truly awesome dad, a very knowledgeable man with a great love for his family which shines through in all his actions. I really noticed Andrew's great admiration for his dad after he told me he had leukemia. Over time I learned more, and through this my friendship with Andrew blossomed.

It was hard for Andrew to have his dad sick and in and out of hospital. Andrew would often mention the great times they had tossing around a football, and how he wished for the day when he could do that again. Andrew also told me he loved having his dad at all his hockey games. Nowadays it's not always easy for Andrew to get up for school, but in the days of hockey Mr. Dorricott only had to open his bedroom door, whisper "hockey time!", and Andrew would bolt out of bed ready to play. From these stories I could tell that Andrew's dad played a significant role in his life.

It must be hard seeing someone whom you love suffer; actually I know it is hard. I know it because I've been there and I've watched Andrew. Andrew was always willing to talk to you about his dad if you asked; he was always grateful for that support. Many times the listener had to speak no words - just listen. Often times when I talked to him about his dad, I wouldn't know what to say; I wished for the perfect words to come to me so I could offer words of comfort. However, I learned that many times words aren't needed, that just your presence and your listening ear can do more than 1000 words.

Some days I could tell Andrew was more bothered than other days. There was something missing from his cheerful self. This wasn't noticeable to all his classmates. Andrew never liked to dwell on the fact that his father was ill; the last thing he wanted was everyone to feel sorry for him and be nice to him just because not all was well with his dad. Andrew is sincere and he wants friends who are sincere. He didn't want any attention drawn to himself. Andrew did not hide the fact that his dad had leukemia; he knew he could not wish it away; he was ready to fight it! He used whatever resources would help him in this fight, and I think they were friends and prayer. I'm glad I could play a part in both of these. Andrew is a strong believer in the power of prayer and it was uplifting for me to see that. Sometimes it can be really hard to leave all the tangles in your life in the hands of God, and trust that he knows best. I saw in Andrew a sense of calmness among all the upheavals that came his way. Andrew has faith and trusts that his Lord and Saviour knows best and will always care for him.

Andrew told me that when his dad went into hospital he wasn't scared or worried so much about himself as he was about his family, that they would be okay. Andrew also remained strong at school; many people commented on how Andrew held together through the good and bad times. Those people were right. Andrew's awesome smile was seen every day and he remained to be the spectacular person he always is.

As a friend of Andrew's, I have watched him struggle with his dad's illness. I ached inside when he told me of the bad times, and I rejoiced with him when his dad did well. Andrew has taught me many valuable things - how to be a great friend, to put your trust in God and believe He knows best, and to be thankful for everyday things like health and loved ones. I thank God that today I can rejoice with Andrew and his family over the health of Mr. Dorricott."

I am very deeply affected by each of these expressions of pain and agony, anxiety, and personal reactions to each step of their own individual journey by the people I care about so much. There was nothing I could do to protect them from the hurt. I am devoted to them and indebted to them. Thank you to each of you, for <u>all</u> you have done while you were undergoing such deep and lasting suffering yourselves.

For myself, believe it or not, there was never a time during these past almost ten years when I thought I would die as a result of my leukemia. Not that I was always certain if or how I would be healed, but I always knew that God was in control and I wouldn't go until He intended it. There were certainly times when I wondered about it. The prospect didn't frighten me but it greatly saddened me; it seemed like such a waste.

As I look back, the past ten years seem to fall into three phases. The first four years were quite quiet (and so don't take up much space in this book). Only the doctors and my immediate family knew, and my life, externally at least, was very little affected. Then from early 1992 to mid-1995 I was on treatment, my appearance changed, and many people knew. But I was still working full-time and life continued fairly normally, although things were clearly getting worse. During this time I was just trying to get through it and "back to normal". The full implications of being fatally ill hit me only gradually. But the last two and a half years have been quite different and very acute - and I recall that it was around that time that I "waved the little white flag". I spent many months off work and many weeks in hospital. Household life was overturned, and the stress level on the family was very high. But it has been during this last period that so much has happened to affect our lives, and that has been such an intense learning experience for me. Had this learning begun in 1988, would we have been spared a lot of the suffering? I don't know, but I wasn't ready. Sometimes it takes a lot for my heavenly Father to get my attention. And when I don't respond, He has a way of turning up the heat. I know He's not going to give up on me. He cares enough about me to have put me through all this, because it matters to Him how I turn out. As Thomas Moore once said, "When the pain of changing becomes less than the pain of staying the same, we begin to change".

As I read back over what I've written in this book (and there's much more that could have been written), I'm amazed myself at all we've been through and how well I'm doing. Twenty-one chemotherapy cycles, many of them experimental; countless infections and complications and days in hospital. I should be dead by now. But I'm not - and it's no coincidence. And I want to live. I didn't take it all in my stride, even if it might have looked that way to some others; I wasn't always strong throughout it. Whether or not the leukemia will come back I don't know, but I'm in better health today than I've been in a long time. And I mean that physically, emotionally and spiritually. It feels so good to feel well.

For all of that the credit goes squarely to the Lord, with an assist to all those people who for so long have been praying in faith and encouraging us. I still shake my head and don't know quite what to say when I think of all the consistent, earnest prayer by so many people, for so long. They trusted in God. He does hear, He does intervene, He does work in our lives if we truly let Him - but always according to His great purpose for us. He is a God of love, but not someone to be ignored or toyed with.

James 5:11 in the Bible talks about a man who is famous for all that he suffered: *"you have heard of the perseverance of Job, and seen the end intended by the Lord - that the Lord is very compassionate and merciful."* Job's affliction wasn't a random event; he wasn't a statistic - and neither am I. His experience had a purpose to it - the "end intended by the Lord", and so has mine. Learning what that is, and bringing it about in my life, is what has given meaning to this ordeal and has sustained me throughout it. It's a lot easier to see what that is in retrospect; it's much harder to trust God for what hasn't happened yet. Many people suffer affliction in their lives, whether illness or other kinds. We often pray for their deliverance, and that is right, but we can go beyond that to pray that the purpose of it all will be realized.

I have so far come out of this experience a different person than I went in. These differences may not always be apparent to other people, although I hope they begin to be. I find it frustrating when I realize that they are still far from complete or permanent. And so this is all about change - me changing - God drawing me always closer to Him to be more like His own Son, who delights Him totally. It's too easy when things go wrong to just ask Him to "fix it". Do I really want to be changed? It's a tough ride.

I have benefited from the best in professional medical and psychological care. I know that many people are far less likely to accept the latter type of help than the former, as I was. But when I now see others struggling with public or private ordeals of their own who could benefit from such help, I just hope they won't dismiss it without checking it out.

As to my immediate future, I don't know. (As to my eternal future, I am in no doubt.) But for the next few months or years, at this moment I am no more in the dark than anyone else is. And I can sure *live* with that!

And so I put down my pen (as they used to say). My story is not yet finished, but I must go. I have things to do. I have a life to live...

Supplement – "Ten Years Later..."

It's a beautiful day in September 2007. I'm standing in our back garden, at our home in the country near King City, north of Toronto, where we've lived for the past almost six years. I'm watching our three grandchildren playing happily (and noisily) – Emma, just turned 8, Grace aged 5, and Liam 2 and a half. My thoughts go back to how I finished the book I had written back in early 1998, "I Want to Live". I had referred to the man Job in the Bible, and had quoted the scripture: "You have heard of the perseverance of Job and seen the end intended by the Lord - that the Lord is very compassionate and merciful." And now as I stood there I remembered that, after all his suffering, the story of Job ended with him enjoying the rich blessings of God, including his children and his grandchildren. Thinking back over the ten years since my bone marrow transplant in July 1997, I said to myself "God is so good. He is indeed compassionate and merciful."

The book

Writing that book had been so therapeutic for me during my enforced isolation in 1997 after the transplant. Finishing it and getting it published gave me a goal, something to work on. My wife Sandra had helped me immensely, reminding me of things I had forgotten, and making sure it properly reflected the roller coaster of emotions we had both experienced. I had given copies of the draft to all three of my children, Adele, Jennifer and Andrew, because they were so prominent in it. I think they found it hard reading – it brought back so many difficult memories for them. But on one of her visits from Vancouver, Adele sat me down with it at the kitchen table. She had highlighted several parts where I had finished a sentence with an exclamation mark, but had not elaborated on it. She said, "Dad, you don't go below the surface. Clearly this situation meant a lot to you, but you don't let us in on it. You could have been writing this about somebody else. You need to tell us what was going on inside." And so she took me through each part she had marked and asked me "How were you feeling then?" I found that I had no trouble at all recalling exactly how I had felt. It was riveted in my memory. And as I told her about it (and felt the emotion all over again), she just said "Write it down". And so I went back through the manuscript and added the italicized paragraphs that told the story of what was going on inside me at the time the outside events were transpiring. Whenever I go back now and read some of the book myself, as I do from time to time, it is always those parts (the feelings, rather than just the facts) that affect me the most, sometimes even bringing tears to my eyes. Thank you, Adele, for that.

I also sent copies of the drafts to Dr. Callum, the wonderful resident doctor at Princess Margaret Hospital, to be sure that I had the medical particulars right, and also to Dr. Larry Nussbaum, who had helped me so much psychologically. A while later I phoned Larry to ask for his comments. He told me to phone back in a few days because he wasn't quite finished. "I'm going through it line by line," he said. And so a week or so later I made an appointment and went to see him. Just as he had always done, he welcomed me at the front door and led me upstairs to that familiar room. We sat in the same chairs, facing each other. Then he told me that, when he had wakened that morning, he had thought "Keith's coming to see me today. I wonder how I can convey to him all that his book has meant to me." And so he said that he had decided to sit down and write me a letter. He handed it to me – three long pages of single-spaced hand-writing. Turning the tables on him, I asked him to read it to me, as he had so often had me do when I had written something. He laughed and then read it out loud to me. I watched him intently.

It was an amazing letter. He wasn't making suggestions as to how I could improve the book at all. Instead he was communicating to me the impact that reading it had had on him - even though he was a professional. He reminded me that I had said once that if the book helped even one person it would be worth it, and he said: "It's been worth it". He told me that, unlike many people and religions, I had made God very accessible in the book. He told me that as he had read about me asking my questions of God, he had found himself asking his own questions about God. It was one of the few times he had ever allowed me to see behind Larry the professional to Larry the person. He finished it with "Amen". It was quite a letter. I was very moved by it. Obviously I still have it.

Larry was intrigued at how openly I had described what went on in our sessions. He said that counseling was a mystery to a lot of people and that this book would help to de-mystify it.

He asked for a lot of copies when it was published, as he could think of quite a few people he would like to give it to. Later on I learned that those parts, the descriptions of my sessions with Larry, were a great help to a young friend of ours by the name of Charlene Archibald. They had influenced her in deciding to get some counseling to help her deal with the effects of a stroke she'd had when she was quite young.

I eventually found a printer who was willing to publish the book without wanting to become rich doing it, and I ordered 500 copies. I started giving them to friends and to people who asked for them, each time with a prayer that God would use my little book to His glory and to their good. It amazes me that, even now, over nine years later, I still get frequent requests for copies. I don't sell them; I prefer to just give them away. Almost 900 copies have been distributed altogether. I have no idea where they all are by now. I have none left, but rather than just get more printed, I wanted first to add this supplement to answer some of the questions I often get asked.

What to do?

In February 1998, seven months after my transplant, it began to dawn on me that I actually had a future. I had become so used to living day to day with tomorrow just being a blank sheet. But now I began to wonder what I should do with the rest of my life. It felt like I was coming back from the dead, that my new life was a gift, a bonus. I knew that I had been healed for a purpose and I didn't want to miss it, whatever it was.

I began to think about a second career, perhaps going back to university and learning something totally different. Professional counseling was one of the things that interested me. I had been so impressed with Larry Nussbaum and so helped by him, and there certainly was no shortage of need for that out there. I began to send out enquiries and search for information. But as time went on the conviction grew in me that I should return to what I had been doing all along. It was what I was good at. I hadn't made a mistake in my career choice. Plus I felt a debt of gratitude to my employer, Bank of Montreal, who had been so good to me during my prolonged illness. And so eventually I decided to return to work at the Bank. But what exactly would I be doing?

I found that the Bank was immersed in the possibility of a giant merger with the Royal Bank, another major Canadian bank. But it would have to be approved by the Minister of Finance later that year and there was a lot of work to be done to get ready for that. Matt Barrett, the Chairman and CEO, asked me to head up our relationship with the Office of the Superintendent of Financial Institutions, the regulatory body for banks in the country, and one of the bodies whose support would be required. I'd had a good working relationship previously with the Superintendent himself, John Palmer, and so this was a good fit. As I became involved in the work, it felt so good to be useful, to have a role and to be needed again. I had so missed that.

Shingles

One day that spring I began to feel a severe pain on the right side of my forehead. I tried to just ignore it and stick it out, but the pain became worse and worse. I phoned Princess Margaret Hospital. "Oh yes", they said "you've got shingles. We're not surprised." They said it was the result of my suppressed immune system, and was quite common with people who had gone through what I'd gone through. I'd had shingles twice before, on both sides of my back, but never in my head. Over the next few days it got so bad that I couldn't stand any light at all in my right eye. I had to be taken numerous times to hospital, where I was told I was in danger of losing my eyesight. (I can remember one occasion in particular when Sandra was driving me there. I was covering my eye with my handkerchief as tightly as I possibly could, but with the eye still being in excruciating pain because the tiniest bit of light was still getting through.) Every few hours a pain attack would strike my head. When it started I knew exactly what was going to happen but I couldn't stop it. The pain would begin on the crown of my head and move slowly but inexorably down through my right eye and down my face. It only took about two minutes each time but it seemed like two hours. I writhed in pain until it was over.

Eventually the shingles largely went away (they never totally leave your nervous system), but they left a permanent ulcer in the cornea of my right eye that still blurs my vision. Even to this day I have to take prescription drops in that eye three times a week, and no eye glasses are strong enough to overcome it. How grateful I am that God gave me two eyes. They considered a cornea transplant, but then thought it would be too risky with my compromised immune system. And so I added an ophthalmologist to my list of recurring doctors' visits. But if I was ever inclined to complain, I would quickly remember that the only on-going medication I was on from my illness and transplant was daily thyroid pills, which many people have to take. All things considered, this was truly amazing.

I meet Dr. Butler again

One day, shortly after I returned to work full time, I walked into the Toronto Board of Trade for lunch with two colleagues. On the way in I noticed a familiar face at one of the tables. It was Dr. Butler, my original doctor at St. Michael's Hospital. He was the one who had told me, in my final visit to him in 1991 before he retired, that I had "one to two years to live". And here he was, looking very tanned and relaxed, and here I was, very much alive. I went over to his table. "Dr. Butler", I said, "I don't know if you remember me - I'm Keith Dorricott." He looked up at me, and I thought he was going to fall off his chair. He had obviously never expected to see me again. We had a nice chat.

I got such a kick out of this happening. I went back to my table chuckling to myself. "I'm not dead. Leukemia didn't kill me. It's God who's in charge here."

Remission!

I knew that July 1998 would be a critical point in my recovery, the date of my twelve-month checkup at Princess Margaret Hospital – another bone marrow biopsy. As the day approached I was outwardly calm but inwardly very apprehensive. This would go a long way towards telling whether the transplant had been a success, or whether I still had leukemia. I asked Dr. Lipton what I should expect. He said that in all probability they would find quite a number of leukemia cells in my bone marrow, just as they had done six months before. But hopefully there would be no new ones (although they are sometimes hard to distinguish). The old ones can take two or more years to go away, he said. And so he carried out the familiar procedure – drilling into my back hip bone, extracting marrow and sending it off to the lab for analysis. They would phone with the results in a few days, he said. I felt like leaving the phone off the hook.

The few days passed. It's a long time to hold your breath. Sandra and I were up at our condo at Grandview with my Mum for her 85th birthday. My sisters and their husbands were coming later, to join in the birthday celebration. I was sitting outside on the deck when the phone rang. Sandra went in to answer it. It was Princess Margaret calling with the results! Everything stopped for me. After a few minutes' conversation Sandra came out to give me the news. The bone marrow test showed not a single leukemia cell in my body – not one! I was in complete remission! The leukemia was gone!

I just sat there. I was stunned. I showed no reaction at all. Around me they were rejoicing, but I just sat there. Not a single leukemia cell – old or new. They were gone. It had happened. It was real. I was well – for the first time in ten years. What a proof that it was God's handiwork. No more dreaded chemotherapy. I had a life again. It was all over. It was too much to take in.

Gradually I came out of myself to begin to interact with those around me – hugs, tears, happy words. Then the others arrived and joined in, delighted to hear the news. Later some of us went out for a round of golf and I played the game of my life.

Sandra

But Sandra's ordeal was far from over. She had been my primary caregiver for all those years, and now that the pressure was off, the toll began to tell on her. Her migraine headaches became even more severe and she felt deeply depressed and at loose ends for a long time. With the kids grown up now, and me so much better, what was her role in life going to be? Eventually she decided to take a course she'd always wanted to take - to obtain a qualification in interior design, for which she is naturally gifted. She has an innate sense of colour and layout, and great taste. After a lot of work she completed the course and passed – first in her class! She was surprised, but I wasn't. But it would take a lot more than that for her to deal with what was happening. It would be something she would continue to work through over the next few years.

Emma

In September 1999 Adele and Bruce in Vancouver had their first child, and our first grandchild, Emma Claire Robinson. One of my great desires had been realized, to live long enough to have a grandchild. I wasn't sure I was ready to be called a grandfather, but I sure loved having a grand-daughter. However it was a very difficult birth, with emergency surgery having to be performed on Adele. Sandra was out there in Vancouver with her at the time, and it was very traumatic for her and for Bruce, as well as for his family. I was 3000 miles away, at home in Toronto, and it made me realize how difficult it had been for Adele being so far away when I was so ill. I can remember prostrating myself in prayer before the Lord that night, pleading with Him to save my daughter's life, and waiting for the next phone call to hear the outcome. I don't think I had ever prayed so fervently, even for myself. Little Emma was hardly breathing when she came out. I flew to Vancouver as soon as possible, to see them all. I was so relieved to see Adele looking as well as she did.

I remember being amazed at how instantly I felt a bond with little Emma. I had known it when my own children were born, but I hadn't expected it to be so strong with my grandchildren. And to look at Emma nowadays, as a lively, bright eight-year old, you'd never know how difficult her start in life was. I love it when she comes running up to me shouting "Grandpa!", as though she hasn't seen me for ages.

Jennifer and Martin

That summer we'd had a visit from two young men from England, Angus McIlvenna and Martin Jones. They'd come across for a church event and were staying with us. Right under my nose, with me totally unaware of it, a romance began between Martin and our daughter Jennifer. Over the years she'd had several opportunities for a serious relationship but none had seemed right to her. Whenever I had thought of the possibility that marriage and family life might never happen for her, it had made me very, very sad. It was what she wanted. She was obviously very good at her job, as a chartered accountant with PriceWaterhouseCoopers, and she had great career potential, but she wasn't overly ambitious about that. Other things were more important to her.

Martin was different from the others. It became clear that they were very much in love. He was a chartered accountant also, but he lived in England. Earlier Jennifer had talked about possibly spending a year or two in England on an exchange program with her firm, for the experience, but now the planning became much more serious. As a result she arranged to spend two years with the firm in their Manchester office, near Leigh where Martin lived. And so she prepared to leave home for the first time, and to move three thousand miles away, in the opposite direction from Adele.

I will not forget leaving her behind at the train station in Stockport, near Manchester, that September. I had been in England and was with her in her new apartment when she first went there. But then I was leaving for a meeting in London and she would be on her own - in a new country for the first time. As I boarded the train I looked out of the window and saw her sobbing on the platform, with

Martin trying to console her. I felt like I was abandoning her, but she was a big girl now. It was lovely to see Martin's tenderness for her. When I arrived at my hotel in London a few hours later, I phoned her, and her cheery voice made me feel a lot better. She's a strong and courageous woman and I knew she'd be all right.

My calling

The reason I had been in England at that time was to teach a week-long residential seminar called Training for Service. It's an intensive Bible Study program for young adults and others in the churches of God, and it was right up my alley. I had been invited to join the other two course leaders, Phil Brennan and Andy McIlree, who had taught it for several years. It was a work that I felt called to by the Lord and I was grateful for the opportunity. It was to be one example of what would become my principal occupation after I retired from secular work - Bible teaching. I have been privileged to be engaged in Training for Service each year since then, as well as in other similar activities.

I now travel to Great Britain about four times per year for various assignments. I often stay with our very good friends David and Rhoda King in Davenport, south of Manchester. Their home has been a home-away-from-home for me for a long time now, and it had been a great boon to be able to go there and relax when I was in England during my illness. This traveling also now gives me the opportunity to visit both of my aunts from time to time. My Aunt Olga Ferguson is almost 93 years old (as I write this), living in her own place in Paisley, Scotland, and keeping remarkably well. She still drives her own car, and does very well at it. My Aunt Sheila Beadsworth, nine years her junior, is not doing so well, however, as she is increasingly suffering from Parkinson's disease. Life is very difficult for her, and earlier in 2007 she had to give up her own place and move into Eothen Homes, an assisted-living home in Whitley Bay in north-east England.

Tracing my roots

In 2001 I was in England again, and once again I visited Jennifer. Then I flew up to Scotland on a private mission. For a long time I'd had a strong desire to try to locate the place where I had been born, back in 1943, although I had no idea if it even still existed. All I knew was that I had been born during a blackout in World War II in an old people's home in the small town of West Kilbride (as I described in chapter 3). When I arrived at Glasgow I rented a car and drove down to West Kilbride. It only took a few minutes to drive through the town, but I could find no clues. I wasn't even sure what to look for. Then I noticed a building marked "The West Kilbride War Museum". I stopped and went inside and met the couple in charge and told them what I was looking for. To my amazement, the lady told me that she had worked at that home years before, but she didn't know if it was still there or not, as they were now building new houses in that area on the edge of town. She told me it had been called the "Cubrieshaw Home for the Elderly". She gave me directions, and so I got in the car (it was raining) and I drove to where she had told me to go. I saw the homes being built and some construction workers nearby. I got out of the car and spoke to some of them, but they didn't know anything about there being a home for the elderly. I was just about to give up when one of them said that there was an old house up the hill, and that the people who lived there might know about it. And so I drove up the hill and down the long treed driveway to the big old house. It was locked, but I saw some other workmen some distance away. By this time it was raining hard. I got out of the car and called to them, asking if they knew about a home for the elderly. One of them, an older man, turned around and pointed to the big old house and said "That's it, right there".

I could hardly believe it. This was the place of my birth. I felt a strange connection with the past, of my being part of the continuity of time. I stared at the place and felt a kind of affirmation of who I was. As I remembered what my mother had told me of my shaky start to life, not expected by the doctor to live, I thought again of God's hand on me throughout my life. I walked all around the house, tried the door, and looked in the windows. No one was home. But around the back I saw an old sign leaning against the building - "Cubrieshaw Home for the Elderly". This was it. I drove away contented – mission accomplished. When I returned home I was able to tell my mother about it, and this triggered some more of her recollections of that momentous night, which helped to round out the story even more.

Resuming my career

Meanwhile, at work, I found that I didn't have quite the same motivation as I'd had previously. I always made sure that I did my very best work, but my interests in life had changed. I had changed. As I became involved in one business matter or another I found myself thinking "I've already been there; I've done that". The staff seemed still to be wrestling with many of the same issues that I had been involved in a year or more before. My employment contract with the Bank entitled me to take early retirement as soon as I reached age 57, which would be in February 2000. And so eventually I spoke about it with Tony Comper, the Bank's new CEO. He asked me to stay on for another twelve months, to again take responsibility as Vice

Chairman, Corporate Services. And so I agreed. However, one year later, I was finally able to take early retirement.

I was ready for it, although I'm not quite sure Sandra was so ready to have me around the house all the time. I was so heavily involved at the time with various matters in working for the Lord that I really felt like I had given up two full-time jobs to concentrate on one. And it was the one that mattered. I explained this to my fellow-executives at my retirement reception, explaining that I thought they were quite able to increase the Bank's stock price without me, while I moved on to the next chapter of my life.

From time to time as I think back on my professional career, I feel very satisfied. It was constantly fascinating and energizing. It was never conventional or routine. I met some wonderful people, traveled the globe and used my talents to the full. I was always on the cutting edge, and I left things better than I had found them. My ethical values were never compromised. And so I truly have no regrets. Since then I have never missed the work itself (nor the commuting), although I do welcome every opportunity to renew acquaintances with colleagues that I came to know well. My personal identity had never been bound up in my job or my position, and so I found it fairly easy to "walk away".

In January 2001, around the time I was leaving the Bank, I was contacted by Rod McQueen, a business writer at the National Post, a national daily newspaper. He had heard about my story and wanted to do a feature article on me in his weekly column. I was a bit reluctant at first because I knew him to be a tough writer, and I didn't know what his angle might be. We had always been cautioned at the Bank about talking with reporters. But then I remembered my vow about taking every opportunity to tell what the Lord had done in my life so that He would get the credit. And so I agreed to do it.

Rod came to our house, sat down with me and turned on his tape recorder. I asked him if I would be able to see the article before it was published but, as I expected, he told me "no". He then just started asking me a few questions and I felt a freedom talking to him about my experiences, including the spiritual dimensions, although I had no knowledge at all about his own beliefs. But there was no hint of him being at all skeptical.

The following Monday I was to fly to Chicago for my final meeting with my colleagues there at the Harris Bank. At the Toronto airport that morning I picked up a copy of the National Post and turned to the business section. There on the front page was a large picture of me and a headline that read "Trusting the Power of Prayer". As I read the article I realized that it could not have been more honouring to God no matter who had written it. I was again so thankful for His over-ruling in what could have been a difficult situation. The article concluded as follows:

"In December, 2000, Mr. Dorricott retired, but not before declaring his love for the Lord in front of fellow employees at his send-off parties.

He has no difficulty reconciling his spiritual and professional lives. 'It's totally scriptural to work for your living, to earn your keep. I have observed shady practices, unethical practices, but I've had no part of it. I don't know whether I've lived a charmed life, but there have been very few episodes in my life when I've ever felt like I was put in a situation where I was compromised.

'I feel sorry for people whose career or business objectives become so all-encompassing that they miss the more important part of life.

My top three priorities are: No. 1, God and His purpose in my life; No. 2, my family; No. 3, my career. I've never been out to make every penny I can:'

He believes his 10-year battle has given new hope to countless others. 'To see what God has done has really strengthened their faith. It encourages them to pray for other people. I've been able to help people with cancer or who are trying to care for people with cancer just by telling my story. I can't prescribe for them. Everybody's situation is unique. But there is real power in people's stories and experiences.

'I'm much more clear about my mission in life and why I'm here. I just want to be used to help people come to find the reality of God in their life in a very real, personal way. It's been an amazing experience for me. I'm ready to get on with the next chapter in my life. I'm not exactly sure what it entails, but I didn't know what each of my previous chapters entailed either. I'm so grateful to have my health. It's amazing what God can do when we get serious with Him.'"

In February Sandra and I made our annual visit to Barbados. I would be chairing the annual directors' meetings of the Bank's companies there for the last time, and it would be my last official act for the Bank. We had a delightful outdoor dinner with the directors and their wives, all of whom were such good friends by now. Some very nice things were said about me (some of which may even have been true). But the evening before had also been special. They had arranged a retirement reception for me, also outdoors, at the home of Brad Bellis, the Managing Director, and his wife Jane. There were many people there and I was enjoying it thoroughly when Brad called everyone to attention and told them that they had a presentation to make, and had someone special to make it. Out of the crowd came a gentleman that I realized was the legendary Sir Gary Sobers, probably the greatest international cricketer of all time. He had grown up in Barbados, and still lived there, and was well known to many of them. He presented me with an autographed cricket bat. They had all known about my interest in cricket, despite living in Canada, dating back to my boyhood in Scotland. I had a very interesting chat with Gary that evening, and later read his autobiography. (Whenever I told my British friends about this, they were suitably impressed, but my Canadian friends had no idea who I was talking about.)

Live TV

A few weeks later I received a phone call from David Mains of the television program "100 Huntley Street". He had read the article in the National Post and wondered if I'd agree to be interviewed on their show. It would be a live interview, which would then be re-broadcast on various stations around North America throughout the day. Again, as I thought about it and prayed about it, I agreed to do it. And so they scheduled the interview for a few months later, in July.

When the day arrived I drove to the Crossroads studio in Burlington, not knowing quite what to expect. I was welcomed warmly. Without any briefing, when the time arrived they sat me down on the set across from Lorna Dueck, who would be interviewing me. She had read my book the previous weekend for background. Again I felt very much helped by the Lord as I responded to her questions on live TV. I wanted so much to be a genuine and effective witness for Him. I was very impressed with Lorna's professionalism, and I felt that the right emphasis had been expressed in the interview.

Towards the end of the interview, Lorna asked me about my perseverance throughout my illness. She said many people are tempted to give up in situations like that. She asked me what kept me going. I told her about one time in hospital, before I was about to go into Intensive Care, as I looked around and saw Sandra, my family, friends, doctors and nurses. And I had said to myself, "They're all doing everything they can for me. I've got to do whatever I can do for me." Their support was such a constant encouragement to me.

I told Lorna: "I never thought this disease was going to kill me. I always thought God had a plan for my life. I didn't know what it was, but I had to see what was involved, and where He was going to lead it. I had to trust Him for that. Don't ever give up", I said, "because God knows the end from the beginning, and He will take you where He wants you to go if you allow Him to."

Another opportunity had been given to me to tell what God had done in my life, and I had kept my vow to Him.

The inside story

This was to become a pattern in the months ahead. As I traveled around to various churches of God and other places within Canada, the Unites States, the Caribbean and Great Britain, and met people who had prayed for me so faithfully over the years, I was able to thank them personally and show them in the flesh the result of their prayers. On one occasion I began my talk by saying "I'm glad to be here. Actually, after what's happened to me, I'm glad to be anywhere", and it was so true. By now I even felt free to tell some stories that I had purposely left out of my book, such as the following:

In late 1996 I was in very poor condition and was running out of treatment options. I had been told earlier that year that I wouldn't be able to have a bone marrow transplant, and yet my white blood count was getting astronomically high (540, instead of a normal 4 to 11). However, as I recounted in chapter 12, as a result of my salvage chemotherapy early in 1997, the count came down to 1 – yes, one! It was as a result of this that they reconsidered me for a transplant, which I eventually had that July. However there was another factor that God may have used in all this, that I hadn't mentioned in the book…

In November 1996 a business colleague of mine, Bryan Smith, had given me an article written by two California doctors. It described great success they'd had in treating AIDS patients by applying a small do-it-yourself device that emitted a slight electrical impulse to their pulse points. This impulse disturbed the passing blood cells sufficiently to break off the protective immune coating that had prevented drugs from penetrating and doing their job. As I read the article it reminded me of a conversation I'd had with Dr. Brandwein two years previously as to why particular chemotherapy protocols stop working. He had told me that the body's immune system recognizes them and builds a protective coating around the cells. If that coating could be removed, the drugs could reach their target and continue to work. Bryan even had one of these devices, and so he sent it to me – to use at my own discretion, he made sure I understood.

At this stage in my illness I was ready to try anything. The instructions said that I firstly had to detoxify myself for two weeks (including no tea or coffee), and then spend one hour per day with this gadget switched on, attached to the pulse points on my wrists or ankles. I decided to try it. The first day, since Sandra wasn't home, I had to go next door to my neighbour, Mary Edwards, who was a nurse, to see where to attach it. When she heard what I planned to do, she said "Not in my house you don't". She didn't know if I would keel over dead – and neither did I! Her husband Mark, who is a lawyer, *reacted differently. He said "If this thing works, we could make a lot of money". We had a laugh about that and then I went home to do it. For two weeks I applied it faithfully. I didn't feel a thing. After two weeks (it was just before Christmas) I developed a cold, and so I thought it wise to stop. And then two weeks later I started the chemo – which worked so spectacularly on my white blood count. Whether this little gadget helped or not I have no idea, but I wouldn't be at all surprised if it did. God is not limited in what He can use.*

Often as I met new people, such as on the golf course or on holiday, we'd chat about ourselves. Often in the context of why I had retired, I'd have the opportunity to briefly mention my healing from leukemia. I made sure I always brought the Lord's name into it. Sometimes the conversation didn't go anywhere, but other times people would become quite interested and want to know more, and another opportunity would be given to me to testify. In some cases it resulted in requests for my book, and another copy would be sent out, with the usual prayer.

Our family

In September 2001, I was in England again and staying with Jennifer, who was now engaged to be married to Martin later that month in Toronto. That was when the 9/11 terrorist attacks happened in the United States. The destruction of the World Trade Center affected me greatly. I had often been in New York City on business, and the offices of my old firm Deloitte & Touche had been high up in one of the Twin Towers. I had been up there in the early 1980's and I didn't know if the firm was still located there or not (it turned out they weren't). When I heard about the attack I felt I just had to make contact with Sandra by phone and find out what had happened. I learned that even the building in Toronto I had worked in, First Canadian Place, was evacuated that day. And along with countless other people, my return flight to Canada was cancelled and there was chaos trying to arrange a flight home.

We were concerned that this event might prevent some overseas people from coming to Jennifer and Martin's wedding. But it went ahead as planned, on September 29ᵗʰ, 2001, and I had the delight of also performing the wedding of my second daughter. It was the realization of another dream I'd had when I was ill. It was so good to look at her on her wedding day and see her looking so happy.

Sandra and I had often talked about moving out of the busyness of the city once I retired, but we had put it off until after Jennifer's wedding. However, the very next week we went looking, north of the city, in the lovely rural area around the quaint village of King City. We found a new house on two acres of property, and before the end of October we'd bought it. We moved in between Christmas and New Year's. The location was good because we were still quite close to my mother, who was living in a seniors' assisted-living facility in north-west Toronto, and also fairly convenient for our son Andrew to drive to college. However Mum was getting near the end, and she passed away on April 15ᵗʰ, 2002 at age 88. In eight days' time she would have been widowed from my Dad for twenty-five years.

Paul Altman, one of the Barbadian directors and a very good friend, had very generously offered Sandra and me the annual use of his villa "Sea Shell", which allowed us to continue our annual visits to the island even after my retirement. That February (2002), we were there with Adele, Bruce, baby Emma, Andrew and Heidi. By this time Andrew and Heidi had developed a very strong and growing relationship, and on this trip something very special happened for them. On the Friday evening they disappeared just before sunset. About an hour later they returned with Heidi having a beam on her face that lit up the room. They had become engaged. Andrew had proposed on the beach very romantically as the sun was going down. He'd had it all planned and had brought the ring with him. The wedding was set for June 2003, which was just after they would both graduate from college – Heidi as a teacher, and Andrew with a marketing degree.

That summer, with Jennifer's two-year exchange almost over, she and Martin relocated to Canada, to live in Toronto, not too far from us. Each of our children was getting on with their lives, building families of their own, and it was good to see.

In July 2002 Adele and Bruce had their second child, whom they named Grace Alexandra – 'Grace' to honour what God had done at Emma's birth, and 'Alexandra' to honour her Grandma (Alexandra is Sandra's real name). They were of course concerned that the problems that had happened at Emma's birth might happen again, but everything went well this time. However Adele suffered very severe post-partum depression afterwards. She had experienced it after Emma's birth, but this time it was even more serious and prolonged. Sandra spent more and more time with her in Vancouver. Eventually Bruce and Adele decided to move house to Ontario, which was a huge upheaval for them. Bruce had owned a dental practice out west, and this meant uprooting and starting all over. It wasn't easy for them. In June 2003 they arrived, and after spending some time with us, settled in Aurora, less than ten minutes away. How ironic – they had been by far the farthest away of our children from us, and now they were the closest. Then in late 2005 Bruce bought the dental practice in King City where he had been working as an associate.

In May 2003, with the end of the school year, and with his wedding just about a month away, Andrew and I took another three-day golfing holiday to Florida, just as we had done a few years before. We even went to the same place. He had bought new clubs the year before but had not yet used them. He took great care packing them and quite reluctantly checked them in at the airport. They were the last items to come out on the carousel, by which time he was getting very nervous. We had a great time together, played three rounds of golf, and then returned home. It was a milestone for us - he was about to leave home and become a married man. God had provided a wonderful partner for him, as He had for our other two children.

We still play golf together every chance we get. It pleases me so much to be able to go and enjoy a game with him, and he's very good at it. I remember all those times when I was in hospital and couldn't be with him, couldn't be a father to him, and so these times are very sweet. Recently he told me that there was no one he'd rather play a round of golf with than me - great words for a dad to hear. The wedding took place in June and again I had the honour of performing the ceremony. That made it three out of three. May God continue to bless our children's unions, as He has blessed ours.

Erhard

In early 2002 I had been invited to go to Northern Ireland that coming summer to be the spiritual leader at the churches' camp for young adults. I agreed to go, as again it was the kind of teaching ministry that I knew I had been called to. The camp is held at a beautiful spot on the north Antrim coast, very close to the famous Giant's Causeway. I agreed to go just that one time, but I have now been there six years in a row. What has kept me going back is that I have seen the Lord at work among those young people, and that is a great thrill.

In July 2004, two days before I was due to leave for the camp again, I received an Email from Anthony Irwin of the church of God in Armagh in Northern Ireland, a young man whom I had met at one of the Training for Service courses. He had heard me tell the story of my conversion to Christ as a boy, where I had mentioned the name of Erhard Nessler (as referred to in chapter 7). To my surprise, Anthony told me that his wife Karen was Erhard's grand-daughter. Erhard had married a lady in one of the churches of God in Northern Ireland, although years later he had left his family. Occasionally however he would visit Northern Ireland to see his grand-children.

This Email told me that a few weeks previously Anthony had given a copy of my book to Erhard, who had apparently read it and had said he would like to talk with me. This was surprising, as previously he had not wanted to talk with anyone about his past. Anthony was asking me whether I would be willing to talk with Erhard on the phone from Essen, Germany.

Would I? I'd be absolutely thrilled to do it. Both my sister Shirley and I had wanted for a long time to make contact with him and to hear his side of the story. He had been an important person in our lives. I Emailed Anthony back to say that I would be delighted to talk with him but that I was due to leave the following afternoon for England. I suggested 8 a.m. Toronto time (2 p.m. in Essen) the next day as a good time. I sent off the Email not knowing if anything would happen.

The next morning I was lying in bed thinking about it, and praying about it, when the phone suddenly rang. It startled me. A voice with a very proper English accent said "Is this the

Dorricott residence?" I replied that it was. Then he said "Mr. Keith Dorricott, please". I asked "Is that Erhard?" He said "It is". We then proceeded to have a wonderful conversation for about half an hour, although he told me that I had mis-spelled his name in the book, which I apologized for. He also told me I had some of the facts wrong, that he hadn't been shot down in Scotland, but that he had been captured by American forces in France and sent to the Scottish prisoner of war camp. He was just a new recruit at the time. He was now eighty years old and confined to a wheel-chair. He was not in good health. But he told me that my book had been good for him.

Knowing how his life had wandered away from the Lord, I marveled at that statement. This man who had been used, through my sister, to bring about my salvation and start my spiritual career, had now been helped by something I had written decades later. Imagine that. Here was more evidence of God at work - the great orchestrator.

I asked Erhard about Shirley being brought to the Lord through him in the car that night in 1948. He remembered it well and said that it had been a good experience for him also. I asked him if he remembered my aunt and uncle, the Fergusons, and he especially remembered Aunt Olga singing around the house. "She was a good singer, wasn't she?", he said. He even remembered the title of one particular song that she often sang – "This is My Task". I told him how wonderful it was for me to finally be able to talk with him, after fifty-six years. I told him that I considered him to be my spiritual grand-father. He said that I should get his address from Anthony and that he would like to keep in touch.

After I hung up, I called Shirley and told her. She was ecstatic, and wanted to get his address so that she could be in touch with him as well. I then called my Aunt Olga Ferguson in Scotland, aged 88, and she was almost speechless. She remembered the song he had spoken about and sent me a copy of the words, which I sent on to him. A few days later at the Irish Camp I met up with Anthony and Karen. I was eager to tell them about the phone call, but they had already heard. "After he talked with you", they said, "he called to tell us about it." Wow – another connection had been made with my past, this time relating to my second birthday.

I sometimes tell people about my three birthdays. My first one was February 6, 1943 when I was born and preserved miraculously during the blackouts of World War II. The second one was August 25th, 1948, when I was "born again" – when I came to know the Lord as my Saviour at my bedside in Fairlie, through talking with my sister Shirley. She had just been saved through Erhard who was a Nazi airman, like the ones who had been bombing us when I was born. And the third birthday was July 8th, 1997, when I received the bone marrow transplant from my sister Hilary that saved my life. Those are three important chapters in the story of God's intervention in my life. (Although I have three birthdays, I only get gifts on one of them.) For several years, Shirley and James, Hilary and Bryan, and Sandra and I got together to celebrate July 8th. It is an important date for all of us.

Annual check-ups

Meanwhile, each year in July, I go downtown for my annual checkup at Princess Margaret Hospital. In the early years I was a bit apprehensive as the date approached. It reminded me of those many times when I had been sitting in an examination room waiting for the doctor to come. When he arrived and began to read my chart, I would watch intently to see if his eyebrows went up or down. I read so much into his facial expression. But in later years I looked forward to these annual visits, for the chance to see again those wonderful professionals, Dr. Lipton and Dr. Brandwein. (Dr. Brandwein had transferred to Princess Margaret not long after my transplant.)

At a checkup a couple of years ago, I said to Dr. Lipton "That didn't take long". He replied "It doesn't take long when someone is as healthy as you are". What great words to hear from your doctor. He told me that one of his patients had recently told him he was going to write a book about his experiences. "It's been done", Dr. Lipton had told him. And then he asked me if I had any more copies of my book, as he wanted to keep giving them to some of his patients. I replied "For you, anything". And so the next day I went back downtown and delivered him a dozen more.

Liam

In March 2005, Jennifer was due to give birth for the first time. Sandra in particular was quite apprehensive, remembering what had happened to Adele at Emma's birth. She and I went down to St. Joseph's hospital that day to be with Martin for the arrival. Andrew and Heidi arrived later. The delivery went well, and Jennifer gave birth to a healthy baby boy, Liam Hayden Jones, our first grandson. But then things started to go horribly wrong. Jennifer was hemorrhaging, and they couldn't get the bleeding stopped. We were all shooed out of the way and the nurses and doctors started running, with grim looks on their faces. Then they rushed Jennifer down to the Operating Room, not far away, and closed the door. It was agonizing for all of us, but especially for Martin. Sandra suggested that I phone our church hall where our assembly prayer meeting would be just about ending, as it was almost nine o'clock at night. I did, and we learned later that they then stayed for quite a while praying fervently for our daughter. Martin kept going outside the hospital to phone his mother in England on his cell phone. She was standing by at that end desperately waiting for news. Every once in a while Jennifer's doctor, who was wonderful throughout it all, would come out and give us a status report. Things were getting steadily worse and decisions needed to be made. We were all constantly and fervently in prayer to God, together and individually, in rooms, in the hallways, even in the washrooms, everywhere and anywhere. We knew Jennifer's life was in great danger. Was it possible in this day and age in a modern hospital that she could die in childbirth?

Eventually the doctor came in to ask to Martin for permission to do a partial hysterectomy on her to save her life. What a decision to have to make on the spot. In one way the answer was obvious, but it would have profound consequences. It would mean that she could never give birth to any more children, and she wasn't even conscious enough to be consulted about it. Martin looked grim but he was so strong. I can't imagine the thoughts that must have been going around in his mind - that he might be left without his wife, and yet with a young son to bring up by himself, in a country far from his own, and far from his own family. We were never closer to each other than that night. Martin gave his consent and the doctor ran off to carry it out.

After four or five hours the crisis was over; the bleeding was stopped, and Jennifer was taken down to the intensive care ward overnight. We all tried to bunk down in one of the rooms, with little Liam in a crib in our midst. We didn't sleep much that night. The next morning we were able to take him down to see her. I carried him in, all bundled up, to let his Mum see him for the first time.

I will never forget the sight of her lying in that bed in Intensive Care after what she had been through. But she was alive. We laid little baby Liam in her stretched out arms. She couldn't even move them because of all the intravenous lines she was hooked up to. But she just looked down at him and smiled. But then her doctor had to deliver the news about what they'd had to do. I just stood at the end of her bed and wept for her. It was a terrible burden she would have to carry with her for the rest of her life, and she had done nothing to deserve it. She had always been strong in character, but never more than that day. The good news is that little Liam is just a great little guy. He is all boy, with reddish hair, and into everything. He is a delight, and Martin and Jennifer just dote on him (and so do we).

Reconnecting with Matt Barrett

In July of that year, 2005, I flew across to Britain to work at the camp in Northern Ireland again. Sandra came with me this time, and we spent a few days in London on the way. The first day we were there she traveled into the city to go shopping. That was the day of the bombing in the London underground. The whole system was shut down and she had to take a taxi cab from downtown back out to our hotel near Heathrow Airport. It took her several hours (and, I told her, used up all her shopping money). But it was a very unnerving experience for her.

Before I had left Canada I had arranged an appointment to meet with Matt Barrett, my previous boss at the Bank of Montreal. He was now chairman of Barclays Bank in London, and I wanted to say hello to him again after five years. When I phoned his office they didn't know who I was, of course, but they agreed to give me five minutes in his very busy schedule. And so the day after the bombing I went into town to the headquarters building in Canary Wharf for my appointment. I waited for him, and then Matt came into the room to meet me, smiling. He said "Did they ever find out what cured you of your leukemia, or was it just a miracle?" I replied that I didn't think there was any other explanation.

We had a great chat for over half an hour and he seemed in no hurry to end it. We reminisced about a number of things, but mainly I wanted to convey to him my sincere gratitude for how he had treated me throughout my prolonged illness. I had reflected on it several times after I retired. "There was a while there," I told him "when I wasn't much use to you." I reminded him of his remark to me one day when I showed up at a meeting after a prolonged absence. He had said "You're a tougher out than Pete Rose" (referring to the legendry Cincinnati baseball player who got safely on base more often than any other player). But he seemed genuinely pleased that I had come to see him to express my appreciation. And I felt very good afterwards that I had been able to do that when we were no longer boss and employee.

As I thought about it later, I recalled one time when I had been telling him about my latest doctor's visit. I had happened to mention what Dr. Brandwein had said about the possibilities for me of potential new research, how expensive it was and the problem of lack of funding in Canada. Matt had immediately asked me "How much do they need?", and I had told him - it was a very large amount of money. He replied "Write me out a requisition and they'll have the cheque by tonight." And they did! It was unbelievable. That was the kind of thing that wasn't publicized about Matt, the compassionate and generous personal side of him that few other people knew about. He was another instrument in God's hands.

In spring 2006 Martin and Jennifer moved into a new house in Etobicoke, not far from where we had lived on Poplar Heights Drive, and about half an hour from where we were now living in King City. It was familiar territory to her, near to where she had grown up. And then a couple of months later Andrew and Heidi bought their first house in Dundas, outside Hamilton, about an hour away from us. It was great to see all three of our children and their families settled in homes of their own (not far from us) and getting on with their lives. In each case they are also giving their lives to the Lord and serving him in the ways they each do best.

Shirley and Hilary

Shirley and James, my sister and brother-in-law, live in Cobourg about an hour to the east of us. They travel a great deal. James, despite being eighty years of age, still loves to go on international work assignments, and Shirley sometimes goes with him. They are both also very active in volunteer work. Shirley recently returned from two months in northern China, where she was teaching English at a Chinese university. Every couple of days she would Email us all a fascinating account of her experiences. I told her that she should write a book about it – it was quite an adventure.

Hilary and her husband Bryan moved to Bolton, north-west of Toronto a few years ago, and then more recently bought a home near Trenton. Bryan completed his counseling degree at university, while still working in leadership education, and he travels a great deal as a senior consultant with the Hay Consulting Group. Hilary is very involved in rescuing pugs which have been abused, rehabilitating them, and finding homes for them. Recently Hilary has volunteered to take on a very challenging task – editing and circulating a family newsletter from time to time, to help keep us in touch with one another, despite our busy lives. What a great idea. She just issued the first one.

One day in August of last year (2006) Andrew and Heidi got us alone and gave us some great news - they were expecting their first child. They were so excited about it, and so of course were we. Andrew gave the baby a nickname – "Jellybean", and we all started following Jellybean's progress with great interest.

The idea of this supplement is born

Also in the summer of 2006 we received a phone call from a man by the name of Dennis Seeley, who had made contact with us through a friend of theirs who knew me at the Bank of Montreal. His wife Gerri had cancer and was being treated at St. Michael's Hospital. A nurse there, Marlene, who had also looked after me years before, had recently given her (of all things) a copy of this book "I Want to Live". Gerri had read it and said she was very helped by it. Dennis and Gerri, who are both active Christians, wanted to contact us, and so began an on-going communication between us. Dennis wanted as many copies of the book as I could give him, as he said he knew many people that he thought could benefit from it. I was delighted for him to become, in effect, a distribution agent for this little message from God.

It was through talking with Dennis that I decided to add this supplement to the book. So many people who have read it have asked about how my health is now after so many years, and about how Sandra and other members of my family are doing. I was running out of copies anyway. And so rather than just reprinting some more, I thought it would be better to add this update first. In talking with Gerri recently, she told me that she is in remission and doing really well, and they are praising God for that.

Prompted by that contact, last December Sandra and I decided to go back and visit the ward in St. Michael's Hospital again. It was a Saturday morning, but four of the nurses who had so diligently cared for me nine years earlier were there. We spent almost an hour chatting with them, recalling various events. It amazed me that they still remembered so many details of my case. After all, I am only one of dozens and dozens of patients they had ministered to over the years. It was good to be able to show them that their work in my case had not been in vain, that I was alive and well.

Another book

For the past many years, perhaps going as far back as twenty years ago, I've had a notion in the back of my mind to write a book on certain teachings in the Bible that are very precious to me. Over the years I have been shown wonderful things about the teachings of the Lord, as practiced by the churches of God that I am part of. I believe that they have come to us as a clear revelation from God, but I see little evidence of them in the writings and speaking of many of my fellow-Christians. And yet as I read my Bible I see them as being central to what God is looking for in the life and service of followers of Jesus Christ in these days. What should I do? And so was born the idea of another book.

Actually I initially thought someone else should write it, someone who was a better writer than I am. I did speak to one man, the late Reg Darke of Victoria, British Columbia, about fifteen years ago. But over the years this exercise of mine has strengthened rather than weakened. It just didn't go away. And so finally, late in 2005 during a visit to the church in Victoria, while staying with our friends Jack and Pat Young, I actually started to get down to it. Over the next several months I put in many hours writing and rewriting it, not knowing whether I would be able to produce something that I would find satisfactory. Eventually I did. I gave it to one of my fellow-overseers in the churches to review, Edwin Neely of Brantford, and also asked my daughter-in-law Heidi to review it. I thought she would understand the reaction of other Christians who, like her, had not been brought up in the churches of God. Not surprisingly, she gave me many very helpful comments.

Then, with the help and guidance of Nigel Berrisford, who had been an executive with W. H. Smith and then Chapters bookshops, I sent out a number of proposals to major Christian publishing organizations. Nigel knows how the publishing business works, and knows many of the senior people personally. I then made an arrangement with iUniverse, a subsidiary of Chapters, to have it published. It is due to be out by the end of this year. It is my fervent hope that it will stimulate serious enquiry from thoughtful Christians who are seeking to do God's will completely in their lives. But I'm quite content to leave this in God's hands to see what He plans to do with it, while being excited at the possibilities. God's ways and God's timing are always best. The title of the book is "Are We Missing Something?" It focuses on some key scriptural truths regarding "Discovering God's house, God's church, and true worship". Its sub-title is "How Scripture Can Guide Christians to Unity in the Twenty-first Century". [Information about it is on the website: www. kdpublications.com, which my son Andrew developed.]

Hobbies and friendships

In my spare time I still play my five-string banjo and enjoy bluegrass music, play a bit of golf (but not particularly well), and drive my little sports car, now a 2007 Mazda MX-5. Sandra and I, and other family members, still enjoy our condo up at Grandview, although we don't make it up there as often as we'd like to. Life just seems too busy. Our good friends Ron and Jenny Thomas of Hamilton bought a unit up there a while ago, and this gives us the opportunity to spend some time with them when we are both there.

Late last year our friends Bruce and Bev Archibald put on a surprise celebration at their home for our long-time friend Laurie Williams, who had just turned 60 years of age. Because of our strong connection over so many years, I could not let the occasion pass without writing a poem for him. It began this way:

> *I first met Laurie Williams back, I think, in '63;*
> *At one of Becks' great parties (he was courting Brenda B.).*
> *It wasn't very long until we became the best of friends;*
> *So I'm pleased to give this eulogy – long before it ends.*

And the last verse went as follows:

> *So now my friend, in the great game of life, you are just about rounding third;*
> *So don't take your eye off the coach's signs as He keeps giving you His Word.*
> *If you don't deviate, you'll be safe at the plate, when the Lord will finally appear;*
> *Meanwhile as we wait, my trusty teammate, it's awfully*

good to be here.

Good friendships are very precious, and Laurie and Brenda, and Bruce and Bev, and Sandra and I have all been good friends for a long, long time.

Jellybean

Over the years Sandra and I have enjoyed many holidays together, including several cruises, although we usually look for those that don't involve a lot of open water, as Sandra suffers from seasickness. We have been on ten cruises altogether - in the Caribbean, Alaska, California, Europe, and the Erie Canal. The last one, in September and October 2006, was on a paddle steamer on the Mississippi and Ohio Rivers.

However at the start of that cruise we received some very sad news. Andrew and Heidi phoned to tell us about the results of one of her pregnancy tests. It showed that the baby had problems with its heart. Over the next few days the news got worse and worse. The doctor said they did not expect the baby to survive; even if it did, it would need an immediate heart transplant at birth, and another a few years later. We were all devastated and were so sad that Andrew and Heidi's joy had been snatched from them. Yet their faith in God remained amazingly strong, while they struggled with all that was going on and the uncertainty of it all. The nickname "Jellybean" became such a term of endearment for all of us, as we waited to find out if we would ever meet our little grandchild alive. Day by day we (and many others) looked to God to do what the doctors could not do and heal that dear little one completely.

Sandra and I had planned a two-week trip to Britain in November. She had wanted to visit some aunts of hers that were getting on in years, while she still had the opportunity. Then we intended to be at the Northern Irish Camp's 40th anniversary celebration and stay with our good friends John and Hazel Hutchison. Finally we planned to cross to Manchester where I had a two-day meeting, and would visit with David and Rhoda King. However as the time drew closer Sandra just knew that she should not go. She did not want to be away in case anything happened with the baby, and so she cancelled the trip. I shortened mine to one week. It was a good thing that we did.

On Friday, November 17th I flew to London, and then the next day to Belfast to attend the camp reunion. On the Tuesday I was to fly to Manchester.

As I was leaving for the airport for the Manchester flight, my cell phone rang. It was Sandra, calling from Toronto. "Heidi's been taken to hospital. She's hemorrhaging. Pray!" She couldn't stay on the line, as she was rushing to the hospital with Amy Hart, Heidi's mother. I didn't know how serious it was, but it sounded bad. Was Heidi's life in danger? I prayed fervently: "O God, don't take his wife......"

When I arrived at Manchester airport I was able to phone again. Standing outside the terminal building in the rain with my cell phone, I reached Sandra at McMaster hospital in Hamilton. We were only allowed to talk briefly. The baby had been born (three months prematurely)…a little girl…Jadyn Belle Dorricott (meaning: "God has heard…and she is beautiful"). But she was only expected to survive for a few minutes. With a heavy heart I turned back inside to try to arrange an immediate flight home to Toronto. David and Rhoda came in to be with me, which was a great comfort to me. Then I flew to London's Heathrow Airport, and immediately phoned Jennifer in Toronto while I was waiting for my luggage. She told me that little Jadyn had died an hour earlier. I grabbed my suitcase from the carousel and ran through the tunnel to the other terminal building to try to catch the 9 p.m. flight to Toronto. The gate was already closed but they let me on. I arrived at 2 in the morning (7 a.m. British time). Jennifer met me at the airport and we drove straight to Dundas, to Andrew and Heidi's house, where Sandra was staying. After a very short sleep we went to the hospital, where the nurses had allowed Andrew and Heidi to keep little baby Jadyn overnight until we could get there, even though she had passed away at noon the day before. I held her in my arms. It just seemed like she was sleeping. She was so beautiful. And then Andrew and Heidi had to take the heart-wrenching step of giving her up.

As I looked at my son and daughter-in-law in that hospital room, with her family and ours around, I felt a mixture of deep emotions. There was such an enormous sense of sorrow for what they had lost. Would they ever get over it? Sandra and I would have given ourselves to have spared them that ordeal, but of course we couldn't. But there had been blessings also. For one short hour they had held and talked to their little daughter that they loved so very much. She was a real person, and they were her parents. Nothing could ever take that away. Little Jellybean had become known to us as beautiful little Jadyn Belle, our grand-daughter. And Sandra had held her when she was living. The love that Heidi and Andrew showed each other, and his care for her, were inspiring. And all of us in that room felt a special bond with one another, a bond that little baby Jadyn had given us.

A family funeral was held, with a tiny white casket. And then a week later, on December 2nd, 2006, Andrew and Heidi arranged a celebration service for her in the church of God hall in Hamilton. The place was packed, standing room only. This little one had touched a lot of lives. We sang the hymn "Safe in the Arms of Jesus" and family members spoke what was on their hearts. It was the most beautiful and authentic service I have ever experienced, and in it God was glorified. When it was my turn, this is what I said:

"There are a lot of things we just don't understand... And we can torment ourselves trying to find answers. But we have such a small window into the God of eternity, and we don't see very clearly when our eyes are full of tears.

It hurts so much to see your children hurting so much, and not being able to fix it, the way you've done so many times. Andrew & Heidi had so much joy of anticipation of their firstborn, and that was snatched away from them. They must feel robbed... They didn't deserve this, but we know it doesn't work that way...

We look at Andrew and Heidi's faces, and we see grief, but we also see unspeakable joy. They have suffered a terrible loss, but they have been given an unspeakable gift. They trusted in God...and they still do. Praise His name.

Why, God, did little Jadyn have to die? Isn't parenthood a good thing, a gift from God? Isn't love from you? You were able to heal her little heart, we still believe that, yet you chose not to. And we don't know why. God, we think our family's had enough of these life-and-death ordeals over the past few years. If it's Satan who's behind them, then please, God, shorten your leash on him...

Many years ago, someone said these words: 'And even in our sleep, pain that cannot forget, falls drop by drop upon the heart; and in our own despair, against our will, comes wisdom to us, by the awe full grace of God.'

If a reason for all this heartache was that more good would come from this little girl's passing than if she'd lived longer, then we could begin to understand it, and maybe even accept it... If a reason was that we'd realize a little more of what it cost God to give His own Son for us, then it has worked; because we do... If a reason was to make our prayers and pleadings more meaningful, more heart-felt, more united, then it has worked; because they have been... If a reason was that they'd see greater outpourings of love and genuine caring from friends this way, then it has worked; for they have... If a reason was to help us appreciate even more the ones we already have, our children and our grandchildren, then it has worked; for we do...

I look at my daughter-in-law and wonder what it must have been like for her to carry that little one inside her all those weeks, knowing how sick she was, and then having to give her back to God so soon... I look at my son who has grown up over the years before my eyes, and I see the man he has become, and I fall down on my knees in wonder and gratitude... I look at my wife and know how much she hurts inside and that she would do anything, anything at all, to heal their hurt. O God, please heal her now...

I am so glad, God, that I got to meet my darling little grandchild, and to hold her for a little while. She is so precious. She lived for an hour; she'll be loved forever. She's engraved herself permanently within our hearts. I am her grandpa, and that makes me feel very, very good.

If a reason was, God, that we'd understand more of You this way, then that has worked... For above all, God, we know that you yearn that we would really come to know you, our one true God. For God is great, and God is good. God is loving and God is kind. He is almighty. He is holy and He is faithful. He does everything right. He is the God of the living and the God of for ever. And our God is here with us now, and He will never ever go away. 'For Jehovah God is our Sun and our Shield. He gives us grace and glory. No good thing will he withhold from those who walk uprightly.' (Psalm 84:11)

God, we don't doubt you (how dare we?). But we admit we do not understand it all... And so we simply bow and say to you - "Amen".

Our daughter Adele had experienced serious problems in delivering little Emma, and then suffered very serious post-partum depression for a long time after giving birth to Grace. Our daughter Jennifer almost lost her life giving birth to little Liam, and cannot give birth to any more children. And now Andrew and Heidi had lost their firstborn, and didn't know whether their future holds a family of their own, which they so much want. The doctors can't say for sure that the problem with Jadyn won't happen again. And so my leukemia was certainly not an isolated problem; it was just one in a series of major trials. Life can be very difficult at times, and the ten years since my transplant have proved that for our family. Sandra suffers on-going health problems with her migraine headaches, diverticulitis and other ailments. Bruce has had big uncertainties in his dental practice, and Andrew went months without work. And so this life is no bowl of cherries; we're not promised that all will go well. We're not in heaven yet. But the big question through it all is: "What happens to our faith, our trust in God?" Do these experiences destroy our reliance on Him, or actually strengthen it? We never know until they happen.

Sandra's migraines

In December, just a couple of weeks after Jadyn's funeral, Sandra had had to be rushed into hospital. Her blood pressure and heart rate had dropped precipitously. She was given priority treatment in Emergency. At one point that night her heart rate was down to 28! We didn't know until later how close to death she came. Gradually, as she was hydrated and medicated, she recovered. Later the next day she was released from hospital, but not until the doctor in charge had thoroughly investigated her condition, even to the extent of tracing her long history of migraine headaches and all the medications she'd ever been on. As a result, he referred her to the leading migraine neurologist in Canada, a Dr. Gladstone of Sunnybrook Hospital. The earliest available appointment with him was not until the following May.

Sandra and I both went to her appointment with Dr. Gladstone in May. She had completed before-hand a lengthy questionnaire he had sent her. He had obviously thoroughly reviewed her case, and he spent well over an hour with us. He confirmed to her that all her headaches were migraines, that they were largely hereditary, and that she had herself already figured out most of the things that triggered them. However he also prescribed a new medication which he said was successful in about 50% of the serious cases like hers. "Those are the people who sent me those thank-you cards", he said, pointing to a long row of cards on his bookcase. Sandra had to start at a low daily dosage, and gradually increase it to a very heavy dosage. She also had to keep a daily diary.

In September she returned to see him for a follow-up visit. By now she was on seven times the original daily dosage, and had suffered a lot of adjustment symptoms as she had increased it. However it seemed to be working; her headaches were definitely less severe and less frequent. Was this finally the answer that she had been looking for all those years? Dr. Gladstone confirmed that the medication was working, and told her to continue with it, and even increase it further.

This allowed her to be well enough make a trip to the U.K. on her own the next month to make a surprise visit to her friend Rhoda King and to finally visit her aunts in Scotland. She was able to see her Aunt Mona Fisher just two weeks before she passed away.

Skittle

Last June (2007) on Father's Day, late in the evening, Andrew and Heidi handed me a greeting card that he had made. Inside it said:

Dear Grandpa,

Hi, I would like to introduce myself. I'm your newest grandchild. Sorry for the fuzzy photo. This picture was taken when I was 8 weeks old. I'm only 19 mm long. Today I'm 11 weeks and probably almost twice that long. I know that still is small (only 4 cm). Mommy and Daddy saw my heart beating away! It's already full of love for them and you too (I can hardly wait to properly meet you). You'll have to wait 'till the beginning of January though if all goes well. Please pray it does! Happy Grandfather's Day! Love, "Skittle" XOXOXOX

As Sandra and I read this, and looked at the little ultrasound picture on the front, it began to sink in. Andrew and Heidi were going to have another little baby!!!...

Skittle's due date was January 6th, 2008. In August Heidi went to have a echo-cardiogram scan to discover if Skittle was suffering from the same heart problem that little Jadyn had. How we prayed and yearned for a good result, and waited... As Sandra and I were going into Toronto General Hospital that day for me to have a routine colonoscopy, my cell phone rang. It was Andrew calling, with the results of the test. A minute later and our cell phone would have been off, and we'd have missed the news until later that day. But he was able to tell us - all was well. Our hearts just leapt.

Forty!

Sunday, September 9th, 2007 was our fortieth wedding anniversary. It was hard to believe that we had been married that long. It was a natural time to reflect on all that had happened. (It was back in 1988, just past the half-way mark, that I had been diagnosed with my leukemia.) The day before that, we had spent the afternoon and evening looking after Emma and Grace. We had taken them to the Kettleby Village Fair nearby, and then back to their house until Bruce and Adele returned from their appointments. Finally just before 8 o'clock in the evening we arrived back home. As I walked in the back door and into the kitchen, I heard shouts of "surprise". There right in front of me were over forty people - family and friends, all dressed up. Our children had organized a very special party for us both, to celebrate forty years of married life and ten years being cancer-free. Sandra had been expecting the latter, but thought that it would all be for me. Well, she was wrong. While we had been at the fair, the kids had been hard at work at our place getting it all ready.

What a wonderful evening it was. The kids had arranged every detail, including a catered dinner, the three grandchildren singing "Skinamarinkydinkydo…I love you", and a slide show of our "four decades" of married life. Then they added to it by each of them telling us about how much they loved us and appreciated certain things about us as their parents, and lessons learned from watching their Mum and Dad's marriage. Adele spoke about our commitment to God, to each other and to our family. Jennifer spoke about our support for her throughout her life, and Andrew spoke about several fond memories he had. Bruce, Martin and Heidi all added their own comments, and we found it all very moving. Then Sandra got up in response, and read to Hilary the poem she had written to her in 1998 when she gave me her bone marrow. Then I spoke and thanked them all. It was great to see so many good friends there together, and to rejoice in what had been going on in our lives, and their part in it. Usually you only hear nice things like that said at people's funerals; but we got to hear them that night about ourselves. And then later that evening, Sandra topped it off by presenting me with a very special gift – a beautiful new wedding band. She slipped it on my finger, as she had done forty years before.

Back in 1967, when we were married, one of Sandra's dreams had been to go to Bermuda on her honeymoon. We had to borrow money to do it, but we went, and we spent a delightful week there. What better place to celebrate forty years of married life together? And so on September 22nd (Emma's eighth birthday) Sandra and I flew to Bermuda for a week. We had a delightful time, although late in the week Sandra had a bad road accident. We were on mopeds, as we had always done on previous visits to Bermuda. But the traffic was very heavy, and late on the trip Sandra's bike hit the curb hard and threw her to the ground. She just lay there – very still.

Within seconds people were all around, wanting to help. One lady called an ambulance and it was there in five minutes, it seemed. Two police officers arrived and supervised everything. People could not have been more helpful. They put Sandra on a board with a collar around her neck, and took us by ambulance to the hospital. It looked very serious. After a thorough check-up and X-ray, she was released, however. But the next day she was very, very sore. She knew she couldn't fly home on the Saturday and so we had to postpone our flight and find a different hotel, as the one we were in was fully booked. It took several weeks for Sandra to feel herself again. It seems clear now that she had fractured a couple of ribs and the bridge of her nose. And so ended our motor-cycling career. We don't bounce the way we once did.

But, as is so often the case, as we reviewed the events later, there were so many ways in which it could have been a lot worse. For example, she could have collided with the on-coming traffic. Or she could have landed on the paved road instead of on the grass boulevard. God had looked after us again, and we were very thankful.

But there was something else we wanted to do to celebrate this great milestone of forty years of marriage, and so we have arranged a cruise for the entire family to go on - all twelve of us (including Skittle, of course – just listed as "Baby Dorricott") in December 2008 to the Western Caribbean. We are all excited about that.

Looking back and looking forward

I had called my book "I Want to Live". That was based on a deep desire that arose within me during a crisis point in my illness in 1995, when I realized how much I had wanted to stay alive and to have my leukemia taken away. It was a point where I learned to pray more deeply than I ever had before. But to live for what purpose? I had come to realize that if the Lord was going to give me life, it was because He wasn't yet finished with me. He had more that He wanted to do with my life for Him. And so my goal needed to be to discover what that was, and then get on with it, by His strength.

And that is what has in fact happened. The Lord has directed me into a teaching ministry in the churches of God. My stock in trade is God's own Word, and it is very precious to me. And I have found increasingly that the things of the world have fallen away and taken their proper place in my life.

The incidence of cancer is certainly not getting any less in this world. There seem to be very few families whose lives are not affected by someone who has it in one form or another. As I write this, I am thinking of our friends Esther Taylor in England and Andrew Drain in New York, who are both battling heavy chemo treatments at present, and don't know what the outcome will be – as well as those who are close to them who are suffering greatly along side, wishing there was more they could do to help. And I'm thinking of my young friend Stewart McKechnie in Greenock, Scotland who has had two surgeries to remove a brain tumour, and doesn't know if it will return. There are countless more, all with their own agonies and turmoil. May God be good to every one of them as He works out His purposes.

As I look back over the past ten years since my life-changing transplant, I think of the many problems our family has struggled through, our many trials. But I am indeed alive. I do have a life, and I am deeply grateful for it. I thank God for giving me such a wonderful wife, and we're more in love and we understand each other better now after forty years together than ever. Sandra has suffered greatly, both physically and emotionally, from things that have occurred in our lives, and I just long that God would come in for her complete healing also. He has blessed our family in so many ways, giving them families of their own.

And so now, as I finish writing this, it's September 2007, just over ten years since my transplant on July 8th, 1997. And the doctors tell me I am in very good health. As Andrew reminded me, I've been free of that dread leukemia for almost as long as I had it. Praise God for that. I am alive.

Post-script...

It's November 29th. Sandra and I are up north in Muskoka, at our condo at Grandview. The phone rings just after noon, and Sandra answers. It's Andrew calling: "Heidi's going to have a C-section in about an hour". Skittle is about to be born - five weeks early! Heidi has started to have Braxton Hicks contractions, and the doctors don't want to leave it any longer because her previous C-section scar is extremely thin. Sandra tells him we'll leave right away and drive straight to McMaster Hospital in Hamilton (normally a three hour drive). We hurriedly pack up and set off, but the weather is awful. There is almost no visibility for several miles due to heavy snow squalls, and there is an accident on Highway 11. (On the way Sandra comments that the trip is reminiscent of another 29th date - July 29th, 1970 - when our daughter Adele was born. She was also over five weeks early, and that day also we'd had a long drive down from the north.)

Eventually, about five o'clock, we arrive at the hospital and find Andrew in the hallway. He gives us the news – they've had a little baby girl, Lauren Chelsea, six pounds, four ounces. She is healthy and well and so is Heidi. Praise God! Lauren will have to stay in the neo-natal unit for a few days for monitoring because she is pre-mature, but she is completely healthy. We go in to see Heidi. Both she and Andrew are exhausted, but they are beaming.

Sandra and I feel so happy and so relieved. God has given all of us this wonderful gift – again the gift of life. After all the sadness of Jadyn, our son and daughter-in-law have a healthy little girl. Andrew takes us along to meet Lauren, our fifth grandchild. As she lies there in the incubator, I introduce myself to her. She opens her eyes slightly, and then blows me a big bubble. I can tell – she and her grandpa are going to become really good friends...

Printed in the United States
By Bookmasters